Hello all,

My name is Jo Thomas. First, a little  years as a reporter and producer, for to Radio 2's *The Steve Wright Show*. I wrote my debut novel, *The Oyster Catcher*, in 2014 and it was a runaway bestseller in ebook, winning the 2014 RNA Joan Hessayon Award and the 2014 Festival of Romance Best Ebook Award. My novels since then include *The Olive Branch*, *Late Summer in the Vineyard*, *The Honey Farm on the Hill*, *Sunset Over the Cherry Orchard* and *A Winter Beneath the Stars*.

If you've read my other books, you know you're in for a story about food and love, with a splash of sun, a dollop of fun stirred in and a cast of characters I hope you'll fall in love with. If you're new to my world, you're very welcome. I hope you're here to stay!

I was once at one of my favourite restaurants in Puglia, Southern Italy, where I wrote my second book *The Olive Branch*. The owner brought around a bottle of limoncello, a wonderful Italian lemon liquor, at the end of the meal with glasses for us all. As he pulled up a chair, he asked what kind of books I wrote. He didn't speak any English and I didn't speak much Italian, but I explained that my books were about food and love, because I have always felt that the two are intertwined. He told me that for him, life was all about the food that he and his family grew on the land, cooked in the kitchen and served on the table. He held out his arm to the olive grove surrounding us, gestured to the *forno* in the kitchen, where the burning wood was glowing orange and merrily pumping smoke out of the chimney, and slapped his hand down on the scrubbed, wooden table, *la tavola*. 'For the ones we love', he told me as he held his hand to his chest over his heart. And this is exactly the kind of book I like to write: about the food we grow to cook and put on the table for the ones we love. So, pull up a chair at my table.

You can find out more about me and my books and follow my latest adventures at my website www.jothomasauthor.com, on Facebook www.facebook.com/JoThomasAuthor or on Twitter @jo_thomas01. Do get in touch, I'd love to hear from you.

Love Jo x

'Warm and witty . . .
Well worth a read'
Carole Matthews

'Romantic, fun and full of heart,
reading a Jo Thomas novel feels
like being on holiday without
even leaving the house'
A J Pearce

'Jo's trademark
warmth and wit sing
from the page'
Cathy Bramley

'An utterly charming
read full of rustic
romance and adventure'
Woman

'Perfect for those who dream
of a new life in the sun'
My Weekly

'Sun, good food and
romance, what more
could you want?'
Heat

'A warm summer breeze
of a story that's full of
atmosphere and romance'
S Magazine

'Perfect summer read'
Liz Fenwick

Jo Thomas

My Lemon Grove Summer

REVIEW

First published as an ebook in 2019 by Headline Review
An imprint of HEADLINE PUBLISHING GROUP

First published in paperback in 2019 by Headline Review
An imprint of HEADLINE PUBLISHING GROUP

1

Cataloguing in Publication Data is available from the British Library

ISBN 978 1 4722 4601 1

Typeset in 11.25/15 pt Adobe Caslon Pro by Jouve (UK), Milton Keynes

Printed and bound in Great Britain by Clays Ltd, Elcograf S.p.A.

HEADLINE PUBLISHING GROUP
An Hachette UK Company
Carmelite House
50 Victoria Embankment
London EC4Y 0DZ

www.headline.co.uk
www.hachette.co.uk

*To my son Billy for making me smile
and in memory of his friend Luca
who reminds him how special it is to
be able to make others laugh.*

*And to Janice Symons, an inspirational lady
who taught me that no matter where your kids come
from or where they're going Mum is always Mum.
Some people only have to touch your lives
to make a difference to it.*

Grandpa Potts in *Chitty Chitty Bang Bang* said:
'Never say no to adventures. Always say yes,
otherwise you'll lead a very dull life.'

Family is what you make it . . .

Chapter One

'Ghosted? Really? Again?!' I say out loud. I look at the screen of my ancient phone, hoping that Mr Right, from Thursday night's third date, will suddenly appear on there. Like I'm waiting for the genie from the lamp to appear in a puff of blue and green smoke and show me the face of my ideal partner. The one who, on paper, was perfect and delightful when we dated. I thought he might just be the one. But this time, instead of Cinderella running out on Prince Charming, looks like Prince Charming has done the running out on me . . . again.

I seem to have a habit of picking Mr Perfect on the dating app, only for him to think I'm not Miss Perfect once we've met a few times. I'm worn out by it. I'm nearly forty, for heaven's sake. Shouldn't I be settled, with a husband and kids, a home and a rescue dog by now? Isn't that what life promises us all?

'Ghosted?' Lennie repeats. 'Again?'

I nod and double-check my phone. Then once more for luck before finally admitting defeat.

'Yup, ghosted . . . again!' The words ring in my ears and I take a big swig of the warm, slightly sweet rosé wine. 'Ew, Zinfandel.' I grimace and look around at the small make-shift bar for other drink options. But it was either this, warm

Chardonnay or Shiraz. All of them guaranteed to give me a banging headache. The little function room we're in isn't even a room; it's a curtained-off corner of another function room, with a big window looking out over the bay and the city. Next door, a wedding party is in full swing, their disco lights illuminating the curtain that separates us, lighting up the barren, bleak space we're standing in.

'Honestly, Zeld, I can't believe people can be so rude! How many times have you been ghosted now?'

I sigh. It seems to be the way of the world these days. Swiping left or right. Ghosting. All of us looking for the same thing and barely any of us finding it. But I do seem to have a habit of picking the wrong ones. One, two, three dates at the most, and then when I think we might have something going on, I'm dropped, ignored, without a word. It hurts. Never knowing what I did wrong, why I thought it was going in the right direction and they didn't, never understanding the mistakes I've made; just knowing that I have, again.

'What about you?' I take a sip of foul wine. 'How are you and Bridget from House of Dreams getting on? Isn't there some kind of rule about not dating colleagues from the agency?'

'No, Bridget and me were never getting together.'

'Anyone else on the scene?'

He looks uncomfortable and shakes his head.

'Now that Marcus, your boss, he's a catch, but I bet he's taken.'

'Just broken up with someone, I think. Don't imagine it was anything serious. He doesn't seem to be the settling-down type.' Lennie takes a swig of his wine. He looks strangely uneasy, and I have no idea why. There's something on his mind, that's for sure, but I can't work out what and I can't ask him over the loud music; I can barely hear myself think!

I follow his gaze till we're both looking around the nearly empty function room, Lennie's face pink in the flashing light from next door. The buffet table is groaning, as though expecting to feed hundreds of partygoers. Instead there's just a handful of us, including a few bored children playing chase amongst the chairs.

'We said we'd only stay an hour,' Lennie says loudly into my right ear, looking bored and desperate.

'But there's hardly anyone here. We can't just leave; she'll notice.' I lean back and nod towards Lydia, our old college friend. I say friend; we were more like a group gathering around the same table in the canteen every lunchtime just over twenty years ago. But Lydia is an enthusiastic and dedicated Facebook 'friend', even though we haven't seen each other in years, nor do we have anything in common.

I look around at the other guests here to celebrate Lydia's fortieth. There are a couple of colleagues from the school where Lydia teaches, with their children. And one of her sisters is here with her young family; the other sister couldn't make it this weekend. Then there are her college friends – that's me and Lennie. I have this overwhelming feeling of impending doom. Is this it? Is this what the future holds for me? A half-empty room, an expectant buffet table and a load of no-shows?

I glance at my phone one more time, just in case Mr Engineering Company Owner is really Mr Right and he's going to tell me it's been a nightmare of a day, his phone's been out of charge and he's had a flat on the Audi on the way to meet me. But no. Nothing. Just a silence that tells me everything I need to know. I let out a long, slow sigh.

'Let's get out of here,' says Lennie.

'We can't. If we go, there'll be hardly anyone left. We promised we'd come.'

'And we have. We've shown face. Now let's go and find something half decent to drink.' He nods at my glass. 'You hate Zinfandel! And I bet your feet are killing you in those shoes. I know you love a bargain, but just because they were one doesn't mean you should buy them if they don't fit properly.'

He makes me laugh. He knows me too well. My toes are dying to be released from my bargain-buy vintage red polka-dot T-bar heels. I always try to wear heels. It helps make up for my lack of height. Lennie towers over me, making me feel even shorter than I am. Lennie is tall and slim, with dark hair that he loves to keep waxed, to match his sharp work suits; and if he doesn't, it always seems to look like bed hair. He's recently given up on contact lenses and taken up dark-rimmed designer glasses, making him look like a young Jeff Goldblum, with a wide smile that never fails to make me smile back. Whereas I have bright red dyed hair, with lipstick to match, and what you might call the fuller figure; or as Lennie describes me when he knows I need cheering up, curvaceous. But I think I'm more hour-and-a-half than hour glass.

'We can't leave,' I repeat. 'Besides, I can't afford to go anywhere else. Not on the wages I'm earning now I'm a failed businesswoman.' I'm working as an assistant in the clothing department of a big store. It's all rules and clocking in and clocking off, dress codes and company policies. My worst nightmare, in fact, with the wages to match.

'You miss the shop, don't you?' He tilts his head at me.

'I loved it.' I try not to let the crack in my voice show. 'It was my dream.' But I'm no good at hiding emotion. If I'm happy, everyone knows it, and if I'm not . . . well, I'm not great at hiding that either.

'I know,' Lennie says kindly. And he does. We've been friends ever since college, where we met Lydia. He did graphics and design and technology, with the hope of becoming an architect. I did drama and photography. But Lennie didn't become an architect. He went on to uni, partied hard and lost all interest in his studies. He eventually became an estate agent; staying in the housing game, he would say, but I know it isn't really for him. He likes working out how houses can be changed and redesigned to improve them. Dealing with valuations and time-wasters isn't really his thing. But the job does come with a smart car and requires him to wear a suit every day, which his mum, Valerie, is very proud about.

I flitted around between wanting to do set design in theatre and television, stage make-up, or maybe camera work. I think it was all to feed my obsession with fifties black-and-white movies. Really I just wanted to be Audrey Hepburn in *Roman Holiday*. So glamorous! But I couldn't make anything pay. Eventually, after ending up waitressing in an American-style diner in a cheap nylon uniform, waiting for opportunity to knock, I gave up on the dream of working in film.

But when I got the chance to bring Lennie's idea for a vintage clothing shop to life, I grabbed it. There was a pet shop on the high street. The owner was retiring. Lennie was sent to photograph the premises and advertise the lease.

The day I picked up the keys and started sweeping up the stale sawdust was probably the happiest of my life. This was going to be my own glamorous Hollywood-inspired vintage clothing and collectibles shop. I was going to be living my Audrey Hepburn dream in real life.

Lennie and I had spent nights watching and rewatching *Roman Holiday* in our late teens and early twenties, when I was living with him after his mum scooped me up and put my life back on track. We also watched *Rebel Without a Cause* and anything with Marilyn Monroe in. I'd like to say I look like Marilyn Monroe, but I don't. Not really. Though I do love wearing full skirts and wide belts, which I have been pulled up on at work on numerous occasions for not conforming to regulation uniform dress. Honestly, I'm nearly forty! It's like being back at school. I also like to wear a scarf around my hair, which is almost a disciplinary offence. I take it off when I get to work and put it on again as soon as I've finished, imagining I'm walking out on the arm of my very own Gregory Peck.

Ah, the romance of it all! But maybe that's my problem. I'm an old romantic, and perhaps what I'm looking for only exists in films. I've been hoping to star in the feature-film version of my life and seem to have ended up on the cutting-room floor.

'Superspecs are moving into where the old greengrocer's used to be on the high street,' says Lennie, flicking through his phone now out of boredom. 'And Buster's Burgers are coming too.'

'Well, there's no room for independent businesses any more now that the rates have gone up. It's mostly all chains,' I say, feeling my hackles rise. I grip my glass and give an involuntary shudder of fury, and some of the wine slops over the rim. I wonder if I'll ever stop feeling like this.

'You'll get a shop again one day,' says Lennie, glancing up from his screen with a sympathetic expression.

'I'm just so angry.' I can feel my cheeks burning. 'I mean, business was good. I was scraping a living, and with the online side as well . . .'

Lennie looks at me softly. It's not like he hasn't heard this a million times since I had to give up the lease and hand back the keys two years ago. Two years! Time is flying! And if getting the keys was the best day of my life, giving them back was the worst. Having that shop was everything I'd dreamed of. Well, a start, anyway. I imagined it getting bigger and more successful; larger premises for the collectible furniture I'd started to branch into.

'You feel bullied out,' Lennie finishes for me, smiling, though I have no idea what he's finding to smile about. I look down into my vivid pink wine and nod, hoping that one day the upset will ease. My dream, my future was stolen from me. That's how I actually feel.

I take a deep breath and steady myself, and then look around the room at the party. It does nothing to brighten my mood. Who would be at my party if I had one? I have no kids or extended family. It's just me . . . and Lennie and Valerie. I'm not in contact with my mum; we parted company years ago. Her life was chaotic, to say the least. I did meet up with her again some years later, but we didn't really find much in common. We stayed in touch for a bit after that, but it fizzled out. I didn't have any real urge to meet up again. Her world was still chaotic and I wanted mine to be different.

It was Valerie who gave me the stability I craved. She had been our school bus driver when I was at secondary school and we'd always got on. I'd sit up front in the minibus and take control of the radio or the CD player. She knew when I'd had a bad day, and if I wasn't on the bus, she'd check to see if I was in detention. There was always an emergency chocolate bar in the glove compartment for those days when I'd got told off for not doing homework, losing something, not paying attention, or when I lost my rag and had to be sent to sit outside the headmaster's office to cool down. I never really fitted in, but Valerie was always there.

After I left school, with the certainty that I wasn't going to get any GCSEs, I fell in with the wrong crowd. My life started to go off the rails, and when I hit rock bottom, it was Valerie I phoned. She came and found me sitting on a bench in town, bundled me into her car and moved me in with her. To begin with, Lennie and I were a little wary of each other, but we soon bonded over starting at the further education college together, and a love of tea and toast in Valerie's little kitchen, and became the closest of friends.

Eventually I felt I should move out and into a flat share, and have been living this way ever since. Property prices have soared in our area and I'm not sure I'll ever get on the ladder now. Even Lennie ended up moving back home to try and save money.

So I really don't have anything or anyone to show for my life to date. I mean, you get to your twenties and think you've got it all to come. You party hard, certain that life will come together in your thirties. You get to your thirties and expect it all to fall into place – career, home, partner and kids. How has it never happened for me, like it never really happened for my mum? I'm thirty-nine, for goodness' sake – nearly forty! – and I live in rented accommodation with Maureen, my landlady, a list of rules as long as your arm and a cat called Henry who wees in my wardrobe if I leave my bedroom door open.

I mean, there was Nathan for a couple of years of my thirties, when I thought life was finally panning out. But that all finished after a disastrous weekend in west Wales when I found him in bed with the pub barmaid. My thirties seem to have been a constant quest for this happiness we feel is part of life's natural cycle. I've been constantly searching for Mr Right, for the right job, the right house. I thought I'd nearly got it in the shop, with my flat above and the little balcony that I'd filled with geraniums overlooking the high street. All I needed was for the perfect partner to turn up and I was on the way to having it all. And then it was gone.

I don't want to be like my mother. I want my life to be fulfilling, successful. I want a big family to celebrate with when I turn forty, close friends and loyal customers; instead, I know I'll be lucky to have even a few work colleagues, and some college friends I barely know.

'Urgh!' I say out loud. 'It's so depressing!'

'What is?' Lennie says distractedly, checking his phone again.

'This! Life! Well, lack of it . . .' I sigh, my bosom in its V-neck sweater rising and falling. 'If my fortieth is like this . . .'

'Doesn't have to be.' He grins widely. 'We could have it all, be the ones who made it work . . .'

'What do you mean?' I frown. I can't see any way of my life suddenly lining itself up in a neat, orderly queue before I reach my milestone – or should that be millstone? – birthday.

'I mean . . .' He's having to shout to make himself heard. The music has kicked up a gear; clearly Lydia is trying to get the party going. 'The pact!'

'The what?'

'At college? Remember?'

I shake my head and move in closer to him, feeling comforted that I have such a good friend to share the rubbish hand life has dealt me.

'What I mean is, no more ghosting! No more chasing around looking for Mr Perfect!'

I'm still confused. I look towards the door, hoping that he means my date has turned up and he can tell he's the one. In fact, some of the guests are leaving. I'm cross with myself for thinking for even a second that Mr Right had finally arrived to sweep me off my feet. I'm nearly forty! It's time I stopped this nonsense. It's time to stop believing that there is love at first sight out there for me. It's a myth, peddled by smug married people to make others think they've found the holy grail when really their lives are just as mundane as everyone else's.

'What are you talking about, Lennie? Please God, don't tell me you're going to set me up with someone. Although maybe arranged marriages aren't the worst idea in the world. I mean, I bet if you went out to find me my perfect partner, you'd get it a lot more right than I have.' I manage a smile.

'Exactly!' Lennie beams.

'What? You're not serious!' The smile drops from my face.

'I'm not suggesting we find each other dates, no.'

'What then?

'Remember?' He suddenly looks less confident. 'What we said? When we were at college?'

Suddenly I do. 'What? You mean . . . ?'

'The pact,' he finishes.

'The pact!' I throw my head back and laugh loudly and enjoy the feeling it brings. Lennie can always make me laugh. I look at my good, faithful, funny friend and smile affectionately. But Lennie isn't smiling.

'You're serious!' I clutch my glass and my eyes widen.

'Why not? It makes sense. It was the perfect pact.'

I stare at him, then lift my glass and swallow the lot.

'If we didn't find our perfect partner by the time we were forty, we'd marry each other and live contentedly together,' I say, still wide-eyed and with a hint of excitement.

'Exactly! We could have it all. Be Mr and Mrs Content! It's the perfect plan.'

'You're serious? You want to go through with the pact?'

'Why not? The question is, do you?'

I look around the emptying room like someone has just suggested a way out of this wretched event; a way out of the misery that is online dating; a way off the very high and dusty shelf.

Chapter Two

'The pact,' I say slowly, and am immediately transported back to my teenage self, with the help of Britney Spears singing 'Oops! . . . I Did It Again' in the background. It's a tune that seems to have followed me through my life. I turn to see the lanky teenage Lennie standing in front of me. Same daft smile. Same sticky-up hair, refusing to sit one way or the other.

'Yes, the pact.' He smiles widely, as if he's discovered the key to our happiness and it was that simple all along.

'We were seventeen, going on eighteen.' A smile tugs at the corner of my mouth; I can remember it so vividly.

'But we were right! Let's be honest, it's not going to happen. There is no Mr or Ms Right out there for us. Otherwise we would have met them by now.'

'Yes but . . .' I look at a couple leaving – one child attached to his father's ankle and another, clutching a well-worn bunny, snuggled in her mother's arms – and I feel a pang of envy. I'd've loved children. A family dining table. I'd've loved to have been able to cook, but pasta carbonara for one was never that appealing. Instead, I've lived off jacket potatoes with various fillings for years.

Lennie interrupts my thoughts. 'We always said we were the perfect couple, if only we could fancy each other!'

We both laugh, and then we stop and look at each other, a shroud of seriousness suddenly wrapping itself around us. Could I ever fancy Lennie? Could I fall in love with him? I look at his familiar face. I can't imagine him not being in my life. He knows everything about me: how I'm feeling, how to cheer me up. He even knows I like my boiled eggs cooked from cold, and three minutes from boiling! But a couple? Could we? Could I see him like that? There's no fireworks, no spark, no magnetic draw towards his lips, his hips, no burning desire to want to feel my naked skin against his like there was with my date the other night. But my date not only doesn't know how I like my eggs, he doesn't even return my calls! Lennie would never do that. Lennie rings me practically every day, at least once, sometimes more. He sends silly text messages. He's always thinking about me . . . and me him. I chew my bottom lip. Maybe you can't have it all . . .

'I don't think you can have it all, Zeld.' He says what I'm thinking, confirming everything I adore about him. 'Look, some relationships are all gorgeous in the moment, like a burger when you're really hungry, but you've forgotten you've eaten it an hour later. Others are like a slow-cooked meal. The ingredients go in, pretty unexciting at the beginning, but the longer they take to cook, the more satisfying and delicious the meal and the more it stays with you.'

I look at him. He's been thinking about this, I can tell.

'But . . .' My mind is trying to sort out the thoughts tumbling and crashing around in there; trying to make sense of it all. 'We're not forty yet! Well, I'm not. I still have three months to go!'

Lennie looks at me. His eyes fix on mine and I blush.

'It's not going to happen, Zeld; there is no Mr or Ms Perfect. This is as good as it gets. We get on great. We like the same things. We bicker. But we're always there for each other. We *are* Mr and Ms Perfect . . . as perfect as it gets.'

I chew my lip some more. He has a point, I think. Though I'm not sure whether I like it.

'You and me . . . a life and a family of our own,' he says.

'A family?' The word catches in my throat: a final chance at the one thing I always wanted. I shiver, and he slips off his jacket and puts it round my shoulders. 'A proper relationship?' I say. 'Like, a proper girlfriend–boyfriend one?' I want to make sure I understand exactly what he means.

He nods gently.

'It might take a little time to get used to . . . being together like that, but I'm sure we will.' He looks at me, his face open and honest.

'But . . .' and I can't believe I'm saying this, 'how? How would it work? You couldn't just move into mine. And you're living with Valerie still. That's not what it's about. That's not the grown-up dream. Even if we decided to call ourselves a couple, nothing would change. Neither of us has got the money for a deposit on a new place.' I can feel my frustration starting to bubble up again. 'I was cleaned out trying to hang onto the business. I haven't even got enough for another round of drinks at these prices.'

Lennie, though, grins even wider.

'I've got something to show you. Let's get out of here.'

He picks up a bottle of Prosecco from a nearby table laid up to welcome guests, grabs hold of my hand and swoops me out through the fire exit and into the cold night air, both of us laughing like we're teenagers again. We sit on the harbour wall and he holds out his phone to me. The page lights up. I make myself comfortable and slip off my shoes.

'Families, couples, professionals and hard-working individuals wanted to move to an idyllic Sicilian hilltop town for subsidised rents and a relocation fee,' I read slowly, with a finger under each word, trying to stop them from doing their usual thing of jumbling up on the page.

'Think about it,' Lennie says. 'Sun and sea . . . and decent wine! We could both get jobs, and we'd have the relocation fee and a house all to ourselves. That's what they're offering. I saw it on the news. It's a fresh start.'

'But we're not a family . . . or even a couple.'

'No, but we could be . . . The pact! This is it, Zeld! This is our chance to . . .' he glances back towards the party, 'to avoid ending up like that! Hitting forty with only a handful of mates to show for it.' He looks out at the harbour, and so do I. Could it really be our chance? 'And God knows, I could do with the money. What with all this uncertainty over Brexit, people aren't buying houses. Commission's at an all-time low.'

I take the phone from him and try and read the advert again.

'It's almost too good to be true. Where is it again?' I squint at the screen.

'Sicily!' He looks at me, his eyes sparkling.

'Think about it, Zeld.'

'But what would we do, for a living?'

'Anything we want!' he beams. 'We can get jobs when we get out there. See what's around. Doesn't matter what. Maybe they'll need an English-speaking estate agent. But I'll turn my hand to anything. Then you could set up in business again. Find a shop. A whole new start.' He looks at me, his enthusiasm infectious. 'If not now, then when, Zeld? Think about it. You could be spending your fortieth having it all: a home, a new business, a family . . . in the sun. Your very own Roman holiday!'

I take the bottle of Prosecco he's holding and take a swig, and then another. I look out over the lights of Cardiff Bay and try to imagine them being the lights of Sicily.

'I want to say yes . . .' I say, looking straight ahead.

'Then why don't you?' he asks next to me, and I can hear the smile in his voice.

'Because that's what I always do, say yes without thinking things through. Acting in the moment. It's what's got me into trouble over and over again in life.'

'This is different, Zeld. This is me! It's what we always said we'd do. When you think about it, we've actually been planning it all our lives. Nothing impulsive about it at all.'

I look at him. He could be right. But what if he isn't? What if . . . what if . . .

Suddenly my phone vibrates in my bag. As I rummage for it, glad of the distraction from the bouncing thoughts in my head, Lennie takes the Prosecco and swigs without wiping the top of the bottle first. It's a good start, I think. He's smiling, and I know he's doing the same as I was, looking out at the lights, pretending it's Sicily. Maybe, just maybe this is the best idea he's ever had.

I look down at the phone, and suddenly the silly grin slips from my face.

Lennie clocks me.

'Who is it?'

'Mr Perfect from the other night.' I remember it with a treacherous thrill running up and down my body.

'You're joking! Your ghoster!'

'Uh huh!' I nod, slowly reading the message of apology.

Lennie takes another swig of Prosecco.

'It's your choice, Zeld. If that's what you want, go for it. Or,' he nods to the lights across the bay, still obviously picturing our potential future together, 'there's Sicily. Me, you and a whole new life where ghosters are a thing of the past. Where loyalty and sharing our dreams is what's important. Like I say, really we've been planning this since we've known each other. It's not as crazy as you think. This is you and me, Zeld. The dream team!'

My phone buzzes again.

Fancy meeting up later?

My thumb hovers over the keypad, waiting to be told which way to go.

I look down at the screen. Could he be the one?

And then another message pops up.

No reason for us to get serious or anything. We can just hook up as and when, what do you say?

I mouth the words silently, and realisation washes over me like a freezing wave. I'm clearly not qualified to choose my own Mr Right. I ram the phone into my bag and take the bottle from Lennie.

'You're right. Why are we wasting time on losers? We're lovely people, right? We deserve a bit of happiness. As you say, we've been planning this practically our whole lives.'

'Exactly!' he beams back.

I think of all the time-wasters and ghosters I've met on that damn app. The mistakes I've made waiting for my perfect partner to appear, when all the time Lennie's been right here. Lovely, loyal Lennie. My friend, my best friend. Of course this is who I should be sharing my life with.

I take a deep breath. 'Let's do it!' I say, and I feel the familiar rush that making impetuous decisions gives me, the buzz, the excitement of not knowing what the consequences will be. I raise the bottle in a toast – 'To the pact!' – and swig the cheap fizz, because this time, I'm in it with Lennie. We're doing this together, just like we planned all those years ago.

'To the pact!' Lennie replies. 'And decent bloody wine!' and we both let out heads loll back and laugh, enjoying the relief and excitement our decision brings. No more chasing rainbows. It's time to settle for what's here and now, what's been right under our noses all along. Our life together is about to start, and I get a little thrill of excitement in my tummy. I look at Lennie and hope it's the start of the fireworks that will come in time.

I know that I've made the right decision. I had a dream and the dream passed me by. I need to go for this. Get out of the rut I'm in. For all the greedy councillors who put up the rates on the high street and put me out of business; for all the ghosters; for the store managers who make me dress like everyone else – I'm doing this because of you!

I'm excited, terrified, but also feeling a strange sense of release. A huge weight has been lifted from my shoulders. I've found what I was looking for and it was right here all along. Not a spur-of-the-moment thing; like Lennie says, we've really been planning it all our lives. Like the slow-cooked meal, it's going to be perfect!

Chapter Three

I take a last look around the bedroom that has been my home for the past two years, since I lost my lovely shop and the flat. It was Lennie who made my dream come true then, and now he's about to do it all over again. I smile thinking about him. Always there for me. Giving me a leg up when I need it.

I look at the single bed with my case on it. Renting a room from a stranger was not how I expected to end up in my late thirties. But now, well, I might just be getting everything I dreamed about after all. My own home, my own front door, perhaps my own business again, not relying on anyone else, and buckets of sunshine into the bargain.

I double-check my passport and boarding pass in my hand luggage. Organisation is not one of my strong points, but I'm determined not to lose anything or be late. I have one huge case I bought from the discount shop. It doesn't look very sturdy, but then it's only going one way. All it has to do is last the journey.

I check the mirror and give myself a scare. I'll put make-up on as soon as we arrive, but doing it in the middle of the night seems somehow wrong. I do, however, pull out my scarf and tie it up around my head. Then I wrap my waist-hugging cardigan around me and creep out of my room, swerving the cat sitting on the landing, staring at me as if judging me.

I try to bump my case down the stairs as quietly as possible, avoiding the creaking one ten steps from the bottom. The last thing I want is to wake Maureen and listen to her telling me what a stupid idea this is. It's not! Well, maybe it is. But this is me taking a chance to make something of my life again. A second chance to get on life's ladder. To have a home of my own. I don't care if it's the size of a shoebox. I just don't want to have to share with anyone else again . . . apart from Lennie, of course. It's going to be me and Lennie from now on, a couple.

That sense of relief washes over me again. I'm off the shelf. It's going to take a little getting used to, but I smile none the less.

Despite it being the end of May, it's cold and dark and damp outside.

What if he doesn't show? What if he's got cold feet? What if he has suddenly realised he doesn't want to spend his life with me, that there might be someone better out there?

As I'm thinking it, panic starting to rise within me, the lights of a taxi turn into the road. I watch it come towards me and stop. A rear window winds down. Lennie is there, smiling at me. Always on time. Always there. I should never have doubted him.

'Looks like you need a lift,' he says, grinning.

'As it happens, I do,' I whisper, playing along.

'Going anywhere nice?'

'Sicily, as it happens. I'm moving to Sicily!' As I say the words out loud, they suddenly make everything real, and a giggle bubbles up inside me.

I'm feeling light-headed with excitement and a good dollop of nerves too. But not enough to dampen my urge to get going and get there. Since our application as a couple was accepted, I've given my notice to Maureen and my job and spent the past couple of weeks trying to convince everyone that it's a really good idea. Apart from Valerie, who was delighted that Lennie and I were finally getting together. She said she'd hoped all along that it would happen one day, though she thinks we should just have a grown-up gap year and then come home.

Lennie gets out of the cab and pops open the boot, putting my case in there next to his. He looks at me, and I wonder if I'm supposed to kiss him. He's obviously thinking the same. We lean in, and at the last second I opt for my usual big hug while he goes for my cheek and ends up kissing the top of my head. I return the kiss into the breast pocket of his jacket, then clumsily we pull apart. We'll work on the finer details later. I've always been a klutz, so Lennie tells me, but if we're going to have a family, we need to start with the basics and get the kissing right. But we'll get there, I tell myself.

The awkward moment over, he holds the car door open and I smile. Back to our normal selves. I take one last look up at the terraced house and see Maureen standing behind the twitching curtain. As the taxi speeds off down the road in the direction of the airport, I feel like a prisoner leaving behind her cellmate, feeling lucky to be getting out and finding my freedom.

I try and sleep on the plane, but I keep reliving that awkward kiss and hug, and I can't help wondering what it's going to be like when we actually have to sleep together. We once had a drunken fumble at college, when we shared a bed after a party. Afterwards, we both agreed we'd had too much to drink, and that it was a bad idea anyway. Why ruin a perfectly good friendship? But it was always there, the elephant in the room. People assumed we were together or would end up together.

It was after that drunken fumble that we made the pact. And now here we are. I actually think that this time maybe a few drinks will help things along. That and the sunshine. I'm sure once we're there we'll be relaxed and ready to find our way around the bedroom. I don't need sparks and wild passion; just a nice time will do me fine. I look round at Lennie's familiar profile, his head lolling back as he sleeps, and try to summon up some sexy thoughts. But they don't come, and I put it down to tiredness. I lay my head against his firm broad shoulder and shut my eyes.

When I wake, the captain is telling the cabin crew to take their seats for landing.

'Window blinds up, please,' the flight attendant tells me on her way through. I do as I'm told and am immediately dazzled by bright morning sunlight. As my eyes adjust, I look out and catch my breath. There is the imposing bulk of Mount Etna filling my window like she's centre stage in a photograph. She stands tall and proud as if looking down on her subjects below, slowly puffing out smoke that sits like a white crown around her snowy head.

'Wow!' is all I can say, and I feel Lennie's weight leaning in to me to catch a glimpse too.

'Wow indeed!' he says as we finally touch down on sunny Sicilian soil for our new life together.

*

Emerging through the sliding doors into arrivals, I feel like I'm entering a whole new world, and the butterflies in my stomach agree. We stand with our trolley and look around at all the people holding signs, trying to find our names. It's like looking at a sea of sunglasses, on top of heads, on foreheads and tucked into the necklines of jumpers. There are shiny platform-heeled trainers everywhere, and despite the bright light outside, everyone is in coats and puffa jackets. To us, it looks like high summer, but clearly to Sicilians, this is still not hot. There is the sound of little dogs barking from under their owners' arms all around the arrivals hall, and the smell of hot coffee and sweet pastries makes my stomach roar.

None of the signs seem to have our names on them.

'What if it's all a hoax?' I blurt out, doubts and fears suddenly flooding into my anxious mind.

'Yes, but no one has actually asked us for any money yet,' says Lennie, the voice of reason as always. He's right: no one has asked us for money. Quite the opposite, in fact: they're actually paying us to move here. A lump sum when we arrive, and another in three months if and when we decide to stay. And we're being charged a peppercorn rent for a house.

I look around at the friends, families and colleagues kissing each other in greeting, and feel another surge of happiness. I definitely need to practise my kissing.

'I'll text the number I have and find out what's going on,' Lennie says. 'Why don't you get a couple of coffees and something to eat?' He pulls out some euros from his wallet.

'Okay. I'll pay you back,' I say, taking the notes. 'As soon as I get my fee.' Maureen wiped me out when I gave in my notice, insisting on all sorts of costs for cleaning carpet and curtains, claiming it was in the contract.

'No need to pay me back,' says Lennie, throwing out a long arm and wrapping it round my shoulders. 'We're a couple, a team. What's mine is yours!' He beams, and I smile back. It gives me a lovely warm feeling, being a team.

By the time I get back, carrying two strong black coffees and eating a warm deep-fried bun called an iris fritter, filled with sweet and creamy ricotta and chocolate chips, I feel like I'm in heaven. For Lennie I have a ciambella, a sugary circle like a doughnut. He loves doughnuts. The Sicilians clearly have a sweet tooth!

'Here.' I hand him a coffee and the paper bag with his ciambella in it. 'But first you have to try this.' I hold up the iris fritter and he takes a bite. Warm ricotta oozes from the sides of the bun and the corners of his mouth.

'Oh!' He rolls his eyes in pleasure. 'That was worth coming here for!' he says through a mouthful of chocolate and cream cheese.

'So, what's the news?' I ask, reclaiming my iris. 'Oh, I got these too,' I add, pulling out bottles of bright orange juice from my bag and handing one to Lennie.

'I spoke to the mayor himself. He said he was sorry, he'd been delayed and he'd be here shortly. I told him we'd wait outside. He has our photographs from our application, so he'll recognise us. We might as well go and soak up the sun while we eat our breakfast.'

Juggling coffee cups, grease-soaked paper bags and serviettes, we push the trolley out through the glass doors and into the warm, bright sunshine, where we stand and look at each other, neither of us really believing we're here. Mount Etna is there, tall and proud, and I find myself giving her a nod in greeting as we locate a bench and tuck into our breakfast buns, coffee and orange juice. I already feel like everything is working out just as I hoped it would.

'*Mi dispiace! Mi dispiace!*'

We both drop our heads forward from where they've been tipped back towards the sun, sunglasses on and eyes shut. Lennie pushes his glasses onto his forehead like the other men I've seen. See! We're practically locals already! A man in a dark blue suit, a light shirt, top button undone, and a dark tie loosened at the neck is striding towards us, dodging moving cars. He has a dark brown face, with deep lines around his eyes and either side of his large nose.

'Welcome, Zelda and Lennie!' He holds out a hand towards us and we stand to greet him. He takes my hand, shakes it vigorously and then kisses both my cheeks. I deal with it effortlessly. Again, I think, like I was born to be here. Then he does the same to Lennie, who is a little more taken aback but attempts to go with it and makes a loud kissing noise on the second peck. 'Welcome, citizens of Sicily!' The man smiles as warmly as the sun and then smooths down his grey hair across his head. 'I'm sorry for my delay. I had . . . some problems. But please,' he waves a hand towards the car park, 'come with me. I will take you to our town . . . your new home.'

'Problems?' I ask.

He suddenly looks hot, and his forehead shines in the sunshine. Then he fixes a wide smile across his face. 'Nothing that can't be sorted. Now, please . . .' He leads the way to his car, and as we follow, Lennie gives me a reassuring quick wink and a smile.

The car, a dusty silver Fiat, has a number of dents in it. Not quite what I was expecting. Not exactly fitting for the mayor, I think, but then he did say he was late because he'd had some problems. Maybe it was car problems, and this is a borrowed one.

We leave the airport at speed and make our way onto the autostrada, and I watch as my new world whizzes by. At last we turn off onto more narrow minor roads. Everywhere I look, there are yellow flowers, growing on overhanging branches beside and above the bumpy roads.

'What is that plant?' I ask, my curiosity going into overdrive. I want to know everything about my new surroundings.

'Etna broom,' the mayor tells me. 'It grows here and in Sardinia. Where the ground is sunny and open, and on poor stony soil.'

As we career along, the jasmine-like scent wafts into the car, along with dust from the roads. I look up at Etna, in our sight the whole time, as if watching our every move.

'And over in the fields, wild fennel. It makes great pesto,' he says, pointing to the stony mounds in the fields covered in brilliant green and more yellow. And despite my delicious breakfast, my mouth waters at the thought of wild fennel pesto.

We drive through towns – I say drive; more like a constant dodgems ride, or a game of chess, each driver determined to keep their game plan secret as they negotiate roundabouts and junctions – and along narrow streets where cars are parked with their bottoms sticking proudly out into the road, letting other vehicles negotiate around them. Outside the towns, there are fields of orange and lemon trees in straight lines, neatly tended, making the whole area shine like gold.

As we wind our way higher and closer to Etna, away from the coast, the road signs become more and more dilapidated. Finally, after an hour or so, we reach an ancient-looking town. The walls are crumbling, the lemon groves here as dilapidated as the roads and houses. Left to fend for themselves, by the looks of it, overgrown and abandoned. Pine and palm trees grow happily side by side, along with huge fig and walnut trees, spreading their branches over the faded salmon-pink walls of the houses. No one is stopping to park here in this town perched on the side of a mountain. Everyone is driving on through. Except, it seems, us.

'*Benvenuto!*' the mayor beams. 'Welcome to Città d'Oro!'

Lennie and I look at each other, both of us wondering if this is some kind of joke. It's certainly a far cry from the photographs we've been sent. And I'm sure even the mayor's smile slips as he looks for our reaction in the rear-view mirror. We watch other cars pass us and carry on through the town, along the narrow cobbled street and out the other side as fast as they can.

'They go to visit Etna, and the vineyards higher up,' the mayor tries to explain. But I can see no one is interested in stopping in Città d'Oro. Why would you? I think as I get out of the car and look around the street we're parked on. It's dark and cool. There are houses with overhanging balconies on each side of the road, and at the far end is Etna herself.

'Our grocery store,' the mayor announces, indicating the lone shop, under a battered green and white awning. A woman with long, wavy hennaed hair comes out and stares.

'*Ciao!*' I call, and raise a hand and smile.

She glares and ushers someone else back inside, to the sound of protests and disagreement. A single canary sings out from the dark interior. I lower my hand slowly and turn around. The occasional net curtain twitches, but no one comes out of their house.

I can tell the mayor is looking around for other points of interest to show us. 'Straight ahead is our town piazza,' he says, 'and above that our church and town hall.'

My gaze slides further up the hillside. At the top of the town is a big red property, standing tall and proud, gazing down over the rest of us.

'And a market?' I ask hopefully.

'No market, sadly, not any more.'

'Oh.'

'These cobbles look to be lava stone,' says Lennie, inspecting the worn street and the walls.

'Yes, indeed,' says the mayor, grasping for positives. 'And we have a restaurant. It's very good. Just not many customers, but he opens if we book . . .' He tails off and shrugs, seemingly running out of enthusiastic energy. 'It's about all we have these days,' he adds, and I wonder if he knows he's said it out loud.

I look at the town's dilapidated state – the worn walls and terracotta roofs, the peeling green shutters and listing gates, the neglected, overgrown lemon groves – and wonder what I was expecting. Everyone said it was too good to be true. And it looks like they were right. Everything is sadly neglected; presumably the mayor has brought in people like us to introduce new life to the place. But with the best will in the world,

I'm not sure you could revive this town. It looks like it has been dead for some time.

'Come, I'll take you to where you are staying. It's my family house,' he says as we get back into the car. 'Il Limoneto. You can make yourselves at home.'

I look around the silent streets, the crumbling buildings, the closed-up shops and wonder if I could ever really make this my home. Maureen and all the others were right. This is possibly one of my more stupid, impetuous ideas. I'm tired, hot and wondering what on earth we've let ourselves in for.

Chapter Four

As we get back in the car and set off over the worn cobbles. Lennie places his hand over mine. It's more reassuring and brotherly than anything else, but it's welcome either way. We pass the piazza on our right, with stone steps so worn they have indentations where feet have trodden over the years. They lead up to a huge church with a big brass bell overhead, and next door, the town hall.

We make a really sharp U-turn at the end of the high street and go back in the direction we've just come, heading out of town. We pass a row of houses, completely deserted but with amazing views across the town falling away down the hillside – quite literally by the looks of it – and out to sea.

Finally we pull off the potholed road onto a track. The car bumps and sways, as do we, and I grab hold of Lennie's hand tightly for support. Either side of the track are more over-grown fields of what I think are lemon trees. In amongst them are wild flowers, and there's a beautiful wisteria growing over one tree that must have been there for years. These lemon groves seem a far cry from the ones we passed on the journey up here from the coast. Maybe it's some kind of organic farm-ing, I think, but I'm too busy clinging onto the handle above the door to ask about it.

We stop at some large rusting gates, and the mayor gets out, looking a little anxious, to unlock them and push them open. As we carry on up the track, I notice that the lemon groves on either side are surrounded by electric fencing, with small stickers on the posts, though we're going too fast for me to work out what they say.

Eventually we pull up outside the farmhouse.

'Welcome to Il Limoneto!' says the mayor, waving a hand. Clearly the house was once a bright and sunny yellow. Now it looks like the rest of the town, faded and neglected, like an ageing movie star whose star has lost its shine, her heyday a thing of the past.

Slowly we get out of the car. My joints are shaken by the journey and feel like they're trying to slot themselves back together again.

The mayor goes to the boot and insists on carrying my case to the farmhouse. Inside, it's fantastically cool on the worn but very clean terracotta tiles. In front of us is a big wooden table laden with cakes and tarts, cheese and cold meats, along with a bowl of oranges and another of lemons, fat and bright yellow on a bed of green leaves. But mostly it's cakes and tarts. The Sicilians certainly do love their desserts.

'Please, pour yourselves a glass of wine and have some food. I have to go to some meetings.' He flattens down his hair again nervously.

'Thank you, er, Signor, er . . .'

'Please, call me Giuseppe.'

'Giuseppe,' we both say, and smile.

'We are family now, part of the same community,' Giuseppe says. He holds out his arms, but I don't step forward or hug him or anything. That would be weird. We're not family. We only just got here. 'After my meetings, I will be collecting the rest of our new residents from the airport. I will come back and see you later. Relax, eat, enjoy,' he instructs us, and then disappears out of the door.

Lennie and I look at the dark-wood kitchen and the groaning table, and then at each other.

'Wow!' we both say together, then I grin and try to go in for the hug again, like we're a proper couple, and this time end up clutching at his arm. I'm just not used to this with Lennie. We've always been quite tactile, linking arms when we walk anywhere, him rubbing my feet when I buy impractical bargain shoes, and he's forever ruffling my hair. He thinks it's a sign of affection. I think it's annoying. The hugging thing is new. But it's something I think we should do as a couple. Practice, everything comes with practice, I tell myself again, and look around at my wonderful new home.

'When they said we were getting a place to stay in, I didn't expect it to be like this!' I say.

'No, I thought we were going to be in one of those dilapidated houses we passed on the way here. This could be amazing with a bit of work!' he says, sounding like an estate agent who's just found a gem.

I think I will be very happy here, very happy indeed! Whoever doubted us and said this was a silly idea was so wrong.

'There has to be a catch!' I say suddenly. 'You always tell me that if something looks too good to be true, it usually is.'

'I hate to admit it,' he grins, then shrugs, 'but maybe I was wrong!'

I hold my hand to my chest in mock horror. 'You? Wrong?

I can't remember you being wrong since, oh, since the last time we played Trivial Pursuit. You vowed never to play again when you lost, and said it had to be Twister from now on. And you always win at that because you've got longer arms and legs than me and your mum!'

We're back on home turf. The hugging is a whole new world we'll have to just try and get used to. Especially if we're going to take things to another level and actually sleep together.

Lennie starts looking in cupboards. 'Maybe it's the town that's the catch,' he says. 'There's nothing going on there at all. Even the tourists don't stop, just keep driving through.'

He's right. The town may not have much going for it. But I didn't come here to be part of a big, close community. I came here to start up a business – online if I have to – and to create a home for me and Lennie. Maybe, just maybe we have hit the jackpot after all.

He finds two glasses and pours the wine.

'Now, let's eat,' he says, looking at the feast in front of us.

'*Benvenuto!* Welcome! Come in!'

Giuseppe's voice makes us both sit up from where we've dozed off on the settee in the big open-plan kitchen diner, me with my head resting against Lennie's shoulder. After a delicious lunch and a good old look around with glasses of glorious red wine in our hands, we took our bags upstairs and started to unpack. There are five bedrooms up there, and another two doubles in a converted barn outside. Lennie suggested we have a room each and spread our stuff out. We might as well with all this space. It's not like we have a young family . . . yet.

'No need to rush things,' he said, and I have to admit, I felt a sense of relief. I couldn't have agreed more. I didn't want to feel we had to 'perform' this evening. We still haven't got the hugging sorted. 'Let's take our time,' he added. 'Let it happen naturally.'

Once again, I'm grateful for his level-headed thinking. Otherwise I'd just plough on in there, probably make a complete hash of it and put him off ever wanting to go to bed with me again! It could be where I've been going wrong in my quest for Mr Right. Taking our time is sensible. Although if we are to think of having a baby, maybe not too much time. I'm pushing my luck at my age. But a home here with Lennie will be enough if it doesn't happen.

'Meet your new family!' Now I hear Giuseppe laugh, and we both realise at the same time that we have company. I hope they learn to knock next time. I'm not used to people just wandering in. I've never lived anywhere where you leave the door unlocked. And as for this 'new family', it's like he's suggesting a commune!

'Ah, Lennie, Zelda, let me introduce you.' Giuseppe is standing just inside the double doors that lead out onto the courtyard. He's surrounded by a group of people, like a tour guide.

We both jump to our feet, knocking over the half-drunk glasses of wine we've left on the floor, trying not to look like we've had a boozy lunch and fallen asleep, even though that is exactly what has happened.

'Hi, I'm Tabitha,' says a woman maybe my age or a bit younger, in quite a posh accent. 'My mum loved the TV show – what can I say?' she says.

Ah, *Bewitched*, the American sitcom. A witch marries a mortal man and tries to be an ordinary housewife. Tabitha was their daughter. I remember my mum saying she thought I'd been born a witch. Sometimes I believed it. When I was in the children's home, I often wished I could twitch my nose and transport myself to anywhere rather than where I was.

So if her mum liked the series, and mine knew it, I'd say Tabitha is just about exactly my age. She's wearing a leopard-print hat, dark glasses, an oversized scarf, despite the heat, distressed jeans and DM boots, and has a leather jacket slung over her shoulder, showing her muscular shoulders. Very rock chick. We shake hands stiffly.

'This place is very . . . rustic!' she says.

'Yes,' I reply. What was she expecting here in rural Sicily? I think the place is amazing! Okay, it needs some doing up, but the potential is all there. I realise I'm thinking like Lennie and I smile. I like that. We're singing from the same song sheet. I'm dying to ask Tabitha what she's doing here, presumably on her own. But I manage not to blurt it out and feel quite proud of myself.

'And I'm Barry,' says an older man, late fifties, touching sixty maybe, red-faced and sweating. He's wearing a washed-out Stones T-shirt, and washed-out jeans to match, with a belt just about holding them up under his pot belly.

'I'm Ralph.' Ralph is very smartly dressed, as if he's used to holidays in the sun. I can see him happily at home in Tuscany or Umbria, or on a yacht in the Med, in his neatly ironed polo shirt, crisp cream chinos and leather deck shoes.

'And we're Sherise and Billy,' says a smiling woman, late

sixties maybe, in a vest top showing off her strong shoulders and deep mahogany tan. She's in shorts and sturdy boots and a wide-brimmed hat to keep off the sun. She points to her partner, a small, wiry man, also in shorts, boots and a sensible hat. Despite his small stature, he looks as strong as an ox.

I glance around the odd assortment of people, wondering at their reasons for signing up for a new life in Sicily. What are they looking for? Are they all missing something in their lives back home? And then I realise, is that me too? Am I here because I'm missing something? I was, but what makes me different is that I've already found it. I'm here with Lennie – we're a couple, a team.

I look at the mismatched group again. It feels like the first day in a new office, forced together with a bunch of people you don't think you're going to get along with. Well, at least we won't be working together. I look at Tabitha, prowling around and photographing the farmhouse. My house, I think, already feeling territorial. My new family home.

'Welcome to Il Limoneto,' Giuseppe says. 'This was my family home growing up, but now I live in the town, by the church on the piazza.' He looks around at the place and I can feel the pride radiating off him. Then he claps his hands together and takes a deep breath. 'So, we have a few problems. The builders on your new homes are a bit behind.'

'A bit behind?' Tabitha jumps in.

'Yes.' He puts his hands together as if praying, and touches them to his lips before speaking again. 'The houses we have for each of you needed some . . . renovations. A little building work to make them—'

'But they're safe?' butts in Barry, and I can tell there's a touch of the pessimist there.

'To make them more homely. Call it updating,' says Giuseppe.

'Are they habitable?' asks Sherise.

Giuseppe moves his head from side to side. 'Not quite, but they will be. Soon.'

'Oh, we're not staying here?' I say quietly, processing the information and trying to hide my disappointment.

'For the time being, yes.' Giuseppe nods. My spirits lift. 'Until the builders have finished, you will all stay here, free of charge, of course. Please make yourselves at home whilst I organise your new homes in the town. I'm sure they will be ready very soon.'

'We're all . . . staying here together?' I look around the little group.

'Well, this should be cosy,' says Tabitha with an amused smile.

And there's the catch, I think. This house isn't for me and Lennie after all. It's for *all* of us. We're going to have to live with total strangers, just like when I was growing up. I hated it then, and I really don't want to do it now.

'How long will this be for?' I ask.

'Just till the houses are ready.'

'How long will that take? Can you give us a time frame?' Ralph asks, pushing back his shoulders in a business-like fashion.

'It's like being back in boarding school,' says Tabitha, throwing herself down on the settee with her feet up.

'Just till I sort things. It won't be long.'

'And then we will have our own houses?' I persist.

'Yes, yes, just as I promised. The funding is all there for this rejuvenation to happen.' Giuseppe forces a smile, and sweat beads appear on his forehead.

'Well, I'm sure we can all rub along together for a while,' I say cheerfully. At least we are all going to get our own places to live in eventually, and that's why I came here after all.

'Best we pick bedrooms,' says Tabitha, standing.

'And I will organise dinner in the restaurant in town, by way of a welcome and to apologise for your houses not being quite ready. I will call Luca, the restaurant manager, now.'

Dinner! I don't think I could eat another thing after the huge buffet we've put away.

'And we can all get to know each other,' says Sherise.

'Exactly!' beams Giuseppe.

'Can't wait,' says Tabitha, smiling widely and pulling off her hat and glasses to reveal short, funky hair. She rubs her hand over it, making it look like bed hair, and very sexy. I turn to see if Lennie notices. To my relief, he doesn't. I'm so glad I don't have to try and compete any more.

'Great,' says Ralph with what I think may be a heavy dose of sarcasm.

I look at Lennie, who raises an eyebrow, and I stifle a nervous giggle. Not only is this like the first day in the office; it's like the first day in the *Big Brother* house. What if we just don't get on? Am I going to find myself homeless all over again?

Chapter Five

'So, to the restaurant,' says Giuseppe, as we stroll down the track from the farmhouse, avoiding the potholes, and out onto the road into town, bordered by overgrown hedgerows full of wild flowers and Etna broom.

I'm soaking up the last of the rays from the setting sun by holding my face towards it as we walk, basking in its energy-giving rays. Lennie is walking beside me, and I wonder if I should hold his hand, but instead I hook my arm through his, like we always do, with one hand in his pocket. My silk scarf drapes between us as it slips lazily off my shoulder.

Lennie is the only thing here that seems to be making any sense right now. I'm sure the houses will be ready soon and we'll be able to start our life together. For now . . . well, it's just on hold for a couple of weeks, that's all, and we're simply carrying on like we've always been. Me and Lennie, comfortable with each other without having to think that we're anything more, or how our relationship will work in the future.

The occasional car comes down the lane and we all stand in to the side, brushing our calves against the grasses there. There is a smell of warm soil and flowers.

'What are those, Giuseppe?' I ask, pointing to the overgrown orchards all around us.

He looks at them as if suddenly seeing them for the first time in a long while.

'Lemons,' he says. 'They are lemon trees. These are all lemon groves.'

'They don't look very well looked after,' I say as we walk.

'Well,' he shrugs, 'they *were* lemon groves. Not so much these days . . .'

He puts his hands behind his back and his head down as we stroll on. A few battered old cars slow down as they pass, their drivers staring at us as though we are a circus act. Giuseppe raises his hand and greets each one. It becomes a little worrying when two cars meet each other, neither seeming to know which side to pass the other on. They finally work it out, watching us all the time.

'Can we see our houses?' asks Sherise.

'Maybe not this evening,' Giuseppe says. 'Let the builders get on and then I'll show you.'

'How about tomorrow, then? Be good to see where we're going to be living,' says Barry. 'You have got houses for us, haven't you? It's not some scam?'

'No, I have houses. You will see them, I promise.'

'Tomorrow then?' Sherise isn't giving up.

'Tomorrow,' he agrees, although I sense some reluctance.

'Are they near here?' asks Tabitha.

'Yes, just down there.' He points to a side street leading off from where we are.

'We could go now, couldn't we?' she says.

Giuseppe hesitates. 'Well, we have to get to the restaurant . . .'

'Oh yes, could we?' says Sherise.

40

'Well . . .' Giuseppe falters some more.

Tabitha is already striding away. 'Here?' she says, then starts taking photographs with her phone. She seems to photograph everything, like a teenager addicted to their Instagram feed. We all follow her down the narrow street with its faded pink walls. The houses are the ones we spotted on our way here. The ones that need a heck of a lot of work!

'Like I say, in need of some repair, but it will be done.' Giuseppe wags a finger with determination.

I look at the houses. There is no glass in some of the windows, shutters are broken, doors are peeling, balconies crumbling, but even so, my heart skips a beat. It might not be the farmhouse, but one of these houses, full of character and old features, would make me very happy. I can see myself in one already . . . us, I correct myself.

'They're beautiful,' I say, taking in the old stone and worn ironwork.

'They're knackered,' says Barry, sniffing disparagingly.

Ralph says nothing, but his stiff upper lip tightens.

'Will there be room for any livestock?' Sherise asks. 'Any land?'

'Land, um . . . well, land is tricky,' says Giuseppe.

Billy suddenly looks crestfallen.

'These houses will be for you for now, but there are plenty of other properties here,' Giuseppe says quickly. 'You can find something you like and we can arrange for a very good price for our new citizens. As I say, we don't have much land . . . but maybe enough for some vegetables or something like that.'

Sherise nudges her husband, trying to brighten him, but without any luck.

Not much land? I think, confused, looking back at all the fields we've just passed.

We walk on, down towards the main street, and pass through an archway – presumably the old town wall. Giuseppe explains about the dark lava stone used for building roads and walls. All around us the shops are still closed up, apart from the one we passed when we arrived. 'For all your grocery needs.' He smiles and holds out a hand.

The same woman as before, heavily made up, with dark eyebrows and bright lipstick, wearing a tight-fitting top and skirt, comes out to look at us. The mayor greets her but she barely responds. There is a young girl there too, aged about nine, smiling widely and waving. The woman looks at us as if aliens have just landed. And to be honest, that's a bit how it feels. Lennie takes my hand and squeezes it reassuringly. There's no thrill or sparks, but there is comfort, and that is all I need. To feel we're in this together, that I'm not alone any more.

We walk through the cobbled square. Straight ahead of us, there are views out to sea, and Etna can still be seen, her smoky top shrouded. We pass tiny alleyways off to the left, before turning to the right, through another archway and down some stone steps.

'Our trattoria, our restaurant,' says Giuseppe proudly.

We stand and look at the green door in a stone surround with pink mimosa growing around it. The door slowly opens and I find myself catching my breath. There are steps to the right up to a restaurant with a tiled floor and huge windows; in front of us is what looks to be the kitchen, with a big wood-pile by the door. There is a covered terraced area with tables and chairs, leading to another narrow alleyway, which appears to meet up with the main square again in the direction of Etna. And straight ahead, with more mimosa overhead, is the brilliant blue sea. This could possibly be heaven.

I stare wordlessly as I listen to the rest of the party exclaim about how beautiful it is, then slowly follow them through the open door. Whatever this place may throw at us, there are some real gems to be found. Nothing can stop me wanting to make a go of it here, I think.

Dragging my eyes from the view, I turn to thank the person holding the door open, but as I open my mouth to speak, my tongue ties itself in knots and I feel like I've been hit by a bolt of lightning, sending a billion volts of electricity around my body.

I have no idea what has happened. But something in my world just shifted, like my core has tipped on its axis. I'm light-headed and weak-kneed at the same time. I've never had an experience like this before. What is going on?

Chapter Six

'Zeld? Are you okay? Zelda?'

I can hear Lennie's voice, but I'm having trouble drawing my eyes round to him. What am I thinking? Pull yourself together, Zelda! I don't know what's happening to me, but I'm staring at this man holding the door open for me, and I don't seem to be able to stop.

'Zelda?' Lennie says again.

Giuseppe joins in. 'Have you two met before?'

'No, no!' I say, as does the man holding the door. He seems as shocked as I feel, while we stare at each other like we've known each other all our lives. With monumental effort, I drag my gaze away from his dark hazel eyes with their hint of green and turn to Lennie.

'Yes, fine, absolutely . . .' I try and say, though my mouth is as dry as the desert. I'm tingling all over – more than tingling: zinging! There is a full fleet of butterflies in my stomach, and my head feels as if the top might pop off like an exploding bottle of lemonade at any minute. 'Must be the heat . . . and tiredness,' I try and say, but I have no idea how it comes out.

Totally bemused, Lennie leads me to a chair at what is clearly the best table in the house, beside a big picture window looking out over the overgrown lemon groves that seem to surround the town on terraces draping down the mountain-side towards the sea. You can see everything from this seat: sea, fruit trees and tumbledown houses, the whole restaurant, and the kitchen with smoke coming out of the chimney. The smell of woodsmoke mixes with the fragrance of citrus blossom from the trees below the open window. There are olive trees too, gnarled and bent in the direction of the wind, with a blanket of red poppies all around them. It is heaven.

I must be really tired and hungry for it to have got to me like that, though. My stomach rumbles as I'm handed a menu. I don't look up at the man, just in case it happens again. But I can smell him – a citrus aftershave – and the butterflies swoop around my stomach once more. Maybe it's hormones. Last-chance-saloon hormones. Thank God I've got Lennie! I glance at him and the butterflies begin to settle as he smiles at me. I sip the water he pours for me.

'Better?' he asks.

'Much. Thank you. This place is amazing, isn't it?'

He nods. 'Happy we came? Not feeling it's such a ridiculous idea now? You know I'm always right!' he grins. I welcome the familiarity of his teasing, like the secure mooring of a little boat that would be all at sea without it.

I look around the table and catch a glimpse of the man who opened the door. He's handing the last of the menus to Sherise, who slips her glasses out of her bag. Her husband Billy is looking as though this is the last place on earth he wants to be. But a happy beat starts thudding in my stomach and my chest, and I study the man in the baggy white shirt with the thick, curly dark hair, long Roman nose and smoothly shaven tanned face, as if imprinting his features on my mind like a photograph.

'Everyone!' Giuseppe calls for our attention, and I focus hard on him, and only him, just in case I have that strange sensation again. But try as I might, my eyes seem to be drawn back to the smiling olive-skinned man, and weirdly, his gaze keeps flashing back to me.

'This is Luca,' Giuseppe announces, holding out a hand. 'Our host.'

'*Buonasera*,' Luca says, dipping his head, his voice as soft and gentle as the breeze running through the lemon grove below. He looks around the group and his eyes come to rest on me, and I feel myself blushing. I pick up the white napkin and make a point of placing it on my lap, focusing on the stitching at the edges and hoping my red cheeks won't show.

'Are you okay, Zeld? You look really out of sorts. We can skip this if you like, just go back and get a good night's sleep?' Lennie says. I love that he's concerned and I focus very hard on his familiar face.

'I'm fine. Really fine. Happy to be here,' I tell him. And I am. It's a long way from warm rosé in a tiny function room. I want to make this work, here, with Lennie. I keep my eyes on the menu and breathe slowly.

'So, maybe we should take some time to get to know each other.' Giuseppe smiles, seemingly determined for us to all get along.

'We'll be getting to know each other pretty well if we're going to be living together in that house. It wasn't what you promised, you know,' says Barry. 'You said we'd have places of our own,' he adds, and although he's moaning, he does have a point. But how can I complain when I am here, in the setting sun, looking at this view? I gaze out once again at the fruit trees, the wisteria growing over them and the poppies at their feet, the brilliant blue sea beyond. But I can feel Luca's presence as he moves slowly around the table taking drinks orders, getting closer to me. Everything else seems to recede, my whole being focused on him, his low, soft voice, his smell. I'm feeling as nervous as on my first day in school.

It's ridiculous. My body seems to have sprung into life like the wild flowers in the overgrown, neglected orchards all around us. A bit of sunshine and floral scent in the air and suddenly I'm buzzing. Or maybe it's because I'm here as a couple, with Lennie, and my body is suddenly responding to its newly off-the-market state. I smile. I'm not available. I study the menu, hard. That's what it is. I'm just happy to be here, and it shows. Nothing is going to stop us living this dream.

Suddenly I realise that Lennie is saying my name and gently shaking my arm.

'Zeld, we have to move.'

'Move? But I thought the houses weren't ready,' I say, thinking about my big case back at the house. 'Still, the sooner the better.'

'Move tables,' Lennie is saying in a strange whisper. People have stopped talking, I suddenly notice. The contented hum has evaporated and everyone appears slightly bemused. I glance up at Luca, who is looking apologetic and awkward. A far cry from the smiling, confident, happy man we met coming in. It's like a black cloud has descended, blotting out the blue skies and draining all the good vibes.

That black cloud seems to have arrived in the form of a

party standing in the entrance to the restaurant. A group of four men and, behind them, two women. The man at the front is wearing smart dark trousers – a suit, in fact – a tailored coat and a wide-brimmed felt hat, with reflective aviator sunglasses even indoors. I look at Luca again and take a deep breath.

Chapter Seven

'What do you mean, we're going to have to move?' The early start and the long day of travelling are obviously taking their toll. We've already been told our accommodation isn't ready. Now we have to move tables. This is ridiculous, I think scratchily. Maybe getting an early night might have been a good idea.

'I'm sorry, this table is booked.' Luca looks very apologetic as he sweeps round the table, scooping our glasses up onto a tray.

I'm feeling almost pleased that this man has annoyed me, and that the silly butterflies in my tummy have buzzed off. He isn't some god, come to taunt me with what I can't have, to remind me that there might be something else out there. There isn't. Lennie and I are about as good as it gets, and I'm going to cling on to that. This man might have charms, good looks and a lazy smile that could light up a shopping centre at Christmas, but that's all. And he's clearly not very good at his job if he's having to move us.

'I'm sorry, it's my mistake,' he adds.

I wish I could stay cross at him. But he seems genuinely apologetic. I get another waft of citrus aftershave as he reaches for the bread basket, and my treacherous nerve endings ripple like a bunch of gossiping, giggling schoolgirls.

'This table is booked. I'm afraid I'm going to have to move

you to the one over there.' He points to where he's pushed two tables together.

'But you can see everything from here, the whole terrace,' I say.

'Yes,' he confirms. 'It is the best table in the house, which is why it is reserved. I'm sorry, I didn't realise my diners were coming this evening.' He looks at the group by the door, who are standing watching from behind their sunglasses. None of them is smiling.

Giuseppe looks furious, like a bottle of shaken cola, about to bubble up and over. He stands, slowly.

'My apologies,' he says to us all. 'Luca will arrange to move your glasses and will no doubt bring us wine to make up for the inconvenience.' He looks pointedly to Luca. 'This was not the welcome I wanted for you. But please, come and seat yourselves. The food will be coming.' He holds out a hand towards the table at the back of the terrace. There is a slight shake in it, like he's furious but not letting it out.

'I still don't understand why the other party can't sit at the table back there,' I say to Lennie.

'Let's just move, Zeld. We're new. We want to fit in,' he says, guiding me by the elbow, clearly wanting to keep me from starting an argument. He knows me of old. I've never been very good at biting my tongue. That's the great thing about Lennie and me: we know everything about each other. We've had fun playing the field – well, we've served our time, let's say – and now we're ready to settle down. It's like life had a natural path for us.

He steers me towards the table. As he does, I glare at the party taking our place. The man in the suit shrugs a coat from his shoulders and hands it to Luca, who takes it and hangs it up. I catch the man's eye and glare at him. He slowly pulls his sunglasses down his nose and glares right back at me, making my hackles rise further. Then he moves deliberately round the table and sits in my seat, giving me a single nod as if to thank me for doing as I was told. My head feels hot, I'm so outraged. How rude! He doesn't even take his hat off; just removes his jacket to reveal a waistcoat straining over his pot belly.

Luca moves effortlessly around the table, kissing each of the men and women on both cheeks, handing out menus, collecting more coats. The women are wearing red lipstick, tight-fitting dresses and big sunglasses, and have bags of sass. The younger one looks very pleased to see Luca and grabs his face and plants a lascivious kiss on his lips.

As we settle into our seats, he comes over to take our orders. Giuseppe chooses antipasti for us all, then pasta with lemon and garlic for himself, followed by porchetta. Luca nods and tells him it's a good choice. At least I think that's what he says; my Italian is pretty basic. He makes his way round the table. Most people order pizza, though Lennie follows Giuseppe's lead and Luca smiles approvingly.

Then, taking the menu from Lennie, he comes to stand by me. Right by me! I can smell him again, that aftershave making my nerve endings stand to attention.

'I'll have a pizza margarita,' I go to say, but once again my tongue ties itself in knots, so I point at the menu. He leans over me to confirm my choice, and I get a glimpse of a tiny tuft of chest hair at the top of his shirt. I feel like I've touched burning hot coals. I'm light-headed all over again and reach for my water, nearly head-butting his white-sleeved arm.

He moves off and I sip my water, several quick sips.

When he emerges from the kitchen again, he is carrying two big wooden boards. He lays them down along the table and all of us take a moment to stare. On the boards are triangles of smooth cream-coloured cheese, bowls of glistening olives with capers and tiny cubes of raw carrot, mounds of thinly sliced *prosciutto crudo* and small glass bowls of chutney and some sort of amber liquid.

Tabitha takes an olive and turns to me. 'It's Zelda and Lennie, isn't it?' she asks with a slightly odd smile at the corners of her mouth that makes me think it doesn't quite reach her eyes. She sips at the white wine Giuseppe has just poured from a jug.

'That's right.' I smile and smooth down the white napkin on my lap.

'And you're together?' she asks brightly.

'Yes,' Lennie and I say at the same time. He puts his hand on mine in my lap and we turn to each other and smile, reassuring each other that we've made the right decision. I attempt to push any silly thoughts of an attractive Sicilian restaurateur out of my mind.

'Oh, I didn't realise,' says Sherise, reaching out to help herself to bread from the baskets Luca has placed at either end of the table. She rips it in two, putting half on her husband's plate, but he doesn't seem interested in it. He looks like all the wind has been taken out of his sails. 'I thought you were just friends,' she says with a smile, and there isn't a hint of malice there, just interest. But inside, I can feel a bubble of panic.

My mouth goes dry. How would she know? Let's change the subject, I think.

'The farmhouse, Il Limoneto, is lovely. Has it been in your family a long time, Giuseppe?' I smile politely.

'Well that's the thing,' Sherise continues. 'When we got to the farmhouse, I couldn't work it out, because when I took our bags upstairs . . .'

I suddenly catch my breath, feeling like we've been caught out trying to pull a fast one. I know what she's going to say. I feel like I'm in a speeding car, and the brakes have failed.

'. . . I noticed you two were in separate rooms.' She pops a piece of bread into her mouth and looks at me with interest.

'Really?' Tabitha's eyebrows shoot up over her sunglasses.

Lennie and I both look at Giuseppe, and I know exactly what Lennie's thinking. We put on our application that we were a couple. Couples were given the option of a bigger house, especially a couple who might want a family, and were offered a larger relocation fee. What if Giuseppe thinks we're trying to scam him?

I go to speak, not sure what I'm going to say, but Lennie tightens his grip on my hand and stops me.

'We are a couple,' he says, and then he looks at me and back at the table and takes a deep breath. 'An engaged couple actually.'

A little voice inside me squeaks, 'Engaged? I'm only just adjusting to the idea of us being together. We haven't even . . . y'know, got down to the bed business yet!' I find my eyes flicking up to Luca again, and feel myself blushing. I have no idea why. I have never even had a conversation with this man. My head is like cotton wool. I just got engaged! Slightly unconventionally, but I think that's what's happened.

I look down at my bare ring finger and hide it under the napkin on my lap.

'Yes, engaged.' I back Lennie up and attempt a huge smile, swallowing hard.

'So why the separate rooms?' Sherise puts another piece of bread into her mouth. I reach for the basket and try to do the same. Act naturally, I tell myself.

'Well . . .' I begin. I'm planning to tell them it was just a mistake: I thought we were in one room while Lennie assumed it was the other when we dropped off our bags. But before I can continue, Lennie interrupts, clearly not trusting my runaway mouth to sort this out.

'We're waiting,' he says.

'Waiting?!' Tabitha practically shrieks. And all eyes are suddenly on us. Oh God, he's not going to say what I think he's going to say, is he? My heart starts pounding.

'For the wedding!' he announces with a broad smile. Ever the salesman, he's beaming, selling his captive audience the dream. 'Here! We wanted to marry in our new home, here in Sicily!'

There is a moment of silence as I process the information, as does everyone else around the table. Either they're surprised by such an old-fashioned view, or else they just don't believe him. I'm holding my breath. Then . . .

'Oh bravo!' Giuseppe is on his feet, clasping his hands together. 'A wedding! I am so happy! You have no idea how happy this makes me. The town needs a wedding. All we have are funerals. We need something to celebrate. Etna needs a wedding,' he says, and I'm so shocked by the sudden turn of events that I don't ask what he means. 'You are what this project is all about!'

He is round the table, kissing me on both cheeks, and Lennie too. 'The first wedding for our new Città d'Oro family! And then babies too!' His eyes are full of tears and he wipes at them, sniffing. 'This is why I wanted to create this project, to bring life back to the town, and you are doing that. *Grazie.*' He hugs us again, then turns to Luca and orders Prosecco with a big wave of his hand before getting out a big white hanky and dabbing at his face.

I stare, still in shock. Luca pours the drinks and starts handing them round.

'The thing is,' Giuseppe finally composes himself, 'I could only have dreamed of this. When I started the project, it was what I had hoped for, and now it is happening already. Right at the beginning. It is wonderful. We have been blessed.'

'What do you mean exactly, Giuseppe?' Tabitha picks up her glass, despite her fingers seemingly itching to check her phone. She's never off it!

Giuseppe takes a sip of his drink and dabs his face with his hanky again.

'There is a . . . tradition in the town, a . . . how you say? Supercilious?'

'Suspicion?' asks Barry, and glances at the party at the window table.

'Superstition?' I try. Giuseppe points at me and nods.

'Like a legend?' says Lennie.

'Of course. Excuse my English . . .' His English is way better than our Italian. He smiles and sips and carries on. 'It's not something I was going to mention – well, not straight away. Like I say, it's a superstition. But now we have this wonderful news, I feel I can tell you.'

We all lean in, intrigued.

'It is said that a wedding in the town every ten years will bring good luck. Mount Etna will bless us and Città d'Oro will prosper. If we do not have a wedding, Etna will be unhappy and . . . Well, we are nearly out of time. But now . . .' He throws up his hands. 'But now you are here and have brought good fortune back to the town.' He wells up all over again.

'Congratulations,' Luca says as he hands me a glass of Prosecco, his smile not quite as wide as before. My hand is shaking as I reach out and take it. Our fingers touch and I feel like I've been buzzed with an electric shock, so I whip the glass away, taking a huge gulp.

'A wedding! We are blessed!' Giuseppe throws up his arms with a look over to the other table. 'You hear that? Our town is going to have a wedding. Finally!'

The man in the hat gives a gentle nod but doesn't smile. None of the table do. In fact, I might be imagining it, but they seem to be positively glowering. What's wrong with them? This is exciting news. Most people would be happy and congratulating us. I would if a couple got engaged in a restaurant back home.

Engaged! I say the word to myself, then lean over to Lennie and whisper into his ear, 'Engaged, and now getting married?'

He suddenly looks solemn. The joking Lennie gone for a moment and a new, serious man in his place.

'That is okay, isn't it? It's what we were planning – the whole marriage, family, together-forever thing,' he whispers back, looking at me earnestly.

'You could have warned me!' I try and joke.

'Sorry. Maybe your impulsive behaviour is catching,' he jokes back. 'But you are cool with it, aren't you?'

I see Tabitha typing on her phone. She shoves it away quickly when she catches me looking, and raises a smile and a glass to me. I wonder if our news is spreading across social media already. Though why would her friends and family be interested? But then I suppose she's here on her own, and I know how that feels. I'm the lucky one.

I glance at Luca and get that jolt again, and it shocks me. I look back at Lennie and focus on his face.

'Absolutely!' I confirm with a nod and a broadening smile. 'As long as that means I get to plan a vintage wedding.'

'I wouldn't expect anything less.' He laughs, and so do I.

'And as long as that bloke with the sour face isn't on the guest list.' I nod to the other table, and raise my glass to the man in the hat. He still doesn't react. Just carries on chewing his wasp.

Focusing on my own wedding is exactly what will stop any silly thoughts about attractive Sicilian restaurateurs. I'm getting married, I tell myself, still feeling a little stunned, and take another swig of Prosecco. But my treacherous eyes are inexplicably drawn back to Luca, like some uncontrollable attraction.

A younger me would have said that my reaction to him was love at first sight. Ha! That would be ironic. I've been waiting all these years for a man I want to settle down with to come along, then, like buses, two come along at once. But that's where I've been getting it wrong. I know now that instant attraction doesn't last. I want a forever partnership, something solid. I want to marry Lennie. It's just come as a bit of a shock.

Tabitha stands up and snaps a photograph of the two of us and says, 'Congratulations! Okay if I post it on my Facebook page?' And I can't help feeling slightly odd that the world is starting to hear my news before I've even had a chance to get used to it myself.

Chapter Eight

'Please, everyone, enjoy.'

Giuseppe holds out his hands and we dive in, hunger and tiredness suddenly needing to be fed. I can feel the table next to us watching us, but I'm too focused on the soft, melt-in-the-mouth ham to be bothered by them. I take a triangle of cheese, clashing hands with Lennie as we both reach in and laugh. I dip it in the amber liquid as Giuseppe is showing me from his end of the table, and then put it in my mouth. Oh my God! It's honey, warm honey, with just a hint of citrus, coating the sharp, tangy cheese, satisfying every corner of my taste buds. It's probably the most amazing thing I've ever tasted, the ultimate marriage made in heaven.

It's a sign, I think, a brilliant sign . . . Like me and Lennie, not a couple you would automatically put together, but when you do, they work beautifully and effortlessly in tandem. More people need to know about this.

I take another piece of cheese and dip it into the other bowl: a sweet, soft onion marmalade, Giuseppe tells me, and again, a wonderful pairing. But my heart is with the honey and cheese.

We drink red wine from the vines on Mount Etna, poured from terracotta jugs. Giuseppe and Lennie have their pasta course, and I'm impressed by Lennie's stamina as he attempts to embrace Sicilian eating culture.

'Where do you put it all?' I ask him.

'It all goes to my legs. That's why they're so long.' He sucks in a long string of spaghetti coated with pine nuts, lemon juice and Parmesan.

'Good fork work. You're a local already!' Giuseppe tells him.

Lennie lets the pasta smack around his mouth, and the sauce makes his lips glisten. Again I wonder what it will be like to kiss those lips. Lemony is all that comes to mind at the moment.

Our pizzas arrive. Huge and thin, with tiny bits of charring at the edges where they've been pulled from the wood-fired *forno*. It is possibly one of the best pizzas I've ever eaten, I think, as I finally forgive Luca for making us move tables, and fall in love with the restaurant all over again. I look over at the other party. They are all focused on their plates of pasta and the serious business of eating.

Lennie has beautiful pork in a light sauce with green beans and potatoes cooked *al forno*. I have a taste, and he tastes my pizza, just as we've always done.

After the main course, those more valiant than me have ice cream. But I'm too full.

Then Luca arrives at our table with small glasses and two bottles.

'Limoncello and crema limoncello!' he announces, and moves around the table filling the glasses with either the clear lemon-scented drink or the creamy version.

'Oh, lovely, is it home-made?' Sherise asks.

'Sadly no,' he shrugs. 'Our lemon orchards have seen better days.' He glances at the table by the window and then away again, and I find my eyes following his and narrowing.

'A toast,' says Giuseppe. 'To welcome you all. To the success of our relocation project.' He looks at me and Lennie. 'And to a wedding here in Città d'Oro. A real celebration!' He lifts his glass. 'In three months, when you decide to stay, and become official residents? Yes?'

Three months?! I practically choke. But we all raise our glasses and cheer. I sip the strong limoncello and swallow, my mind full of the evening's developments. My wedding. Just before my fortieth birthday. Finally I'm going to have something to show for my life. I swallow again, and look at Lennie. Then briefly at Luca, and my stomach flips over and back again. I don't need stomach flick-flacks; I need to build a future with someone, and that's exactly what I'm doing.

'To us, and to the wedding. *Saluti*,' I say, and sip again. I really am getting married.

When we have all finished, Giuseppe pays the bill, then turns and nods to the man in the hat. '*Buonasera*, Romano.'

Romano nods in response, as do the rest of his table, then he looks at me, and once again I hold his stare.

'*Buonasera*,' I say, fuelled by limoncello. 'I hope you enjoyed your table and your meal,' and Lennie once again has me by the elbow and is guiding me out before my runaway mouth gets the better of me.

Later, I lie in bed listening to . . . well, nothing, apart from what I think might be Barry's snoring next door. Lennie is sleeping in one of the bedrooms in the converted barn across the courtyard, and I find I'm relieved not to have to worry about us sharing a bed tonight.

I think about our housemates, and the *Big Brother* voice-over comes into my head: 'End of day one in the *Big Brother* house!' How did we all end up here? I wonder. How is the town going to take to us arriving? If tonight's other diners are anything to go by, not very warmly. But Giuseppe seems determined that we should stay.

Hopefully tomorrow we can have a look at our houses. I'm dying to get stuck in. I want to start making a home for me and Lennie. Our home. Because, I think, I'm getting married. I let the fact sit in my brain, like the honey and cheese melting on my tongue earlier, enjoying the delicious sensation, and a smile spreads across my face. I've finally stepped out of the last-chance saloon and into the sunlight.

But as I fall asleep, it's not Lennie's face I see; it's a stranger called Luca. A forbidden fruit; a very dangerous fruit indeed.

Chapter Nine

The next morning, it's like I've woken up in the Albert Hall with a live concert going on around me. But I'm not at a concert. I'm in Sicily, with the sun creeping through the shutters along with a deafening dawn chorus. I stand up and go to the window, push open the shutters and stand and stare . . .

There's a knock at the door. It's Lennie, with bed hair, as always, carrying two cups.

'One weak coffee, for the lightweights amongst us!' he jokes, handing me one of them. He knows just how I like my coffee.

We stand by the window and stare at the neglected lemon grove and the birds flying in and out of the wild flowers between the trees. A butterfly flutters right past us.

'I can't help but wonder why no one's looking after this lemon grove,' I say. 'Or any of the lemon groves for that matter.'

Lennie shrugs. 'Maybe there just aren't enough people. I mean, we've hardly seen anyone. That's why we're here, isn't it? We are the young people!' And we both laugh.

'The young engaged couple!' I say, then think I should follow it up with something and slide my arm tentatively around his waist. It feels a bit odd, so I tilt my head and lean it against his arm, as I do when we sit next to each other on the settee watching old films. It feels affectionate rather than . . . sexy. He turns and slings an arm around my shoulder, moving us away from the uncharted territory of physical intimacy and back into best-mates zone.

'So what are we going to do today?' he asks.

'I thought maybe we could try and get into our house.' I lift my head and look at him excitedly. 'We could make a start on what needs doing.' I drop my arm from around his waist and sip my coffee.

'Good idea. The sooner we can make it habitable, the sooner we can be out of here.' He nods to the door. 'Barry was telling us about his time working as a postman.' There's a smile on his lips. Not unkind, because Lennie isn't like that; he's just a tease. 'And we can start thinking about work. We should get our first payments from Giuseppe, which will tide us over, but I thought I'd ask around. See if anyone needs any help. I don't mind what I do. I'd quite like to be outside.'

I think about the town and its empty shops. The lack of business opportunities.

'It's going to be okay, isn't it, Lennie?' I ask suddenly, looking up at Mount Etna. 'We have made the right decision?'

'We certainly have,' he says, pulling me to him and kissing my hair. I lean against him and rest my head on his chest. I hope he's right, I really do.

'Here they are, the lovebirds!' smiles Sherise. 'You don't fool me with your separate-rooms story!' she laughs, waving a spatula at us. She's wearing a frilly apron and cooking what looks to be a full English. 'I always like to make Billy a fry-up,' she tells us.

Lennie slips his arm around my shoulder and smiles. Sherise serves up the bacon and eggs.

'I get my sister to send us bacon,' she says through the smoke, 'wherever we are. Picked up these eggs on our way from the mainland. Wrapped them in a woolly hat.'

'A woolly hat?' says Barry, and Ralph stops checking his phone and looks up.

'Oh, we've been travelling for months now. Working here and there, moving on, haven't we, Billy?'

Billy nods and looks at the plate of food, but doesn't pick up his knife and fork.

'What kind of work?' Ralph finally speaks.

'Mainly caretaking, housekeeping and gardening, general maintenance. We've been staying in France, looking after a big house there. *Gardiennage*, they call it.'

'Sounds amazing,' I say.

'Oh, it was,' she looks at her husband. 'He's a bit fed up. We thought this project . . . well, that we might be able to put down some roots finally. But after seeing the houses yesterday, I don't think it's going to work out for us.'

'Maybe once they get them repaired, with a bit of paint . . .' I try and enthuse.

'It's not that. Billy was hoping for a bit of land. Keep some animals, settle down to what he knows.'

'What's that then?' asks Tabitha, eyeing up the bowl of oranges.

'We were dairy farmers in the UK. Billy's born and bred into it. His father and his grandfather's farm before that. But,' Sherise shrugs, and I can see the pain etched on their faces all of a sudden, 'when the prices dropped, there was nothing more we could do. Supermarkets were bringing in milk from all over. It was costing us more to keep the cows than we were making from selling the milk.'

She turns and clears away the pan she's been using.

I remember staying on a farm once when I was in the children's home. I was terrified. The cows were huge. But it was incredible how even some of the more disruptive kids got stuck in and seemed to find their place with the responsibility that being around the animals brought. It wasn't the animals that did it for me. Something about being outside just made me feel, well, a lot happier. My brain seemed to work better when I was active. Going back to the classroom after that was a big adjustment, and not one I managed very well, I'm embarrassed to admit as I think back.

'What happened to the cows? You sold them?' Tabitha asks, intrigued, and I think I may have misjudged her. She's clearly interested in Sherise and Billy's lives.

Sherise shakes her head, then turns back and places a hand on Billy's shoulder.

'No buyers.'

'Slaughtered?' asks Ralph, quickly and to the point.

Sherise nods her head slowly. 'There didn't seem much point staying on. So we gave up the tenancy and started travelling.' She brightens, clearly trying to jolly her husband along. 'We've loved it. Been all over.' She starts drying the pan vigorously.

Billy's shoulders drop, and he pushes the plate of food away from him.

'Er, if you're not going to eat that, I could help you out,' says Barry. Billy nods, and Barry pulls the plate towards himself and tucks in.

'This could be great for you then?' I say brightly.

'Not really,' Sherise says. 'As I mentioned, we'd hoped to get some land, keep some animals, but from what Giuseppe was saying yesterday, that doesn't sound possible.'

I feel for them. Looks like their hopes and dreams have been smashed before we've even started. There must be a way to help them.

'I think we should all go and look at the houses, see if we can make a start. We can make sure you get the biggest garden,' I say.

'Thank you.' Sherise smiles, but I'm not sure either of them is convinced they've done the right thing by coming here.

'What about you, Ralph? What brings you to Sicily?' Tabitha asks, and once again I'm not sure if she's being a bit too forward and nosy or just interested. But I'm happy to give her the benefit of the doubt. All the time she's asking other people about why they're here, at least I'm not having to talk about Lennie and me.

Ralph looks around at us all. I get the impression the spotlight is the last place he wants to be in right now.

'I left the army. Went into the City. Let's just say I needed to be as far away from the City as possible. Thought this might be the place.'

'Burnt out?' says Barry, nodding and finishing the eggs and bacon.

'Burnt, certainly,' Ralph says into his coffee cup, making it clear he doesn't want to talk any more.

We fall into silence. I'm not great with silence. And Tabitha seems to really be making an effort to get us to find out about each other.

'I had a shop,' I find myself blurting out, attempting to fill the awkward void. 'It was my dream. Everything I'd ever wanted. Had a flat with a balcony overlooking the high street. I loved the buzz I got from it. Then the rates went up and I couldn't afford it any more. I ended up working in a department store.' I feel like I'm baring my soul. Telling my life story to strangers. At least I haven't told them I grew up in a children's home, or that if Valerie hadn't stepped in that day, who knows where I might have ended up. A lot like my mother, I expect. 'So,' I try and move things along, 'I'm hoping to open a shop here, and do online stuff. Set up a website. A vintage treasures kind of place.'

'There should be loads of those around here,' says Barry. 'You could offer to do house clearances.'

'Oh, I don't want people to think I'm here to benefit from an ageing community!' I say in horror.

Thankfully, Lennie steps in and smoothly changes the subject. 'And I'm just looking for work. I was an estate agent, but I'll do anything. Maybe something that will help the community.'

'Lots of empty houses here,' says Tabitha, who appears to be tapping on her phone again. 'You could try and sell them?'

'The thing is, there's nothing to come here for. People don't want to just buy a house, they want the area.' Lennie slips into estate-agent mode. 'As beautiful as this place is, there's a reason they're practically giving the houses away to people like us.'

'People like us . . .' Tabitha looks up and around at the group. 'All here looking for a fresh start,' she says quietly, her eyes darting between us.

'A new opportunity,' Ralph corrects her, pushing back his shoulders.

'Yes, of course, that's what I meant,' she says, and returns to typing on her phone.

Lennie turns to Barry, who is using a piece of bread to wipe up the egg yolk on his plate.

'Barry?' he asks. 'What are you hoping to do here?'

'Well, I don't really know . . . Maybe find a wife?'

'Have you not been married before?' Sherise asks.

'Oh yes. Three times. Each one ended up a disaster. I worked as a postie all my life. When I was made redundant, my last wife divorced me, saying I got under her feet. I didn't have anywhere to live. Couldn't afford to buy. Bloody estate agents.' He looks at Lennie, and for a moment I wonder if there's going to be an atmosphere, but then they both smile and laugh good-naturedly and I find myself smiling too. 'So I thought, why not? Let's see what life in Sicily's got to offer. It's more than I've got back home. I've been sleeping on my daughter's sofa. I think she was glad to see the back of me.'

I look at Tabitha, still staring at her phone, reminding me of myself before I left, waiting for messages that I thought would change my life.

'What about you, Tabitha? What are you doing here?'

She looks up. 'I'm actually here . . . well, because I want to finish the novel I've been trying to write. I have writer's block and I thought that living somewhere like this would inspire me.'

'Wow! That's brilliant!' I say, impressed.

There's a lull in the conversation. Everyone has pretty much explained what they're doing here, and we seem to have run out of things to say.

'Well,' I say at last. 'I think we should go and see how the

69

houses are coming on. Giuseppe said work was going to start. We could offer to help out. I'm okay with a paintbrush.'

'And I can do bricklaying,' says Lennie. I remember that he spent a summer in his twenties working for a local builder.

'I'm all right at DIY,' says Barry, grabbing his belt and pulling it up over his tummy.

'Gardening for me and Billy,' pipes up Sherise with positivity.

'I can just pitch in where I'm told to. Good at taking orders,' says Ralph matter-of-factly.

'I just have some emails to send first.' Tabitha shows her white teeth.

'Instead of searching for inspiration, you seem to be constantly searching for phone signal,' says Barry, echoing what we're all thinking, and we laugh. I feel a sense of relief. Maybe it isn't going to be so bad staying here with these people. They seem nice. We're getting along.

All in agreement, we set out for town like Robin Hood and his band of assorted merry men. Mount Etna has a really smoky top to her this morning, I notice. The white cloud, like a collar around her neck, seems to have doubled since yesterday, and there's a steady stream of vapour rising up like wisps of hair from her head. She looks like an old woman with troubles on her mind.

There's a strange mood in the air, a feeling of worry, which stays with us as we walk into the silent, empty town. The occasional twitch of a net curtain or the squeak of a shutter suggests that there are people around, but they're not coming out to welcome us. The sooner we get into the houses, the sooner the locals can get to know us and we can start our new lives.

Chapter Ten

Turning off the main road towards the street of houses, expecting to see a team of builders working in the early-morning sun, pulling out all the stops, grateful for any help on offer, we stop and stare. There is no one there. No one at all. The houses are as quiet and empty and sad as they were yesterday.

We walk slowly towards the first house, our previously high spirits now dragging behind us. It has broken and listing shutters on the upper floor, over a crumbling balcony. I reach out and try the front door, but it's locked. Not to be put off, I try the next house down, which is in a similar condition. But that's locked too. I rub at the dirty window and try to see inside.

'If we can just get in, at least we can see what needs to be done,' I say determinedly. I'm like this once I get an idea in my head. I find it hard not to see it through, whether it was winning an argument when I was a teenager, or determinedly learning to read when teachers despaired. Some, like Valerie, might call it single-mindedness. Others, like the care assistants in the home I grew up in, would use the word 'stubborn'. One thing I am determined about is that I don't want my life to be as chaotic as my mum's. I don't want to be the mess she ended up. That's why making my future with Lennie is the right thing to do. Maybe her life might have been different if she'd met the right person, who knows?

Things changed for me the moment Valerie scooped me up and took me home. I saw a different way of living then. A warm, inviting one. Not like the rules and regulations and wariness I felt at the children's home. Always on my guard. Never trusting anyone. Life at Valerie's was ordered, but happy, and safe. That's what I want for my own family.

'There's plenty of us,' I continue. 'If we concentrate on one house at a time, we could get loads done, and then the builders can do the jobs we can't fix.'

'Good idea,' they all agree.

'I've been a cleaner all my life!' says Sherise, putting down the bucket she's brought with her from the farmhouse full of rubber gloves, cleaning fluids and cloths. 'Billy worked the farm, I cleaned at the school. Cleaning I can do, eh, Billy? Especially if it's for us.'

He smiles affectionately at her, but there's a sadness in those saggy blue eyes. I can tell he still hasn't come round to the idea of staying here if he doesn't think he's going to get any land.

'The sooner we get in, the sooner we don't have to listen to Barry's snoring,' Ralph says drily, and we all look at him and then realise he's making a joke, as he releases his first, small smile.

'Ah, Barry, it's a sweet noise,' I say.

'My last wife said it was like a warthog.' Barry hooks his thumbs into his belt and kicks at a loose stone on the ground as we all laugh.

'Right, let's try and find a way in,' I say, buoyed up once more and feeling like we can achieve anything together.

'On it,' says Ralph, scanning the buildings in what I assume is a military fashion.

Sherise and I practically clap our hands together in excitement. Our houses might not have been ready for us, but with a bit of 'can do' attitude, we're going to make this happen!

By the looks of it, Ralph has spotted a window with a broken catch on the first floor of the last house, and starts to look for a way to climb up to it.

'Billy, can you just give me a leg-up here?'

Billy moves in to help, and as Ralph starts to scale the wall, we all cheer and clap.

'It's like watching Spider Man!' says Sherise.

'Hey!' A deep voice stops us in our tracks, making me jump. 'Hey!! *Stàtivi! Arresto!* Stop, you all!'

We turn to see a tanned bear of a man in a tight-fitting T-shirt showing off his washboard stomach under a worn leather jacket. He holds up a hand and walks towards us. A huge hand, the size of a shovel. Ralph jumps down from the wall and nods warily.

'Hopefully he'll have the keys,' Lennie says brightly, pointing out the obvious, which I hadn't thought of. He always seems to manage to find the positives, like all the reasons we should come out here for starters, and why we should stop chasing after Mr and Ms Right and realise what's been under our noses all along.

'Hopefully,' says Ralph, brushing dust from his trousers.

I shield my eyes from the bright sun as the man mountain marches towards us.

'*Buongiorno*,' I attempt in my best Italian. '*Parla inglese?*'

But instead of smiling and holding out keys, he seems to be shaking his head and waving a finger in admonishment.

'*Ah, Inglese*,' he says, as if we've told him we're from a well-known gang of troublemakers. He wags his finger some more.

'We've just moved here,' I explain, in case he thinks we're tourists. 'These are going to be our houses. The mayor, Giuseppe, has sorted it. We're from the relocation project.'

'We wanted to get in and start work on them,' says Lennie politely, stepping in and taking control of the situation. Just like that time I got caught buying a child's train ticket when we were on our way to a gig, and he managed to convince the guard not to fine me. And then convinced the bouncers at the venue that we were over eighteen and had had our ID stolen. Lennie seems to have a way with people. 'I'm Lennie,' he says, holding out his hand, which hasn't got even a hint of a shake in it, I notice.

'Matteo,' says the man mountain. Having shaken hands with Lennie, holding eye contact for several seconds, he turns to the rest of us and we all introduce ourselves. 'Matteo,' he says again. 'Or if you cannot manage it, Matt,' he adds without a hint of humour.

'So, Matteo.' Lennie takes the lead again, and I'm happy to let him. He seems to be doing okay so far. 'Are you the builder?'

'*Siiii.*' Matteo draws out the word. 'I am the builder.'

'Great, so if you could let us in, or give us the keys, we can start helping you out.'

Matteo smiles as he understands, then his face drops, '*Non! M'av'a scusari.* Sorry. *Non possibile.*'

'What? You don't have the keys on you? We can wait.' Lennie looks around at us and we all agree.

'No, not keys. Sorry. You cannot have access to these properties.'

I can't bite my tongue. 'Why not?' I cut in.

'It's not safe,' he says sternly.

'Well, they need a bit of tarting up, I grant you, but we're all happy to pitch in and help out,' I say, looking at the crumbling balcony above and imagining what the view must be like from there.

'No, sorry. You cannot get in until the work is done. It's not safe,' he repeats, and part of me feels like there's some sort of veiled threat in there. 'I am looking after the buildings. Guarding them until I am told to start work.'

'But Giuseppe says that the work is all in hand.'

'There has been . . . a problem. A delay. Other jobs have come in.'

'In that case, let us in and we'll make a start!' I'm getting frustrated now.

Lennie puts his arm around my shoulders.

'Look, Matteo – Matt – if there's anything we can do to, y'know, find a way for you to maybe leave a door open . . . ?' he says quietly.

Frankly, I'm impressed. Bribery! Why didn't I think of that? I could kiss Lennie; in fact, I should definitely kiss him soon. If we're going to be married, we need to get over this hurdle and move on from being the best of friends to being, well, lovers.

Matteo looks at him. '*Non*, sorry,' he says flatly, and all thoughts of kissing fall away onto the worn, cobbled street. 'These houses are locked until . . . until work can begin. Their owner would be very unhappy with me if I was to let anything happen here.'

I let out a long, slow sigh. 'I suppose we'd better find Giuseppe.'

'Are you sure, Matteo?' Lennie tries one last time.

Matteo shrugs. 'Sorry, but I have to do as I'm instructed. My livelihood is at stake here. I rely on him for work.' He holds out his big shovel hands. 'But welcome to Città d'Oro,' he says with a genuine smile.

As we walk dejectedly away, I turn back and look at the row of little houses, then up at the road above and the big red villa there. I could swear I see the figure of a man, in dark glasses and wide-brimmed hat, looking out over the terrace and then turning away as we leave. It makes me even more determined to get into our houses and start living the life we came here for.

When we reach the steps up to the town hall, we see Giuseppe walking towards us.

'Good morning, everybody. *Buongiorno!*' he cries.

'We've just been to see the houses. We met the builder. We can't get in. There's no work going on at all,' we all say at once.

'And then there's our relocation fees,' Tabitha pipes up. 'There's not a problem, is there? I could really do with paying my credit card bill.'

Giuseppe holds up his hands. 'No problem. Just a tiny delay. I am on my way to sort things now. I promise I will let you know. It will be soon . . .'

He straightens his tie and bids us farewell, and we watch him walk down the street. He stops at what looks like the bank, and an elderly man in a smart suit comes out, shakes his hand and welcomes him in.

'Come on, let's go and get something to eat. I'm starving,' says Lennie. The others all agree, and we make our way towards the town's only shop.

Inside, the dark-wood shelves are crammed with everyday essentials: oil and tinned foods, processed meat and packaged cheeses. Not what I was expecting at all. I hear the sound of a bird singing, and I strain my neck to peer over the shelves into a small, dark room, where the young girl I saw before is sitting on her haunches, a pen in one hand, writing in a book. She looks up, smiles and waves. I wave back warily, then turn to see the woman behind the high counter – presumably her mother – glowering at me. I scoop up some bread and cheese and cold meats and the best I can find of the salad, and let it all tumble onto the counter. Lennie adds a plastic bottle filled with wine from a barrel in the corner of the shop.

Five minutes later, we are back out on the street. I look down at the small amount of change in my hand.

'Let's hope our relocation fees come through soon!' I say.

Ahead of us, we see Giuseppe leaving the bank building. He's running his hand through his hair. I go to wave and call out to him. Lennie catches my arm before I can open my mouth.

'I'm sure he's sorting it out,' he smiles. 'Just relax. We're on Sicily time now, remember? It'll be fine, Zeld. Giuseppe looks like he's working it out.'

He's right. I do need to relax. I mustn't be in such a rush about everything. It will all get sorted. I'm going to be patient! I think. I'm going to adjust to Sicily time. As we turn to walk back to the farmhouse, I smile at Lennie, who smiles back at me, slinging his arm around my shoulders like he always does. It's all going to be okay.

Chapter Eleven

'It's been a week now, and there's still no sign of our relocation fee or any work starting on our houses!'

I'm standing in the big kitchen, looking at Lennie. Sherise is cooking bacon and eggs for Billy again. Barry is standing with his thumbs tucked into his belt, looking out over the lemon grove full of scarlet poppies and yellow wild fennel. Ralph is attempting to get online, apparently to check the City markets back home. It's feeling more and more like the *Big Brother* house as every day passes, to be honest. None of us know what to do with ourselves. Lennie is getting ready to go job-hunting, as he has done every day this week, only to come back empty-handed.

'Everywhere I go is either closed up, or they shut their doors when they see me coming, or they don't need any help.'

Everyone we meet is guarded and wary of us. No one wants to engage in conversation or make eye contact even. They hurry on past. Everyone in the house has moved to spending more time on their own, in their rooms, away from each other. The original bonhomie has gone and there's a nervous tension in the air.

I am really beginning to doubt Giuseppe, and wonder what we've done. Is this some sort of weird scam? Everyone is getting worried. Even Lennie and I are weird with each other, not knowing really how we should behave. He's trying hard to play the perfect fiancé, but without any physical contact. It feels like he's almost avoiding touching me now, and I just want us to be how we always were. And no, we haven't kissed yet, and I think that might be half the problem. It's like the elephant in the room. We need to try and move on in our relationship. We're supposed to be getting married!

The only one who seems to be getting anything done is Tabitha, typing away on her laptop in her room. At least her dreams are coming true here, I think with a tinge of envy.

'He said everything would be sorted out soon . . .' Even Sherise's optimism is getting low.

'Something doesn't feel right,' I agree, and I can't help but think back to the man in the restaurant with the sunglasses and hat, the man I was sure was looking out from the terrace when we were turned away from the houses.

'If I was weighing up the odds here, I'd say we'd backed a loser.' Ralph puts away his phone and joins in. 'Can't believe I didn't listen to my instincts.'

'Were you good? In the City?' Sherise asks.

'To a point,' Ralph says flatly. 'Until I wasn't and lost the lot.'

'Oh dear.' Sherise stops serving up eggs and bacon.

'My wife left me. I barely got to see the kids. Not that I was seeing them before with the hours I put in. I thought this was going to be a fresh start. Build a life in the sun where I could spend time with them if they came out on holiday. Looks like I've definitely lost my touch when it comes to backing winners.'

Tabitha has joined us at the kitchen table.

'I'm sure it's all fine,' Lennie says, and I love him for his positivity. 'Look, no one's lost any money here. It can't be a scam. We didn't put anything in.'

'No, but we have all been herded into a run-down farm-house in the middle of nowhere, surrounded by a load of neglected trees, with no transport. We can't find any jobs and we haven't even been given the chance to work on the houses we were promised. It feels a bit creepy,' says Barry. 'What if—'

'Okay, that's enough.' I try and stop him before his over-active imagination has us all starting to panic.

'Well, you hear stories, don't you? I mean, why are we all here? Because none of us has anywhere else to go, that's why. If we had options, we wouldn't have packed up our belong-ings and pinned our hopes on a news story and an online ad.'

'He's right.' Ralph joins in again. 'I can't go home because the papers are baying for my blood. Barry here is sleeping on his daughter's settee. Sherise and Billy have lost their liveli-hood. Same for you, Zelda. And Lennie clearly wants a fresh start too. We're all running from something.' Except Lennie I think. I can't imagine anything that Lennie is running from. He just seems to be running towards the adventure of mar-ried life. 'Even Tabitha couldn't do the work she wanted to do back home, and look at her now. Always typing.'

She looks up at us with her big blue eyes under perfect eyebrows.

'Yes, I think I've found all the inspiration I need here,' she says with a smile.

'What's your novel about?' Barry asks, going to look at her screen. She shuts it quickly.

'Pastures new.' She smiles again.

'All I'm saying is that Barry's right.' Ralph is pacing round the room now like a caged animal. 'Something's off. We were promised houses and a relocation fee when we got here, and we've ended up being shoved into a farmhouse in the middle of nowhere and forgotten about. I don't know about anyone else, but I'm not here on holiday. I don't have the money for that. I need to get working, find something to do . . . Right now, I'd take anything rather than this boredom.'

'Absolutely!' says Barry. Billy nods emphatically.

'We have to get into those houses,' Lennie says. 'At least get our relocation fees.'

Everyone murmurs in agreement.

I look around the room. The tension seems to be rising. And suddenly I can't be patient any more. It's like my energy levels just burst through a dam. 'Something has to be done!' I exclaim. 'One way or another, we need to know what's going on and when we can start living here, instead of just this . . . waiting. Let's go and find Giuseppe.'

As one, we head for the door, Billy's breakfast abandoned on the table, ignored and looking quite out of place; in many ways, exactly how we're all feeling.

Chapter Twelve

We march into town, despite the fact that it's hotter than when we first arrived just over a week ago. The wild flowers are bursting with life all around us. The streets, though, apart from the occasional car, are mostly dead. You can barely see Etna's top for the amount of cloud and smoke, and the hazy air seems heavier than ever.

'Tourists, by the looks of it,' Ralph says as a car whizzes through and out the other side of town.

'Heading for Etna, no doubt,' I add. Through the haze I can just make out the towns further up the mountain. There are vineyards up there too, and wine-tasting experiences. At its highest point, the black volcanic rock makes it looks more like a drive across the moon. The wind seems to be picking up, like there's a storm in the distance.

We walk along the main street, and the little girl comes out of the grocery shop and waves to us.

'Good morning,' she says in perfect English.

'Good morning.' I can't help but smile back, despite my anxiety.

'Where are you going? Can I come with you? Practise my English?' she beams, but her mother comes out, scowling, and ushers her back into the dark shop.

We turn and carry on walking, up the worn stone steps towards the big imposing church with its peeling white facade and idle rusting bell above the door, and the town hall beside it where Giuseppe has his office. The tall palm trees planted there sway in the gathering wind.

We try the office. But there's no one there. Nor at his house next door either. We look down the narrow, cobbled streets and the little alleyways.

'Maybe he's at the houses now. Our houses,' says Ralph.

'Or back at the farmhouse, looking for us,' suggests Sherise.

'He could be anywhere,' says Tabitha.

'Or maybe he's taken the money and left. Gone to find a new life of his own.' Barry articulates what we're all thinking.

We look at each other.

'That's that overactive imagination of yours,' Sherise says.

'Still, probably best we find him quickly.' Even Lennie sounds concerned. 'Let's split up.'

Sherise and Billy return to the farmhouse. Lennie goes round to the row of houses with Ralph. Barry searches the streets behind the main square with Tabitha, while I take the ones below it. As I pick my way down the cobbled path to the piazza, past the restaurant, I steal a glance, cross with myself for hoping Luca might be there, and wondering if I'll get a glimpse of him, but there's no one around – just as well, I think.

The wind is starting to whistle through the streets and the air is heavy, giving me a headache like a pressure on my brain. I pass people sitting in chairs in their doorways, watching as I go. I nod and smile. They nod back but don't smile; instead they just look confused by me.

'*Scusi*, have you seen Giuseppe, the mayor? *Il sindaco?*'

'*Non*,' they all say, looking at me like I have two heads.

I walk on, heading down the hill, in amongst the swoosh of swaying pine and palm trees, hoping to find someone who can say *sì*. I hear a voice and follow it.

'Hello? *Buongiorno?*' But there's no reply.

I see a gate in a stone arch, with initials engraved on it: 'F & A'. It's down some steps, and the land seems to drop away more steeply here. There's a barn at the top end and what look to be crates inside, neatly stacked.

I push open the gate and it bangs shut behind me in the wind. My head throbs.

'Hello? *Buongiorno?*' I say, looking around and feeling like Alice in Wonderland entering a different world, because here there's one big difference to the rest of Città d'Oro. Here the lemon trees are all looking lovely and healthy and cared for.

'Hey! Hi!' A voice interrupts my thoughts and makes me start. I glance around, but see no one. 'Up here!'

I look up to see Luca waving at me from a balcony, his thick hair ruffling in the wind. My heart flips over and back again, and I tell myself it's just the surprise of hearing a voice from nowhere.

'Come up. I'm making coffee,' he calls over the rustling lemon leaves, pointing to the wooden steps.

'Oh no, I just . . .' But he's gone inside.

I walk tentatively up the steps, head still feeling like some-one's squeezing my brain. I hold the railing firmly, but for a moment it feels like my whole world moves and shakes. I stand still and focus on the immaculate lemon grove.

'This place is amazing,' I say when I reach the top and the

open front door. I take a big breath of the heavy air and step in through the beaded curtain, which is rattling despite being tied back.

'*Grazie*,' says Luca, pointing to the table on the balcony, where his phone sits. That must have been the voice I heard. 'Come in, please, have a seat.' He carries out coffee and two cups.

'Oh, I really shouldn't stay. I'm looking for Giuseppe. The mayor. Have you seen him?'

Luca shakes his head. The sky is dark, thick and hazy, but it's warm, very warm.

'No, I haven't.' He puts the coffee on the table. 'Please,' he gestures to a seat again, and I have to say, it is lovely here, with the breeze coming in off the sea over the terraced lemon grove.

He looks at me, and we seem to just hold each other's gaze. There's something between us, but I don't know what it is. This man is being kind and welcoming, one of the few here who is.

'Are you okay?' he finally asks, tilting his head. 'Would you like some water?'

My head throbs. I'm not sure if it's all the concerns I have about us being here, the fact that I can't find Giuseppe, or the heavy air.

'Water would be great. Thank you,' I say, and he smiles and turns and goes into the kitchen.

Suddenly I feel my whole world move and shudder again. Like on the stairs, only this time worse. I grip the table, and the coffee cups rattle in their saucers. I hold the table tightly, and the wobbling seems to subside, just as Luca appears with a glass of water, looking worried. I don't know what's wrong with me.

I take the water and drink it down in one. He watches me, his eyes flicking out to the windy lemon grove and then back to me with concern.

'Are you okay?' he says again.

'Thank you,' I finally say, handing him the glass. 'Just . . . a weird feeling.'

'It happens sometimes.' He looks around the lemon grove again. Clearly he's used to people getting light-headed occasionally.

'Thank you again,' I say.

'*Grazie*,' he corrects me.

'*Grazie*,' I smile.

I watch as he pours the coffee. Perhaps he can help put some of my fears to rest, I think. Although he looks as if he has worries of his own as he concentrates on the cafetière.

'Luca?' I go to ask the questions crashing round my head.

'So, Zelda, isn't it?'

We both speak at the same time.

'You first.' He crosses his legs and sips at his coffee, holding it tightly I notice.

'I just wondered, um . . . How well do you know Giuseppe, the mayor?'

He puts down his coffee cup, and looks up at me.

'Very well. He's my uncle,' he says matter-of-factly.

'Oh.' I'm not sure what to ask next. I'm still feeling a little dizzy, and all my thoughts have jumbled up.

'He's a good man. He was married to my aunt. My father's

sister. I have known him all my life. He grew up here, as did my aunt. They were childhood sweethearts.'

'And your aunt?'

'She died. Ten years ago now.' He picks up his coffee cup again.

'You'd trust him then? You think this project to bring us here is genuine?'

'Oh yes, without a doubt. He wants new people here to bring the town back to life, to how it used to be.'

'Not like the sour-faced man in the restaurant our first night.' I give a grimace. 'Thank God we don't need to have anything to do with him. I don't know what his problem is, but clearly he's not happy about us being here, and frankly, I found him really rude.' I take a mouthful of coffee. 'There's something creepy about him too. He was watching us the other day from the terrace of a big red villa. I recognised him from that hat. I mean, who wears a hat in this heat?'

'Ah, the one in the hat. That would be my father,' says Luca.

I practically choke on the coffee.

'I'm so sorry! I always seem to do that. Open my big mouth without thinking.'

He throws his head back and laughs, showing off his long neck, and I watch his Adam's apple bob up and down.

'I'm sorry about that night,' he says, serious again. 'I had to move you. My father insists on . . . well, preferential treatment. It's always been that way round here.'

'And I'm sorry for what I said about him.'

He holds up a hand, a tiny smile lurking at the corner of his mouth.

'Please, there's nothing you can say about my family that I haven't heard already.'

I look out at the lemon grove, leaves and fruit waving in the wind.

'You have a beautiful place here.'

'Thank you. It was my grandfather's and grandmother's, my nonna. That's their initials on the gate. My grandfather wasn't from here; he was from the mainland. But when he met Nonna, he realised how much she loved this place and knew she would never leave. So he gave up his life on the mainland and came here to be a lemon farmer. He used to say, "No one ever became a lemon farmer for anything other than love."'

I want to ask him why his lemon grove is the only one I've seen tended, but my thoughts flip back to Giuseppe and the project, and Luca's father bullying us out of our seats at the restaurant.

'I'm taking it, then, that if your father likes preferential treatment, and that's how things have always been done, he's not keen on change.'

'Exactly,' says Luca, draining his coffee.

'And he's not keen on a whole load of new people coming in?' I suggest.

He takes a moment and then repeats, 'Exactly,' and the town's reluctance to welcome us is beginning to make sense.

'And I take it your father . . .' I try to pick my words as carefully as I can, 'has quite a lot of influence around here.'

Again, he takes a moment. 'He does.'

I'm thinking this might be the hold-up that Giuseppe was referring to. Is Luca's father making it difficult for him?

'And you? What do you think about us coming here?'

He smiles, and something like excitement ripples through me.

'I am delighted you are here.' His dark eyes sparkle as I look straight into them. 'As you can see, the town is dying on its feet. We need more people. My father likes to keep things the way they were, but that can't go on forever. We need change.'

I smile. 'I'm glad to hear it.' I finish my coffee.

'And it means my father will hopefully stop pushing me to marry my second cousin! The superstition says there must be a wedding every ten years, or Etna will be unhappy. Now you are here and getting married, I am off the hook!' he says, and for a moment I have no idea if he's joking or not. And then I remember the young woman in the restaurant kissing him on the lips.

'You're not serious?!' I blurt out.

'Totally,' he says, straight-faced.

'Your cousin?'

'My second cousin, Donatella,' he corrects.

'Was that the woman in the restaurant the other night?'

'Uh huh.' He nods. 'Round here, they like to keep everything in the family – money, business, even marriage. They trust no one, so they think it's safer that way.'

'But . . . I mean, surely . . .'

He shrugs. 'Like I say, it's how things are around here. If I had my way, things would be done very differently . . . But I just try and stay out of family affairs.'

For once, I'm lost for words. It's terrible that people should be forced to marry for all the wrong reasons . . . or the right reasons. My head starts to get confused as I think about my own marriage.

'I have to find Giuseppe. Ask him if everything is okay,' I say, standing and rattling my coffee cup in its saucer. 'Sorry.'

But Luca just smiles again. 'I think Giuseppe is probably praying right now . . . praying for a miracle,' he says with sadness and a shrug, looking out at the hazy, heavy sky. 'Like I say, my father is a powerful man.'

As if confirming all our worst fears. I knew it, something's not right. 'Praying . . . Of course, the church!' I turn to run down the steps from the apartment and back the way I came, the wind circling me as I go.

'Zelda?' He stops me in my tracks, and I turn. 'Please don't tell anyone you've been here. Don't mention . . . this.' He holds out his hands to the thriving lemon grove.

I nod. 'Of course, you have my word,' I say, too worried about Giuseppe and our future to ask why.

Chapter Thirteen

I arrive at the church, hot, sweaty and out of breath. I lift the heavy handle and push the big wooden door open with an effort. There at the front of the church, about three rows back, is a hunched figure. It doesn't look like Giuseppe, but something tells me it is. The smart suit. The way he rakes his fingers through his hair and then clasps his hands together and holds them to his forehead.

'Giuseppe! Here you are!' I step inside. My eyes can't help but be drawn to the ornate high ceiling. It's so cool in here, and quiet.

Giuseppe turns round, clearly surprised to see me. My footsteps echo like bullet shots as I hurry down the aisle.

'We've been worried about you,' I say. 'We went to your house, the town hall, everywhere.'

'*Buongiorno*, Zelda.' He stands and kisses me on each cheek, ever polite. His own cheeks, I notice, are damp. 'I'm sorry, I didn't mean to worry you.' He holds one hand over the other and wrings them together.

'What is it, Giuseppe? What's the matter?'

'It's . . .' He bites his lower lip and looks to the big statue of the Virgin Mary.

'Is it the builder, Matteo? Or Luca's father? I met Luca

when I was looking for you.' I remember not to say a word about the lemon grove. 'He told me about his father. Is he the reason we can't get into the houses? I'm sure we could work around him. Make him realise we're not here to force anyone out of business.'

'It's very good of you . . .' Giuseppe starts, and then swallows.

'Look, we all want to help with our houses. We're a gutsy bunch. We're happy to get stuck in as soon as Matteo gets the go-ahead. Sherise and Billy just want a bit of land to keep some animals. Lennie and Ralph are happy to find work outdoors. Barry, well, Barry doesn't mind what sort of job is on offer, but we're just not getting anywhere. We could do with your help, an introduction at the council offices or some businesses who might want workers. And of course, our relocation fees would help . . .' I raise a gentle enquiring eyebrow.

He says nothing. Drops his head. Then he takes a huge sigh and and stares straight at me.

'Believe me, that is exactly what I want to do. We need people to take the jobs that the older people round here can't do, like refuse collection, maintaining the roads and the buildings. We have already lost two people to falling balconies this year.' He sighs again.

'Great. Let's get going on it, then. We thought you'd done a runner with the relocation fund!' I joke.

But Giuseppe doesn't smile.

'I wanted to set up this project because more than anything I wanted to bring life back to Città d'Oro,' he says. 'I am tired of attending funerals. I want to celebrate a wedding, and a christening! As does Etna. You and Lennie answering the advert made my heart sing.'

I try to smile then. I want to celebrate me and Lennie as a little family too. I hope that if we keep at it, love will grow. We will make it happen. I hope with all my heart that it happens. The long, slow burn, instead of believing that there is such a thing as love at first sight, because there isn't. It isn't real. Whatever I felt when I met Luca the other night, and when I saw him again just now in the lemon grove, that's not love. It can't be. It's just . . . desire. A silly crush. And that's not being in it for the long haul. However attractive Luca is, I'm with Lennie and I'm happy about that. We're here, and this is our new beginning.

I sigh, glad to have found Giuseppe and that he hasn't run off with the relocation fund. We can get things started now.

'Right, maybe we should go and see the others,' I suggest. 'Let them know you're here and still really behind the project. For a moment there, we thought we were being taken for a ride!' I laugh a little too loudly, and it echoes hideously around the big domed ceiling.

Giuseppe looks at me. I smile back. This man has such a good heart, I can almost feel it from here. I want to give him what he wants, give something back. I want him to be at our wedding, just three months from now.

'Okay, let's go.' I turn and step out of the wooden pew, wondering if there is some kind of etiquette I should follow. I sort of nod at the altar, and bob in a curtsey, nearly tripping myself up.

'The thing is,' Giuseppe says as I right myself, blushing, 'like I say, I wanted this more than anything. You have come here, trusted me with your dreams of a new life. But . . .' he swallows, 'I'm sorry, Zelda. It isn't going to happen.'

'What? Of course it is! We're all still here. Still on board. No one is going anywhere. We want this to work. We've just been delayed, that's all. A setback. Let's go and talk to the others and get things moving before we all go stir crazy. The mood in the house is getting a little tense.' Just like in the town, I think. There is tension everywhere, crackling in the air, like the coming storm. I rub my temples to try and persuade my headache to leave.

He looks around the old church, almost as if he's seeing it for the last time.

'I'm sorry, Zelda,' he says again. 'It's over. The project is off. You'll all be going home. There is nothing more I can do.'

I feel like the rug has well and truly been pulled out from under my feet, and my knees buckle.

Chapter Fourteen

Back at the farmhouse, we're all gathered around the long wooden table. Billy and Sherise are sitting together. Tabitha is messaging on her phone. Giuseppe is at the end of the table, his hands clasped as if still in prayer, hoping for a last-minute miracle. Shutters upstairs are banging to and fro.

'So you see . . .' He swallows hard. The air is still thick and heavy, and there's a low rumbling that may well be Barry's empty stomach. My head feels really thick too, as if full of cotton wool, like a real tension headache taking grip. Because once Giuseppe has explained everything to the group, I have no idea what I'm going to do next. I look at Lennie. What *we're* going to do, I correct myself. Maybe this isn't our fate after all. Maybe the pact is just a silly romantic dream, like the rest of my dreams. I thought the answer had been right in front of me all the time, but clearly I was wrong.

'When I set up this project,' Giuseppe explains, 'I spent some time raising the funds for it to happen. I applied for grants and even sold off my own land so that you would have a sum of money when you got here, houses repaired for you to live in and a further payment if you decided to stay on in three months' time.'

We all nod in agreement. That's what we understood and agreed to.

'It was important that you fitted the criteria. In particular, couples looking to start a family here . . .' He looks at Lennie and me and I can feel all our hopes and dreams cracking in two. There is another rumble outside, the sky darkening further.

'The money was put in an account in the bank. But . . .' he looks around the table, big blue eyes sad, 'now it is gone. The account is empty. Or . . .' and this time I can almost see the red mist rising in front of his eyes, 'or maybe someone is stopping the funds from being released. It was money for the community, a fresh start. But I understand there is a new gymnasium being built, and I fear that the money may have been . . . redirected.' His hands are shaking now, despite his best efforts to hold them steady. I put my own hand on his shoulder.

'I have spent a lifetime trying to fight against this . . . bullying. For my town to be like it used to be, full of families, thriving and growing up here. But I fear it's too late. I have lost the battle, and now Città d'Oro will die, along with its last residents. And may those who made it happen rot in hell!' He puts his hands over his scrunched-up face.

Everyone is silent for a moment, his words hanging in the air. It's hot in here. I throw open the French doors and look out at the cloudy sky, shivering despite the heat and the heavy atmosphere both inside and out.

'So we're not getting our money, or anywhere to live?' Barry breaks the silence.

Giuseppe slides his hands down his long, sad face.

'No. I'm sorry. I cannot deliver what I promised you.' He looks like a broken man. 'I hate to let you down, to break my word to you all.'

I feel pretty sure Giuseppe is talking about Luca's father. His family. They've done this! And I suddenly feel a rush of anger. No matter how attractive Luca is, he's like all the other men I've found attractive in my life. They always let you down. That's why it's so important for Lennie and me to work things out, for us to have time to fall in love with each other – because we're meant to be together. We don't let each other down. Luca might have been all charm at the restaurant and earlier today, but his family have put us out on the streets.

'So what happens now?' Sherise asks.

'I'll organise flights home for you.' Giuseppe looks around at the fallen faces. 'Or onward, wherever you want to go. I will personally pay for them. This is my mistake. I should have . . . I shouldn't have trusted . . .' He stumbles over the words and holds his forehead, raking his hands through his hair again.

We all look at each other in disbelief. Tabitha sends another message on her phone, then glances up.

'Looks like we're back where we started.'

'That's okay for those of you who have somewhere to go,' says Sherise. 'All I wanted was a home of our own again.'

'And some livestock,' Billy adds. 'To be looking out for some animals again, *our* animals . . . a family again.'

'But there must be a way!' I say, frustrated.

'The money has gone. Matteo is being "persuaded" not to work on the houses. He has been offered work on the new gymnasium. There is no money to pay for your relocation, or the building work. It's over. The project is finished. I cannot make it work.' Giuseppe is a beaten man.

'So that's that then.' Barry stands up and pulls his jeans higher up his waist. 'Looks like there's nothing to be done.' He puts his hand on Ralph's shoulder, and Ralph drops his head.

We're a mixed bunch; we'd never have met or come together if it hadn't been for one thing: we were all looking for something, a second chance at life, to get it right, to get what we wanted. I feel the tears build in my eyes, hot and angry, as once again I feel the rug being swiftly and firmly pulled from under my feet . . . all of our feet.

Giuseppe stands. His chair scrapes along the terracotta floor.

'I'll organise flights, and then I'll make sure you get to the airport safely. I'm sorry,' he says again, and this time I step forward and hug him tightly, feeling his pain on our behalf and his own.

As I hug him, I hear the rumble again, only this time much louder. Giuseppe lifts his head and looks outside.

'Thunder,' Ralph tells us, as if briefing his troops.

'That's not thunder,' says Giuseppe, moving to the double doors and holding onto the handles firmly.

'What is it then?' asks Sherise.

Giuseppe looks up and into the distance. He raises a hand to his eyes and scans the skyline.

'That's Etna!'

'Etna? As in the volcanic mountain Etna?' Lennie's face drops and my blood runs cold. That wasn't a dizzy turn I had earlier, I realise. That was Etna rumbling. That was a tremor!

I grab his arm and he slips it around me, pulling me close to him for real this time.

'She's not happy, not happy at all,' murmurs Giuseppe.

And as we watch, orange lava spews into the sky, black ash begins to flutter and fall, and the rumbling gets angrier and louder, determined to be heard.

Chapter Fifteen

'No flights?!' Tabitha looks up suddenly from tapping on her phone. 'You're joking me!' She looks around at the group, gathered again at the kitchen table, but no one is joking. Her face falls further. Obviously she has made plans already and is mentally moving on. I look at her with a pang of envy. What it must be like to have options!

Giuseppe shakes his head as he peers out through the door. The wind has died but the sky is still really dark and the air is horrid, thick and hazy and full of black ash. No sunshine seems to be able to get through, despite it being very close and hot, like we're sitting in a sauna and there's no way out.

'I thought we were leaving today,' Tabitha says, glancing over at her huge silver case on wheels, packed and ready to go.

'Looks like Etna had other ideas,' Ralph says.

Thankfully, no one has been hurt. There have been reports of a few fires further up the mountain, but no villages have had to evacuate and none of the fires have taken hold. But Etna is a very real threat around these parts, and clearly everyone is feeling nervous.

'So when *will* we be leaving?' Tabitha looks agitated and frustrated at the delay. She's anxious to leave and clearly has somewhere to go.

I wish I felt the same, but I don't. My fabulous new life in the sun is over before it's even begun. I reach out and pick up a mandarin from the bowl that Giuseppe tells me he fills each morning from the trees in his garden. I peel it, the amazing citrus smell making me feel as though I've stepped out of a reviving shower. I'm trying to think what I'm . . . what *we're* going to do now.

I have nowhere to go back to, just Maureen's if she'll have me. And I am officially engaged now, even though we haven't actually . . . We're a couple, we're together, and that's what counts. But will we still be a couple if we go home? Somehow 'Lennie and Zelda get together and move to Sicily' seems so much more the story I want for my life, rather than 'Lennie and Zelda get together, go back to their old jobs and share a house with his mother'.

'Sorry, looks like you'll be staying, for a while. Just until the dust settles,' says Giuseppe 'All flights are grounded. Holidaymakers from other parts of the island are stranded. It's having a wide-reaching effect. So please, make yourselves at home.'

'But what are we going to do about money?' Barry says what we're all thinking.

'Yes, I was relying on my relocation fee,' says Ralph.

'And my credit card is maxed out,' says Tabitha. 'Always is these days.' And suddenly she doesn't look quite so bright and breezy.

'I . . .' Giuseppe tries to come up with an answer, but fails and shrugs in despair. 'I don't know what to do. This is all of my making. I brought you here. I feel so responsible. I will make sure you have enough to eat and drink. I have plenty of vegetables in my garden. You are most welcome to anything I have.'

The flights home for us all must have cleaned him out. He's clearly not a wealthy man. Only one family around here seems to be that, I think angrily. Luca's family!

'It's not your fault, Giuseppe!' I say, placing a hand on his shoulder. 'The idea was a brilliant one. We all wanted it. We all wanted to come and be part of this town and help bring it back to life.'

I look around. The others are staring at the floor, where presumably their spirits are. We were all looking for something. We're having to leave before we could find it.

'Look, we need to come up with a way of making some cash, just to get us through the next few days – maybe a week if the reports are right. We're here, in the sun; let's make the most of the time we have left and use the opportunity to work out what we're going to do next.'

Tabitha sighs loudly, like a teenager being told she can't go out.

'Anyone got any ideas? Any skills?' I look around. 'I mean, if I'd had a chance to get out and about, I could have maybe found some second-hand clothes at local markets and sold them online, posted them out.'

Giuseppe shakes his head. 'You can't get anything in or out of the island until the dust clears.'

'I could do cleaning, if anyone wants it?' pipes up Sherise.

'And actually, I'm not a bad cook,' says Ralph.

'Oh yes, and I can do a full English,' Sherise adds.

'I can . . .' Tabitha thinks hard but doesn't come up with

anything. 'I could try and write something about our plight, send for help.'

We all look at her.

'There are hundreds of people in the same boat,' says Barry. 'Holidaymakers, tourists, coach parties . . . we're all stuck here.'

'That's it!' I practically shout, scaring poor Billy.

'What is?' Barry asks. 'We try and leave by boat?'

I shake my head, a smile starting to grow across my face.

'We can't leave by boat. The flights from the mainland are still grounded. It's chaos everywhere. So . . .' I look around, 'like Barry said, there's hundreds of people stuck here. All needing somewhere to stay . . . somewhere not costing an arm and leg. Their holidays are over, they'll be spent out.'

'And?' says Ralph. 'If they haven't got money to spend, where's the business opportunity?'

'They need affordable bed and breakfast. Not villas for another week, or hotels. They need . . .' I hold my arms open, 'this!'

Everyone looks at me blankly.

'But . . . *we're* in this,' says Barry, slowly looking around the farmhouse.

'We could make space, clear a couple of rooms, stick them up on Airbnb. Tabitha, you could write a blurb about the setting, in a lemon grove.' I look out tentatively at the overgrown orchard surrounded by the vicious-looking electric fence. 'Ralph, you could do some costings, work out what we can charge and how much profit we could make.'

'Of course,' says Ralph.

'Sherise, fancy cleaning the rooms in the barn? There's two there; they don't even have to come into the farmhouse other than for dinner and breakfast.'

'Absolutely!' says Sherise.

'And Billy, perhaps some tidying up around the farmyard?'

'Oh yes, give me a broom and I'm happy!' He finally smiles.

'We can work out a menu. Make it all-inclusive and . . . well, get in the punters!' I smile, and suddenly everyone seems to brighten up.

'Just one thing,' says Lennie quietly. 'I'm in one of those outside rooms. Where am I going to sleep?'

'You can bunk in with me,' says Barry, taking a bite of an overstuffed sandwich he's made from the leftovers in the fridge, and giving a little burp at the same time.

'Er . . .' Lennie looks at me.

Sherise laughs. 'Oh, you two can share a room – none of this waiting-till-we're-married malarkey. No need for any pretence on our behalf.'

'Okay,' says Lennie.

I swallow. 'Yes, put your stuff in my room,' I tell him. It's not like we haven't shared before, I think, although granted, we were a lot younger then.

'Looks like Etna had the right idea,' says Sherise. 'Doesn't seem right, a young couple like you not being together.'

'Well, between you and me, Sherise, we didn't know how people would feel about it, what with this being a good Catholic country!' says Lennie, winking. Sherise giggles, and I swear her cheeks turn pink.

'Get in there with your lovely woman,' she says, and nudges

him. 'Enjoy life. Nice young couple like you shouldn't be staying apart.'

I swallow again. So, looks like things just moved on in our relationship whether we were expecting it or not. We're not waiting for the wedding night after all; Lennie is moving in with me, into my room and my bed, and I wish the butterflies would come.

I take a deep breath. 'Okay, let's get these rooms cleared out and put Il Limoneto up on Airbnb. People will need somewhere to stay asap.' I'm feeling as though I'm back in some sort of control of my life now. 'Tabitha, can you write a few words describing the place?'

'Sure thing. Words is what I do.'

'Maybe don't mention the electric fencing around the lemon grove. Make it sound lovely and . . . lemony,' I instruct.

'What am *I* going to do?' asks Barry.

'Well, you can help clear any heavy stuff to start with, and then . . .' The idea hits me. 'You could make signs, Barry, and go and put them up. People new to the area will never find us. They need proper signposting.'

'On it!' says Barry with a smile.

'Do you think you'll be able to find your way around okay?'

'I'm a postie. I'll find my way around no problem, and if not, I'll ask!'

I laugh.

'And Ralph, could you work out what would be a good price to charge that will still make us a bit of profit? And what we can spend on food to make an evening meal if they want one.'

'Absolutely.'

Everyone starts cracking on with their jobs. Giuseppe, looking all watery-eyed, hugs me.

'*Grazie*, Zelda,' he says.

'No problem, Giuseppe,' I tell him, and he climbs into his battered Fiat, still dabbing his tired eyes, and bumps and sways down the potholed drive.

Sherise pulls out a scarf from her pocket and tries to tie it like mine.

'Here, let me,' I say, and do it for her. 'And this,' I tell her, and hand her a red lipstick. She giggles. We look like matching fifties housewives.

Lennie is just finishing clearing out his stuff as we arrive at the barn room. Sweat beads are already forming across my brow, and my eyes are stinging in the hazy heat. The dust is making us all cough every now and again, catching in our throats.

'All done?' I ask croakily.

'All done,' he confirms, picking up his case, then he takes me quite by surprise by planting a peck on my lips. And actually, it was really quite nice, making me smile and feel, well, special.

'Oh, I love kissing!' Sherise says. 'Me and Billy used to kiss all the time. I don't think he's kissed me . . . well, since the cows went. Nothing's been right since the cows went.'

'Barry! Hang on,' says Lennie. 'I have just the thing for you!' He disappears into his room again and reappears through the French doors pushing . . . a bike! 'Da-nah!' He beams, and we all join him.

'Perfect!' says Barry. 'Brilliant! Haven't ridden one of these for years.' He takes the bike and swings his leg over. 'My round changed to a van ages ago. Took some of the joy out of the job for me. That and the collie at number sixty-four.' He starts to pedal, tentatively and slowly, and we all take a couple of steps back and watch him. Lennie comes to stand beside me.

'That's brilliant. Fancy you thinking of that!' I smile at him.

'I thought he might like to get back in the saddle, so to speak.' And we both manage a little laugh. 'There's loads of stuff in there, boxes as well as that bike. We'll have to clear it out if we're going to Airbnb it.'

'Best get started then!' I say, pulling on sunglasses to protect my stinging eyes, ready to get stuck into whatever needs doing. Barry is now riding steadily around the courtyard, creating patterns in the fallen black ash, while Tabitha films him and shouts words of encouragement.

'This is such a great plan, Zeld!' Lennie says. 'I knew you'd think of something. You always do. That's what I love about you!' He pulls me close and kisses the top of my head, then releases me.

I smile up at him. This is exactly how it's meant to be. Me and Lennie. A slow-burn love. It's always there, constant low heat. And that is exactly what I want from life. I just have no idea what will happen when the dust settles, quite literally, and we have to return to our old lives . . . but there's a lot of dust to get through and cleaned up first, that's for sure.

Chapter Sixteen

'We've got a booking!' shouts Tabitha from the house.

Sherise and I have moved out all the boxes that were stacked up in Lennie's room and are giving it a good clean, while Barry is tinkering with the bike in the open-sided barn, where there's an old minibus that looks like it's been parked there for years. He's also found some wood there for his signs.

'A booking!' she calls again, and we stop what we're doing as she arrives in the courtyard with her computer cradled in her arms. Barry abandons the bike, and Ralph comes out of the other bedroom wearing rubber gloves and a pinny with a frill around the edge that could well have been Giuseppe's mother's.

'Where did you get that?' I ask.

'It was in one of those boxes,' he says, and I suddenly experience a glimmer of excitement, but Tabitha's news is far more pressing.

'Look!' she says.

We all gather around the computer.

'They want both rooms!' says Sherise.

'And dinner!' I add, suddenly wondering what on earth we're going to offer. 'Ralph, what kind of budget have we got for food shopping for tonight?'

He pulls out pen and paper, does a quick sum and shows me.

'It's not much,' I say.

'Not if we want to make a profit,' he agrees.

I start drying my wet hands on my apron.

'Who's up for cooking? Ralph? You said you could cook, didn't you?'

He moves his head from side to side. 'When I said I could cook, I mean I love food. I do a mean steak. Actually,' he says, as if thinking back for the first time in a while, 'I used to love cooking, but over the last few years I just ate out most of the time. With clients, meetings, keeping them happy . . . probably why my wife left me. Don't expect she remembered who I was. Same for the kids, I suppose. I was too busy making money to appreciate my family while I had it.'

We all fall silent for a minute.

'I'm more of a pop-it-and-ping-it man myself,' says Barry, breaking the awkward silence, and we all smile.

'Okay, I'll go into town, see what I can get. Maybe pasta of some sort . . .' I start peeling off my apron.

'And if in doubt, get them drunk!' says Barry.

'Yes, don't forget the wine,' says Ralph. 'Very important. If it's from the barrel, we can decant it into jugs. It's a bit rustic, but better than plastic bottles.'

'Okay. Barry, you all right on signs?' I ask.

'On it! Just off now.' He's got a couple of the wooden signs under his arm and a hammer in his back pocket. 'Want a lift into town?' he offers, like he's a young man all over again.

I hold up my hand. 'Thanks, but I think I'll be okay walking.'

'Right then, I'm off!' And we watch as he cycles down the long, dusty drive, avoiding the potholes like he's been doing it all his life, whistling as he goes.

Lennie leans on his broom, where he's been sweeping up the black dust that has settled all around us.

'Want me to come with you?' he asks, holding up his hand against the sun, which is getting hotter.

'No, you carry on here. I should be okay. I've got my Italian app.' I wave my phone at him and smile nervously. Clearly we're both wondering what's going to happen tonight, neither of us wanting to ask the other. The subject is like a huge elephant standing between us.

I'm standing at the high polished-wood counter with an armful of dried pasta and cheese, pine nuts, lemons and bacon pieces.

'What? What do you mean, it's not possible?' I say, thinking I haven't understood properly.

The woman behind the counter speaks to me again, very quickly, in Italian, shaking her head.

The young girl is standing my side of the counter.

'My mum says it's reserved. For another customer.'

'But it was on the shelves. If it was reserved, why was it out?'

The woman shrugs, pulls down her mouth and makes a 'pfffff' sound, which in any language means she neither knows nor cares.

From the back room I can hear the canary singing loudly.

'She says Il Nonno loves pasta. Her uncle, Romano, he has reserved it, she says. She can't sell it to you. She cannot serve you.'

Him again! I bristle.

I put my hand out on top of the pasta packet, stopping her in her tracks. She slowly looks up at me from her heavily made up eyes. I'm desperate. I need these ingredients. Without them ... well, I have no idea what we'll cook for the paying guests we have coming to Il Limoneto tonight.

The woman is glowering at me like I've challenged her to a duel. I swallow, not entirely sure who's going to win, and look at the young girl.

'What did you say your name is?' I ask.

'Sophia, but I prefer to be called Sophie, the English way. I love England. I really want to go. I'm half English, apparently, but I've never met my father.'

The woman scolds her, and I think she's telling her off for speaking English. Sophie lowers her eyes. The woman looks at me again.

'Look, Sophie, please tell your mum I really need these groceries. We have guests coming to the farmhouse tonight. Paying guests. I need to feed them. This is business, one businesswoman helping another.' I smile pleadingly.

Sophie turns to her mother and says something, but the woman replies sharply, then tries to snatch the packets of pasta from my hands.

'I'll pay! Whatever she thinks is a good price,' I say. It is the only thing I can think of. To my shame, I'm offering a bribe, just like Lennie did to Matteo.

The woman eyes me like a python sizing up its prey, giving her lips a quick lick.

'Yes, I'll pay,' I tell Sophie, and then I look at her mother again. 'How much do you want for the pasta? I'll give you whatever you're asking. More than your other customer.'

I look in my purse.

She tugs her black nylon top at the bottom, showing more of her cleavage and the nylon trim at the top of her bra, full of promises that presumably never see the light of day with the lack of potential partners around.

'How much for the pasta?' I say, hand still on the corner of the last packet, stopping it from slipping from my clutches. She licks her lips again, and then slowly and clearly names her price.

I'm standing out on the street, my empty shopping bag by my side. Trying to take in what just happened there.

Whatever it was – extortion, bullying, or a quick-thinking business mind – I lost. I didn't get the pasta. There was no way I could pay what she was asking. Even Sophie seemed shocked as she slowly translated her mother's words. The woman held my stare, and slowly I lowered mine, dropping the bags of pasta onto the counter. I was beaten.

'Tell your mum . . . no wonder this is a ghost town at those prices!' I told Sophie.

And now, I have no idea what to do. I look up and down the street. To my right is the square and the town hall. Before that, the alleyway leading to Luca's restaurant with its views out over the town to the sea beyond. And just off the main road, the houses that were meant to be ours. Everything covered in dark volcanic dust.

What on earth am I going to do? I can't go back with no food.

It would be just as cheap to eat out at those prices, I think.

I walk slowly towards the restaurant's green-painted gate. Could I perhaps buy food cooked here and serve it as our own?

Suddenly the gate opens and out steps a man I recognise from our first night here. It is Luca's father, Romano, the man who, if I'm reading between the lines correctly, has managed to appropriate our relocation fund. As he climbs into a badly parked car, I go to march forward, words springing up in my mind but not quite forming themselves into the right order for all the things I want to say to him. But then Luca steps out behind him, stopping me in my tracks.

My stomach twists and knots. I feel furious, I can barely speak. I glance up the hill to the big red mansion and realise this must be his house, and judging by the sound of building work coming from it, the new gymnasium is being built there too. My mood darkens even further.

I shout, 'Hey! I want a word with you,' and take off after the car across the uneven cobbled street. 'Hey! Come back!'

The window is rolled down and he clearly hears me, but he doesn't stop, just holds up a hand by way of goodbye, infuriating me even more. The arrogance of the man! The battered old car lurches off down the road, clipping the wing mirror of another badly parked vehicle, but he doesn't stop and no one seems to notice. It just about sums Luca's family up! They seem to think they can do anything they like.

I march angrily towards Luca. 'Did you see what just happened there?'

His face drops. 'Is it your car?'

'No, but it belongs to somebody!'

'I know. The people round here, they're terrible drivers,' he says, as if it's perfectly normal. 'How are you? Settling in? Sorry that Etna has not given you such a good welcome.'

'No, we're not settling in,' I say crossly. 'In fact, we're all getting ready to leave, as soon as the dust settles. As I'm sure you must know.'

'Oh no! You don't like it here? Not that I can blame you.' He shrugs. 'It must seem very quiet to you. I'm not surprised you want to leave.'

I take a deep breath. 'We don't want to leave,' I say as patiently as I can. 'We have to. All the money for the project to help us set up home here . . . it's gone!' I glare at him, and then up at the sound of building work coming from the mansion on the hilltop.

'Oh no! Not again!' He throws up his hands.

'Not again?'

'Well . . . I mean, yes, there are some people who think that the best way to make money is to take the easiest money. As you can see, I'm not one of them.' He indicates the restaurant.

'But that is your father's house, isn't it?' I point to the red villa.

He sighs heavily. 'Yes, that is my father's house.'

'And you work for your father?'

'Not directly. But he does own this restaurant – well, the family does. It originally belonged to my uncle who died. I run it with the help of a chef, Valentino, though he is very old now. My family, well, it's a difficult situation. My father has not been a well man since . . . He's not been well for some time, and so we try not to create any upset. No one wants to be responsible for causing his heart to give out.'

'And you, are you like them? Do you do what you like?'

'I do not.' He holds my gaze and shakes his head. 'No. Apart from growing lemons.' A slow smile spreads across his face and then, infectiously, across mine as I think about the smart lemon grove I saw the other day. I'd love to ask more, but I have other problems on my mind.

'Well, I'd better get on. I have to find a way of sorting out this next mess . . .'

'What mess? A problem? Can I help?'

'We have paying guests coming to the farmhouse tonight. We need to make some money to keep us going until the dust settles and we can get our flights home. But the woman in the shop wouldn't sell me any groceries.'

'Ah, my cousin Carina.'

'Another relative?' I roll my eyes. 'Working for your father?'

He nods, and has the good grace to look embarrassed. 'The uncle who owned the restaurant – it's his daughter. She's close to my father, as is Sophia, her little girl. He took on the role of grandfather to her. We all call him Il Nonno, The grandfather. Carina won't like the idea of competition.'

'But we're not competition. We're bringing business. All right, only a little bit, but it's still business for the town.'

He shakes his head. 'My family will do what my father says, and if he says you're competition, they'll all follow his wishes.'

I frown. 'But Giuseppe has worked so hard to get this all sorted. To bring new families to the town to keep it going.'

'My father won't look at it like that. He and Giuseppe haven't seen eye to eye for a long time. They haven't spoken for years. He'll think Giuseppe's trying to put him out of business.'

'But aren't they . . . aren't they related? Brothers-in-law?' I try and keep up with all the family connections.

He nods.

'You look hot . . . Some gelato?' he suddenly asks. 'It will help with the horrid taste in the air from Etna.'

I look at him. I'm supposed to be cross with him. It's his family putting us out on the streets. But somehow, my mouth says otherwise. The idea of ice cream on my dry throat is very tempting.

'Gelato would be lovely,' I find myself saying.

I follow him through the gates and down the steps into the wonderful cool restaurant. I sit at a table, and he brings me ice cream in a bowl.

'Here,' he says with a wonderful smile. 'It's the least I can do to make up for my family's bad behaviour. But you have to guess the flavours.'

I take the bowl from him and taste a green scoop.

'Pistachio?' I guess.

'*Pistacchio*,' he says, and I smile and repeat it.

'Good, and the next?'

'Strawberry,' I say confidently.

'*Fragola*,' he tells me.

'*Fragola*,' I repeat.

'Good! And finally, to complete the Italian flag, the white one.'

'Lemon!' I announce. '*Limone!*'

'My favourite,' he tells me. 'The taste of Sicily, the taste of Città d'Oro . . . well, it used to be. Certainly the taste of my childhood.'

We both tuck in and I suddenly find myself asking the question that's been playing on my mind.

'Luca, why do you stay here? Don't you want to leave, get away? I mean, you said about marrying your cousin. Don't you want to find someone for yourself?'

He puts his spoon into the ice cream and it stands upright.

'It's not easy getting away from a father like mine. As I told you, he's not well, and upsetting his plans would mean pressure on his heart. It's very hard. But yes, it was my plan to get away, before . . .' he takes a breath, 'before my mother left.' He looks down and then up again. The words hang in the air. He doesn't expand and I don't feel I should ask.

'I'd better get going,' I say. 'I need to find somewhere to buy some food, away from the town by the sounds of it.'

'I can give you something if you like.' He stands up. 'Name it.'

'I can't take food from you! That would be wrong.'

'Call it payback, to make up a little for my family's behaviour.'

'I couldn't.'

'You could. Tell me, what can I give you?'

'Well . . . I was trying to buy pasta from your cousin. If you have any that I could use, that would actually be great.'

'Pasta it is!'

'Really?'

'Of course. I have the night off. No bookings. I will bring it over to you.'

'So they don't see you mixing with the enemy?' I raise an eyebrow, teasing and testing him.

'Yes,' he says, cocking his head, stating the facts.

I smile. Somehow I seem to smile a lot around Luca.

'I'll be over later,' he says. 'It will be my gift. And I'm sorry about my father.'

I hope he's true to his word, unlike his father. I hope I can trust him. At the thought, my insides melt anyway, just like the ice cream at the bottom of my bowl.

Chapter Seventeen

By late afternoon, the farmhouse is a hive of activity, just like the bees returning to the scarlet poppies, yellow wild fennel and Etna broom in the overgrown lemon grove surrounding us.

All around the yard the black dust has been swept into piles, like mini Etnas.

The outside rooms are looking great, beds made up with military precision, thanks to Ralph's exacting standards. They've been scrubbed, cleaned and swept to within an inch of their lives. All the boxes that were stored there have been moved up to my room, along with Lennie's belongings. The heat is starting to go out of the day, as I've noticed happens here once the sun goes down.

Everyone is in good spirits – hot, and a bit sweaty, but feeling so much better for doing something and pulling together.

'Don't know about anyone else, but I'm nearly ready for a cold beer,' says Barry, as he finishes tidying up in the barn and gives his bike a final dusting-down, with what I'd say is a look of affection.

I'm gathering up cleaning equipment to put back in the farmhouse, and Sherise is emptying a bucket of grey water over the fence surrounding the orchard.

'There we go. Looks like they could do with a drink, poor things,' she says looking at the trees. 'I wonder what they are?' She points to some small light green fruit on the branches.

I shrug. 'Maybe limes?'

I'm leaning on a broom, wearing a set of overalls I found on top of one of the boxes that were moved to my room. I'm wondering what else might be in there. I can't wait to get stuck in and see if there might be some clothes I could use to start my vintage clothing business . . . Then I remember we're not actually staying and my spirits plummet again. But I'm going to go through the boxes anyway. If there are some gems in there, I'll ask Giuseppe if I can buy them from him and use them wherever I end up.

Lennie walks over. He's so tall, but then I'm also pretty short. He gives me a big hug, pulling me close. As I'm standing there, head nestled against his chest, eyes shut, drawing strength from him and realising my life is so much better now that he's in it and we're making a go of it, I hear a shout.

'Who's that?' I hear him say, and my eyes ping open.

A little green and white moped is coming down the dusty drive. The driver wears an open-faced helmet and is balancing a bulging bag between his tanned bare ankles on the running board.

'It's Luca!' I stand up straight and smile, feeling my stomach do its usual flipping-over thing, so much so that I put my hand to it.

'What's he doing here?' asks Lennie. 'Isn't it his family trying to stop us from staying on?'

'No! Well, technically yes. But Luca's helping us out. I told you I couldn't get food from the local shop. Well . . .' I don't know why I blush at the thought of my ice cream date with Luca. It wasn't a date. Just ice cream. 'I met Luca and he said he'd bring some.' Still don't know why I didn't mention the ice cream.

Lennie's frown turns to a smile.

'He's bringing food from the restaurant?'

I nod and beam. That's it. No need for any further explanation.

'Isn't that going to cost a bit?' Lennie frowns again.

'Let's just say he's doing us a favour. To make up for his family's behaviour.'

Lennie shakes his head, smiling. 'You always find a way, Zeld!' He pulls me to him and kisses the top of my head.

After I told Lennie about my encounter with the woman in the shop, he was all ready to go down there and give her a piece of his mind. But I stopped him, told him I had everything organised. I crossed my fingers and prayed that Luca wouldn't let me down like the rest of this town has. Hoping he'd stick to his word. And he has! But that hasn't helped quell the butterflies in my tummy.

'I brought pasta!' he calls as he parks the moped on its stand.

'Brilliant! *Grazie mille*, Luca.'

Lennie gives a nod and pulls down the corners of his mouth, followed by a smile, impressed by my attempt at Italian.

'Two of the things I love about you, your ingenuity and your have-a-go spirit! Even if you haven't a clue what you're doing or saying!'

'Hey!' I nudge him playfully in the ribs and we both laugh as he holds his chest, feigning injury.

Luca makes his way over to us holding the bulging bag.

'I brought pasta,' he repeats.

'That looks heavy for pasta,' says Lennie.

'I brought pasta machine . . . and ingredients. To make fresh pasta.' Luca beams.

'Fresh pasta?' I say.

'Of course. It's much better. And cheap, too!'

'But . . . I don't know how to make fresh pasta.' I look at the bag and realise my brilliant plan has suddenly hit a pothole in the road to success.

'I will help,' he says, and pushes the unruly hair from his face. 'We'll cook together. Come!' He nods towards the kitchen, as if this is the most natural thing in the world.

'*Buongiorno.*' Luca greets everyone gathered in the kitchen, shaking hands and kissing the women on the cheek. 'So, we make pasta, *sì*?' he smiles.

'Are you a chef, then?' asks Tabitha, with what looks to be a glimmer of flirtation. She's put down her laptop, so that's something.

'No, not a chef. I run the restaurant you came to but I don't do the cooking. Valentino is the chef. He's been doing it for years.' He stops and thinks. 'Years and years. Since I was a boy, anyway.' He laughs. 'Everyone here has been doing what they do for years and years. And the younger ones, they all left, years and years ago!'

He starts pulling out the contents of his bag, and despite his cheery manner, I can't help but think how sad it must be to live in a place where everyone is old and dying and there is no one the same age as you, apart from the odd cousin.

'Maybe one day you'll get to leave too,' I say, and then realise how blunt that sounds.

He stops. Shrugs. 'Maybe. One day,' he says, his smile slipping, and he stares at me and I get that sudden electric-shock feeling again.

I look away quickly and he bends down and pulls something very heavy from the bag. A large metallic object that lands on the table with a thump.

'My grandmother's pasta machine!' he announces proudly.

'We're really making proper pasta?' Sherise asks in awe.

'Not from a tin?' says Barry. We all turn to look at him, and he mouths, 'What?' and shrugs.

'Right, let's start. We need to attach this to the table – Lennie, can you help me? And Zelda, can you flour the table? Tabitha, please go and find some lemons from the trees out there.'

'I thought they were limes?'

'No, the small green ones are verdello. Smaller than the ripe ones. We get them more in the summer or when the trees don't have much water. The less water, the more verdello. But they have amazing smell and aroma.'

'Are you sure I'm allowed in there? It seems to be all fenced off.'

'Don't worry, a few lemons won't make any difference. No one will notice they're gone,' he says, attaching the pasta machine to the table with a final tight screw and shaking it for sturdiness.

'I'll switch off the electric fence,' says Billy.

'*Buon!* Good!' Luca smiles at Billy, who nods and smiles

back. 'Now, to work ... To start, we put the flour into a mound and make a well in the middle, then crack the eggs into the well. I brought eggs from the hens in my neighbour's garden.' He puts a box of them on the table.

'We used to have hens,' says Billy wistfully. 'The eggs have a lovely flavour.' And then he nips out without another word to help Tabitha.

'Here, I brought these too, olives from my garden.' Luca holds up a jar. 'You can serve them with a drink. And cheese, with home-made onion marmalade. Oh, and tomatoes.' He takes out a bunch still on the vine and hands them around for us to smell. 'We can make a caprese salad. It has all the colours of the Italian flag, white, red and green. We have mozzarella for the white, and for the green we need basil. There will be some outside. Can you go and look?' Ralph turns to go.

'With the pasta, we will keep it simple, like the salad: a lemon and garlic sauce. I will show you how to make it. And then ice cream.' He takes a tub of the lemon gelato out of the bag and smiles at me. 'Simple food, but very special. Your guests will be happy, I'm sure.'

'Thank you, Luca,' I say, and once again I feel like my eyes are in some way locked onto his when I look at him. He smiles and I find myself blushing. I hurriedly push up my sleeves and start to rub the flour and eggs together as he has instructed. I have to stop feeling like this every time he speaks to me. It's ridiculous! Well, that's one good thing about the fact that we're leaving here soon. I won't have him distracting me when I want to put all my effort into being with Lennie.

'Here, Luca, lemons!' Tabitha arrives back in the kitchen slightly out of breath. 'That fence isn't easy to get over.'

'Not lemons, verdello,' he corrects her, and smiles. She smiles back.

'Verdello.'

'*Magnifico!*' he announces, and takes them from her. '*Grazie, perfecto!* Now you say *prego*,' he tells her.

'*Prego!*'

'Now we are all speaking Italian,' he beams. 'Next we will try Sicilian.'

'You mean there's a whole different language just for Sicily?' asks Barry.

'And you speak English!' says Sherise.

'Of course! Why use just one when we can use all three?' And he starts to explain the differences between the languages while we all cook together.

'Ralph, here, open this wine.' He pulls out two bottles. 'Keep one for your guests; let's open the other and have a glass. It comes from higher up the mountain, close to Mount Etna. The vines thrive on the sloping mountainside. And the earth is rich from the volcanic dust. It's why our fruit is so good too. Only in Sicily do we have blood oranges, made so from Etna's ash. It is rich in nutrients. That's why we were known for our lemons,' he says, handing round a verdello for us to smell.

'*Were* known?' Tabitha picks up on what he has said.

'In Sicily we had lemons everywhere. It was discovered that citrus fruit stopped scurvy, and so when boats passed this way they would be filled with lemons to keep the sailors healthy. It's how this island became so rich.'

'And now?' I ask.

'And now, well, let's just say that there are lots of places that sell lemons. Supermarkets want them at the lowest price, not always the best quality.'

As we prepare the food, we take sips of the glorious, rich red wine and pick at the glistening olives with crunchy raw carrot and fennel seeds. Eventually we stand back and look at our work. Sherise and I have laid the table outside, under the fig tree in the courtyard. Beyond that, the rooms are ready. We all smile and take our wine into the courtyard as the sun begins to drop in the sky.

'Ready?'

'Ready. And *grazie*,' I say to Luca, clinking glasses. I look at Lennie, who holds his own glass up and joins in.

'*Grazie*, Luca,' he says. 'We couldn't have done this without you.'

'It's the least I could do,' Luca says.

'I must post a picture on Facebook,' says Tabitha, and runs inside to get her phone.

'This place . . . it was a beautiful farm. I used to come here as a child. It's my uncle Giuseppe's family home. It was always full of laughter and fun. It's been a long time since I was here.' He finishes his glass of wine. 'Good luck with your guests. I will leave you now,' he says.

'Whaaa!' We hear Tabitha's squawk from inside the farmhouse, then she appears in the doorway, clutching the frame.

'What is it, love?' says Sherise.

'They're not coming!'

'What?'

'The guests. They're not coming. They say they've tried to find us and keep going round in circles and getting lost.'

'But my signs were perfect!' Barry says.

'They say they asked in the grocery shop and she's found them alternative accommodation.'

'With one of my other cousins, no doubt,' mutters Luca.

'They're not coming!' repeats Tabitha, and we all fall silent.

'Now what are we going to do?' I say at last. I feel like I've been punched in the stomach. All our hard work, for nothing.

'We could try and find them,' suggests Sherise.

'I'll go and meet them on the bike and direct them here,' says Barry.

'We could insist they've entered into a contract.' Ralph joins in.

I let out a huge sigh and shake my head.

'We can't force them to stay here,' I say, dropping heavily into a chair, feeling totally beaten.

'Zeld, you did brilliantly getting this together. Don't beat yourself up.' Lennie puts a hand on my shoulder.

'But we've got everything ready.' I look at the long table. 'It's such a waste. And we needed the money. Now what?'

'We're going to eat,' says Luca decisively. 'Nothing is ever wasted. *Tutti a tavola!* To the table!' he says, taking control.

We all look at him in surprise, and then we do exactly as he says. Nothing should be wasted.

We sit under the big fig tree and eat the caprese salad, with creamy, soft, melt-on-the-tongue mozzarella, tangy, juicy tomatoes and peppery basil. Then we clear away, and cook the pasta, making sure we save some of the water for the sauce. We twist the pasta onto our forks, mopping up the last of the lemony garlic sauce in the bowls, and finish with gelato.

If it wasn't such an infuriating situation, I'd say it was just about perfect.

I gaze up at Etna, quieter now, almost serene, pushing out gentle smoke from her peak. Then I look around at this table of people who came here bravely looking for a new start in life, and a feeling of rebellion starts to bubble up in me.

Chapter Eighteen

At the end of the meal, we clear away. I feel gloriously contented and happy, despite the circumstances. Luca kisses the women on the cheeks and shakes the men's hands, and wishes us all goodnight. I can't help but smile as he rides away on his moped, gently letting my fingers touch the place where he left his kiss.

I climb the stairs with a smile still on my lips and head for the bedroom. It is only when I push the door open and find Lennie there, his trousers halfway down his legs, that I suddenly remember: we're a couple! Sharing a room!

He freezes, and pulls his trousers back up. Clearly he's as unsure about our new arrangement as I am. I walk in, shut the door and start to take off my scarf. It's not like we haven't seen each other in PJs before. We often have coffee in bed together after a night out. But somehow this feels different.

'Look, Zelda.' Lennie once again gets to grips with the situation quicker than me. 'I don't want to rush this, and ruin it by it not feeling right. We have all the time in the world to get to know each other. Let's not feel pushed into anything just because we've ended up sharing a room. Let's take our time. I want it to be special, not some grabbed shag because we feel that's what we should be doing. I don't want it to be like all our other relationships. Let's take things slowly. Being together is what's important.'

I find myself breathing a huge sigh of relief. See! We *are* singing off the same song sheet! We both feel exactly the same.

'Besides,' he adds, sliding his trousers down his long, hairy legs once more, 'I'm not sure I'd be up to much after all that pasta.' He puts his hand to his stomach and lets out a little burp, and we both burst out laughing. Then we tumble into bed and snuggle down, and as he slings his arm around me contentedly, I think I love him even more than before.

But as I lie there listening to his gentle snores, I realise time is exactly what we don't have. Once the dust clears, we're leaving, and the romance of moving somewhere new and making a future together will be gone. Will we still feel the same about the pact when we're back to a life of rented rooms and dead-end jobs?

Chapter Nineteen

'They've been turned around and re-drilled . . . looks like the work of a professional!'

Barry is standing in the courtyard below our window, where Sherise and Ralph are drinking coffee. He's been out on his bike for an early-morning ride through the mist rolling around the abandoned lemon groves as the sun rises through their boughs. But now he's back, and he's furious.

'What? Matteo, you think?' Ralph asks.

Barry shrugs and shoves his bike against the tree. We make our way downstairs to join them.

'What's happened?' we both ask, rubbing our bed-head hair, and Sherise gives us a knowing smile. I'd hate to disappoint her by telling her that nothing but a good's night sleep went on in our bed last night.

'Must have been him!' says Barry, ignoring us. 'Not sure how many other people round here would have the know-how to do it.'

'What?!' Lennie and I say in unison.

Tabitha joins us, looking just as bleary-eyed. This is early for her. She's carrying her phone, searching for signal.

'Someone has turned around all my signs, every single one of them,' Barry explains.

'That's terrible!' And we all voice our disgust at what's happened as we take in the information.

Fury bubbles up, and just for a moment I wonder if Luca knows anything about this. Was last night all an elaborate decoy?

'Readvertise the rooms,' I tell Tabitha. 'Let's see what tomorrow brings. And this time, we'll meet them from the main road. It's time someone took that family on at its own game.'

The rest of the week runs smoothly. Barry goes out on his bike to meet the guests who booked online. We fall into a routine – cleaning, cooking and bed-making – and our household kitty is starting to look pretty healthy. We make pasta and Luca gets the other groceries we need and we pay him back. We can even afford decent wine from the vineyard Luca recommended.

We've put Ralph in charge of the money and the budgeting.

'Are you sure? There's plenty of people back in the City who would advise you against letting me anywhere near the children's dinner money, let alone a week's takings.'

'Absolutely sure,' I tell him. 'Whatever happened in the UK was left there.'

He looks like I've entrusted him with the Crown Jewels.

'It's what we have to go back to that's the worry,' he says quietly.

At the end of the week, the last guests leave, the dust has all but gone and the flights are preparing to take off once more.

Tabitha is on her phone, talking intently, sitting under the fig tree, where we've left the table and chairs all week. Her laptop is in front of her. The weather has been weird. There's still a haziness in the air, and there have been occasional black ash showers, which has meant more cleaning of tables and chairs, sweeping up and dusting. We've felt the occasional tremor too, but on the whole, things seem to be settling down. The air is clearing, there's a hint of blue in the sky and life appears to be slowly returning to normal – whatever that might be.

Ralph is doing a final check of how many guests we've had, and our incomings and outgoings.

'We've done remarkably well,' he says. 'If only I'd managed this kind of profit back in the City. Low-risk, but lots of hard work and effort,' he muses. 'Might have kept my wife and kids . . . and my home. So, any other guests due?' he asks.

I look at Tabitha and try and catch her eye to let her know that I want to check her computer for Airbnb bookings. She's been in charge of all the online stuff and has been brilliant, I have to say. She has one finger in her ear and is pacing up and down now, talking animatedly. We're all feeling the stress of trying to make arrangements. Ralph has been looking at helping at a bird sanctuary on a remote Scottish island, trying to get as far away from London as possible. Barry is going to stay with his brother. And us? Our only option is to go back and stay with Lennie's mum, and much as we love her, that's really not something we want to do if we can help it.

I try and get Tabitha's attention one last time, but she is oblivious. 'Oh, I'm sure she won't mind,' I say. 'Pass it to me, I'll check.'

Lennie reaches over and hands me the computer. There's a

document open that I presume must be the novel Tabitha came here to write. It would be rude to look, so I go to close it, but before I can do so, something catches my eye on the screen. A name. I blink and and reread it. It's there on the page. Not just any name. My name!

Tabitha is now tapping furiously on her phone. My head snaps up to look at her. She appears deep in thought. I can't take my eyes off her. Suspicions and accusations are tumbling through my mind.

'You all right, Zelda?' Ralph asks, and I feel like the colour has drained from my face and my eyes are flashing red.

I'm still staring at Tabitha, and slowly she seems to sense it. She looks up from her phone and straight at me. She knows, I think. She knows that I know.

'Okay, Zelda?' she asks, and I can hear the wobble in her voice.

'I was just checking the Airbnb bookings,' I say as evenly as the fury in my voice will let me. 'I didn't think you'd mind.'

'No! Of course not!' She goes to grab the computer. 'I'll get it up for you.'

I put a hand on it and move it out of her reach.

'No need,' I say. 'I've seen all I need to see. Ralph, could you call everyone out here. I think they should all hear what Tabitha's been working on and why she's always so busy on her phone.'

'Sure.' Ralph looks confused but does as I ask. I don't take my eyes off Tabitha. She doesn't move. It's a stand-off. Neither of us knows what the other is going to do next.

The others start to fill in around the table. Tabitha checks her phone with a big sigh, then looks at the computer.

'I'd like my laptop back, please,' she says firmly, holding out her hand.

'No,' I say. I won't back down.

I take a deep breath, my bosom rising and falling in front of me.

'I think,' I say, 'you'd better tell us all exactly what's been going on and what you've been doing here.'

She looks around, and the atmosphere feels just like it did before Mount Etna erupted.

'What's going on, Zelda?' asks Sherise.

Tabitha looks like a rabbit caught in the headlights, frozen and with no idea in which direction to run. I haven't a clue what I'm going to say, or how I'm going to tackle this, but every cell in my brain is telling me I've got to do something. She can't get away with this!

'Zeld?' Lennie looks concerned. He knows me of old. Shoot first, ask questions later, and right now, I'm about to shoot!

'I'll help you out, shall I?' My voice sounds calm and collected, despite my racing heart and the betrayal and anger thundering through my veins. 'It seems you've been doing a lot of writing whilst you've been here.' I look up at her. 'Would you like to tell us what it's about?'

'Look, just hand me my computer, will you?' She thrusts out a hand again, but I ignore it.

'Not a novel that you've been writing, is it, Tabitha?' I persist.

Everyone is staring at her. She swallows.

'No,' she says, and lifts her chin as if ready to face her fate.

'So what is it?' asks Barry.

I raise an eyebrow at her, but she doesn't speak.

'It looks to be a piece of . . .' I struggle to say it, 'journal-ism. If that's what you can call it. A newspaper column.'

'About life in Sicily?' Sherise asks.

'About us, Sherise: "a bunch of saddos in the last-chance saloon".' I'm struggling to read from the screen, the words shaking as much as my hands and voice.

'Look, it's just a bit of fun,' Tabitha attempts.

'I wouldn't call this fun,' I say quietly, holding back the tsunami of fury building in me. '"Lonely Barry, three times divorced and I'm not surprised . . . Sherise and Billy, on the scrapheap of Britain's farming industry, more used to talking to animals than humans . . . Lennie and Zelda, a naïve couple who think marriage and sex still come in that order and haven't a hope in hell of making it last if they don't know how things are beneath the sheets before they tie the knot . . . Ralph, the City fraudster who's run out on his family after losing millions and robbing the elderly of their pension funds, come to live a life of luxury in Sicily"—'

'What? Not true!' Ralph exclaims.

'Bloody cheek!' Barry says at the same time.

I look up at her. Everyone else is staring with the same disbelief and disgust.

It's Sherise who breaks the silence.

'Trouble is . . . it's true, isn't it?'

'What?' We all turn to look at her.

'Well it is. We're all here because we were looking for something – a second, third, fourth . . . final chance to find some sort of happiness in the chaos of our lives, some sort of sense and order.'

We fall silent again, no one able to argue with her. Lennie puts his hand over mine, and I can feel the support there and am so grateful to have him by my side.

Tabitha finally speaks.

'If it's any consolation, that's me too.'

'Which bit?' I snap.

'All of it really.' She flops into the chair at the end of the table and holds her head in her hands.

'Oh Tabitha. Why did you do it?' Lennie asks.

She looks up at him, clearly surprised by his kind tone.

'I'm in the last-chance saloon too,' she admits. 'I was the young, bright, eager journalist, waiting for my big break, watching opportunities come and go, passing me by. Now younger, brighter journalists are coming up, snapping at my heels, getting ideas past the editor, whilst I'm pushed further and further down the ladder. I'm clinging on by my fingertips here. If I don't come up with something, I'll be pushed off for good, and I have no idea where I'm going to go.'

'Doesn't excuse what you wrote about us,' Ralph says. 'If you'd wanted to know the truth about the money I lost, you should've asked. I might have given you the interview all the other journalists have been hounding me for. Yes, I lost a fortune. Yes, I lost my family. But it was never pension funds, and I'm certainly not living in any kind of luxury. In fact, I'm living with you, which looks pretty much like hell from where I'm standing right now!'

Tabitha looks as if all the fight has been knocked out of her.

'Well you'll be pleased to know I've got my comeuppance,'

she says. 'That was my editor I was talking to. My column has been sidelined, relegated to a tiny slot at the back of the magazine to make space for a new young chef from one of the reality shows.'

'We have to be thankful for small mercies, I suppose,' I say coldly.

'Even so, my kids could read it,' says Ralph. 'And my wife will be in no doubt as to why she left such a loser.' He drops his head. 'I couldn't even back the right project out here; I put all my eggs into a basket that's fallen apart before we've even got started. That's me, just a big failure . . . I think that's how you were describing me, wasn't it?'

'Look, I'm sorry. I didn't want to hurt any of you. I saw the advert, and if I'm honest, I could see myself applying if I couldn't get something off the ground. This was my last chance to bag a headline column.'

'But you were right about all of us,' says Sherise. 'And what have we got to go back to? The same mess we left behind.'

I look around at the defeated faces, and at Lennie, and think about the life *I* left; and my mouth seems to start working before my brain has a chance to catch up.

'Then let's not go back,' I say quietly.

'What?' Lennie looks up.

'Well, Sherise is right. That column, that *is* us! We're all searching for something, and we're leaving before we've even had a chance to start trying to find it.'

'But the project's off. There's no money,' says Lennie, looking at me as if I've had a bang on the head.

'There's no relocation fund at the moment, no. But we've done okay this last week, haven't we? It may not be a fortune, but it's enough. Enough for us to stay here and try to make a new life for ourselves.

'Barry, you wanted a fresh start, a life where you were you, not half of a couple. Ralph, you wanted to build a home your kids would be able to come and visit you in. Sherise and Billy, you wanted land where you could keep animals. Lennie and I, we wanted to join the grown-up club, to get married and put down roots.'

'Yes, but—' Sherise says.

'But nothing. We still have those dreams, and if we go back now, they'll still be exactly that: dreams. At least here, doing what we're doing, we can try to make them come true. Giuseppe wanted to breathe new life into this town; he wanted a community, a wedding. Isn't that what we all want?' I look at Lennie. He smiles at me, so fondly, and I feel warm and happy here with him.

'Yes,' he nods.

'Then why are we leaving?' I look around at the group. All we have in common is the fact that we have lost our purpose in life. Why else would we be here? 'We should stay . . . all of us. What have we got to go back for? I was bullied out of my business and my future once; I'm not going to let it happen again. So what if we have to stay at Il Limoneto until we can find a way to finance our own homes. Let's give it a go!'

I stare at their blank expressions.

'Billy, you don't want to go back to travelling again, do you? Working for other people's dreams of a life abroad? Don't you want to get that dream of your own back?'

Billy shakes his head sadly, and Sherise lets out a little sob. 'I just want a home of my own again,' she says. 'To be able to open the fridge and know what I'm cooking. To sleep in my own bed every night.'

'Let's ask Giuseppe if we can stay on. Run the Airbnb whilst we make new lives for ourselves, set up businesses of our own, find homes here. I know how it feels to lose everything you've worked for.' I look at Sherise and Billy, and at Ralph and then at Barry. 'And I'm not going to let it happen again. I want to stay. I want to fight for my right to make my dreams work out!' I look at the confused faces around the table. 'Just give it a try! For three months. Don't let Tabitha's words be true. Don't let us be that bunch of losers she's written about.'

Tabitha looks mortified. And so she should.

Suddenly Giuseppe appears from inside the house.

'Good news! The dust has settled. You can leave.'

We all look at him.

'What? What's happened?' he asks.

'We're staying, Giuseppe. If you'll let us. Aren't we?' I look around the table.

They all nod, slowly to start with, and then more emphatically. All except Tabitha, who has her head dropped forward.

'I'm in,' says Barry.

'And me!' says Ralph.

'And us.' Sherise and Billy speak together.

Tabitha raises her spiky blonde head. 'And me, if you'll have me.'

'Only if you promise not to write any more columns,' says Sherise sternly. Barry nods in agreement, but Ralph can't look at her. He stares straight ahead, as if blanking her out completely.

'I promise.' She smiles a watery smile.

'And the wedding?' Giuseppe asks.

'Back on! Definitely back on!' I tell him, and he flings his arms around me and Lennie.

'Let's tell everyone!' he cries.

Chapter Twenty

I stand and stare at the yellowing wedding dress in the shop window. There are three mannequins dressed in elaborate gowns. The one at the front, faded lace, is very low-cut. I could never wear that. I'm not sure I want to wear any of them. To be honest, I'm feeling a bit dazed.

Giuseppe arrived back at the farmhouse this morning as we were clearing up after breakfast.

'*Buongiorno!*' he announced with a big beam on his face. 'Look!' He bent down to pick up two loaves of bread from the doorstep.

'Where did those come from?'

'A gift, I would think,' he said. 'People are grateful you are here and that there is going to be a wedding!'

I found myself blushing as I took the loaves.

'They must be from the baker in town,' I said. 'He's never been open when I've tried to buy bread there.'

'And . . .' announced Giuseppe, 'you have a visitor. A guest! Arrived on the first flight this morning.'

'Mum?' said Lennie, staring at Valerie in her big sunhat and with a large suitcase by her side.

'I hear there's a wedding to plan!' she beamed.

'But I only rang you last night!' he said.

'Yes! Got the first flight I could! It's so exciting!' She rushed forward and hugged Lennie and then me.

'How did you get Giuseppe to pick you up?'

'His number was on the contact details you left me. I rang, said who I was, and asked if there was a local taxi. He said he'd collect me. And here I am!' She spread out her arms. 'A wedding! It's everything I could have hoped for, and I'm here to help.'

'Well, we were thinking of quite a quiet affair,' I said.

'Rubbish! My only son and my Zelda are marrying. I want to tell the world. First of all, the dress! You need a dress that makes you feel amazing.'

And so here I am, looking in the window of the bridal shop. The two dresses at the back look more like maid-of-honour outfits – one that would fit Valerie and the other in turquoise satin, with a big sunlight stain right across the front of it. I think about Valerie. She's moved into one of the outside B&B rooms at the farmhouse, insisting on staying as a paying guest. Which on the one hand is great for the house. But I'm worried she's spending all her money and wonder how long she's staying. Surely not until the wedding itself, in eight weeks.

But there may not be a wedding at all if I can't find anything to wear.

I think about the boxes we cleared out of the B&B rooms and which are stacked in my bedroom . . . our bedroom. Maybe there's something in there I could customise. I mean, that is what I do. Take old things and give them a new lease of life.

'Good morning.' A clear and well-spoken voice behind me

makes me jump. I turn. At first I don't see anyone, then I look down. It's the little girl from the grocery shop.

'Good morning,' I reply, and I can't help but smile. 'Sophia, isn't it?'

'Yes, but I prefer Sophie, the English way, remember?'

'Ah, yes, sorry. My mistake.'

'Yes, I like it because it's an English name. My mother doesn't like me speaking English, but one day I'm going to live in England. I'll come and stay with you if you like.'

'Well, I think you have a nice place to live here. In fact, I'm planning to stay, so I won't be in England.'

'Oh, that's a shame. Do you have family I could stay with?' She cocks her head and looks at me seriously.

'Um . . . well, no, I don't. It's just me and my . . . and Lennie. And he's here. Listen, are you sure you're allowed to be out talking to me? I don't want to get you in trouble.' I look at the shop. I'm sure I can hear the canary singing loudly.

Sophie shrugs.

'I'll just say I was out with friends.'

'Do you have a lot of friends in the town?'

'No, there's no one of my age around here.'

'What about school?'

She shrugs. 'I'm home-schooled. I love to read. I'd love to go to school in England. A British boarding school! Did I tell you my father was English?'

'You did. Tell me, do you know the owner of this dress shop?'

'Yes.'

'Oh, right, well maybe she has some other dresses I could look at.'

Sophie shakes her head. 'I don't think so.'

'This can't be all she has. Maybe she could make me one.'

We both look into the deserted shop window.

'She can't make you one. She died, three years ago.'

'Oh, that's awful. I'm sorry.'

'Not really. She was ninety-seven. It's a good age.'

'And who has the shop now?'

'No one. Like most of the shops. The owners have died and there is no one to take them over.'

I look at the window again.

'Sophia!' The familiar yet unexpected voice makes me jump. Luca steps out of the grocery shop, under the battered green and white awning. 'Oh, hi!' He smiles and raises a hand. 'Sophia, your mamma is looking for you.'

'I was just out chatting with my friend.' Sophie beams at me.

'Well, you have studies to do.'

'Ugh, biology and maths, no doubt. Why can't I go to school in England? Can you teach me?' She turns back to me. 'I just want to study English.'

'Oh, I'm not sure. I'm no teacher, and I don't think your mamma would be very pleased . . .'

'Besides, Zelda and her friends are leaving us, sadly,' says Luca.

'Actually . . .' I look at him. 'I'm surprised you haven't heard.' I lift my chin. 'We're staying after all. Perhaps you could pass the news on to your father.' I speak more tartly than I meant to. 'He hasn't got rid of us that easily. Tell him we're here and we're staying.'

Luca's face breaks into a wide, lazy smile.

'Actually, I had heard, but I wanted to hear it from you. That is good news, very good news indeed,' he says, guiding Sophie by the shoulders back towards the shop.

'Like I say, I'm not sure your father would agree!' and I wish I could bite my tongue. Why can't I just let it lie? He hasn't run us out of town. We'll all have to learn to live alongside each other. Not *with* each other, clearly. He doesn't want anything to do with us, and frankly, I don't want anything to do with him. But we do have to find a way of existing in the same town without bothering each other.

'Does that mean you can teach me now?' Sophie says, head turned back over her shoulder.

'I'm sure your mother is doing a much better job than I could,' I say, trying to sound diplomatic but thinking that really this girl could benefit from being in a school with others, making friends. She's clearly very bright.

I hear her mother call her name and shoo her towards the shop before the woman finds another reason to pick a fight with me. Reluctantly she goes in, and Luca turns to me with a smile.

Infuriatingly, butterflies buzz around my stomach. I lift my chin again, trying to regain control of my senses. I have no idea why this man makes me feel like this. Why that smile has this ridiculous effect on me.

'So I hear that the wedding will happen, here in Città d'Oro?' he says, raising an eyebrow.

'The wedding is going ahead, yes, mine and Lennie's,' I say, hoping that repeating this will send the butterflies on their way, along with that lazy smile. It doesn't. 'We're staying,' I say firmly, reminding myself that it's this man's family that nearly put an end to all our plans. 'We're not going to be bullied out by your father. We came here with hopes and dreams and he isn't going to stop that.'

He smiles even more widely, causing the butterflies in my tummy to go into overdrive.

'I'm glad,' he says.

I swallow, look down, and then say the words that are crashing round my head, demanding answers, making me feel stupid, a fool. And, strangely, betrayed.

'Tell me, I need to know . . . When you helped us with the cooking that night, was that all part of your father's plan to get us out? You distract us while someone else turns the signs round and puts our guests off?'

He looks straight at me, and I wish he wouldn't. I actually feel my knees give a bit.

'I promise you, Zelda, it wasn't. I knew nothing of that. Matteo was probably acting on my father's instructions, yes. But I give you my word, I wasn't involved.' And somehow, here, right now, his word seems to mean an awful lot. 'My father holds the purse strings around here,' he continues. 'People might not like it, but they do what he says.'

'Well, I refuse to be run out of town by him,' I say, wishing I didn't feel more than a little uneasy about making an enemy of his father. 'Just tell him we're determined to make a go of things. All of us. The B&B is working, and we're going to look at ways of starting our own businesses. Lennie and I are going to get married here,' I reiterate. If I say it enough, I think, it will become real. 'We're here to stay,' I finish.

He looks right at me with those dark hazel eyes with their green flecks.

'Good,' he says. 'I'll tell him,' and I physically shiver with what feels like pleasure. 'I'm pleased. Etna will be too. And the town. They want a wedding. Even my father wants a wedding – *my* wedding,' he adds with a smile and a raised eyebrow. 'There are many things I've done for my family. Returning here when my father needed me, for starters. Staying here and not returning to the mainland. But you are right, I should not marry just to keep him happy. I won't act on orders. I believe you should only marry for true love.'

He stares at me, and I feel a hot flush start at my chest and run all the way up my neck and over my head.

'The town may want a wedding, but I do not think Etna wants it to be a sham.'

'You don't really believe that legend, do you . . . about having to have a wedding to keep Etna happy?'

He shrugs. 'Who knows. But the town believes it and we do need new families. You saw how unhappy Etna was when she thought you were leaving. Maybe she really does want this wedding as much as the town does.'

'But not your father.'

'My father is a suspicious man, and greedy. Like I say, he doesn't want anyone coming in who will take any profits away from him.'

'He needs to learn to share,' I say flatly. I turn back to the shop. 'And I have a wedding to plan. First, I have to find a wedding dress.'

'Let me make it up to you,' says Luca.

'What? Again? You've done that already,' I remind him, 'when you helped us make pasta.'

'Again,' he says firmly, and holds my gaze.

'Do you know a dressmaker, then?' I ask, worrying that I probably can't afford one even if he does.

'No, this one closed down when the owner died.'

I look at the yellowing dress in the window.

'There's no real call for a shop like this now,' he continues.

'Then how can you help? Is there a shop in a nearby town you can direct me to?'

'There is, but it's a journey and there are no buses here.'

'So how?'

'I'll make the dress for you,' he says.

Both my eyebrows shoot up. 'You're a dressmaker?' I say, astonished.

He dips his head, and I suddenly feel foolish, worrying that I've embarrassed him.

'A tailor, actually. I studied in Milan. Before I had to come back and run the restaurant. I will make a dress for you . . . if you'll let me. But first, I must get to know you. Will you join me at the lemon grove? We can talk there without anyone seeing us. These walls have eyes everywhere.' He looks around and I see net curtains twitch. 'I have to get the lemons in, and,' he laughs, 'to be honest, I could do with the extra hands.'

'And you can make me a dress?' I think of our tight budget.

'Yes, of course. A gift . . . to make up for my father's bad manners.'

I look at him. I think of our dwindling finances again. I couldn't expect him to do it for nothing. That seems unfair. He's trying to make a living like we are in this ghost town. But I really couldn't afford to pay a lot and I can't imagine hand-made dresses come cheaply. I don't want to feel indebted to him. I mean, why else would he do this for me if he doesn't want something in return? Is he really just offering to make my wedding dress or, like his father, am I going to have to return the favour? I think of Matteo turning around our signs on Romano's orders, mistrust creeping into my thoughts.

'I have some boxes of clothes at home,' I say. 'I'm going to see what's there. But thank you for the offer.' Thinking how much I would love to say yes, but it seems too generous a gift to accept. If only there was a way I could pay him for it.

'If you don't find anything, you know where to find me. And for the rest of your party, suits. We are a dying community; suits are often handed on. I can make alterations.'

He smiles, and again I feel lit up. The wedding, I tell myself firmly; it's the thought of the wedding that's doing that.

'I'd like to help,' he says softly. 'We are all happy there is going to be a wedding,' and my excited nerve endings stand to attention.

Back at the farmhouse, Valerie is sitting in the kitchen wafting a cheap-looking Spanish fan in front of her face.

'Ooh, it's hot! Don't know how you can stand it.'

'So what made you come out to Sicily, Valerie?' Barry asks. 'What with you not liking the heat.'

'Well, when I heard the news about Lennie and Zelda, I was just so excited. I want to enjoy every minute of it. I mean, I've always thought they would be perfect for each other. Always hoped it would happen . . . they've been so close for so many years. They drifted apart a bit when they first left college, but they were soon back to being the best of friends. And now this!' She beams, her red rosy cheeks positively gleaming.

'My parents didn't come to my wedding,' Barry says.

'Really?' She looks sad.

'Well, the third one anyway.'

'Three weddings?' Valerie's jaw drops.

'Yup. Nothing to be proud of really. I was just waiting to find the one I'd stick with. I think even I wasn't sure when I married the last time, but I hoped.' He looks wistful.

'I only married the once. Lennie's dad. He was older than me. Much older. But he was the only man for me,' she says, a little misty-eyed.

'I never really got that feeling. I just thought that if we stuck at it, well, it would come. We'd love each other deeply. I thought all the right ingredients were there, but it seems there was something missing.'

'The chemistry. You have to have chemistry. You never know who it's going to be with.' Valerie beams again.

I cough, and they look up and see me.

'Oh, hello, love. I was just telling Barry how thrilled I am about the wedding. So thrilled.'

'Looks like the town are too!' I say, holding up two tomato plants. 'Found these on the doorstep. Another welcome present.'

'We didn't hear anyone, did we, Barry?'

He shakes his head. 'They obviously don't feel they can be seen mixing with us. How about I take those and plant them up?' he says, and takes the plants from me. 'That should give us a nice crop. I'll see if Billy wants to help.'

'And what about dresses? How did you get on?' Valerie smiles at me. 'I'd offer you mine, but it's back home in the attic. Probably not your style anyway,' she sighs.

'Actually, I was just going to go through the boxes where I found my overalls. See if there's any gems in there.'

'Oh, lovely, I'll come and help.' She heaves herself to her feet and follows me upstairs.

'You can't wear that. It's your wedding, not a funeral,' says Valerie.

I look in the mirror. If I ask Luca to let it out a bit, maybe lose a bit of weight, add some trim . . . I turn left and then right. Maybe add a jacket. I pick one up from the box and slide it on. Valerie's right. The dress is too tight, and it's not for a wedding.

I've been through several of the boxes. There's lots of stuff there, though I'm not really sure who it all belongs to. I must ask Giuseppe. It's his family farm after all.

'I'll get us some drinks,' says Valerie. 'Don't know how they stand this heat!' She fans herself and heads towards the bedroom door, then stops. 'I'm so pleased about you and Lennie, dear. I wish his father could be here to see it. You've made me a very happy woman.' I smile. What with Valerie, and Giuseppe, and now the townspeople leaving gifts, it looks like lots of people are delighted that Lennie and I are getting married. Including Luca!

I look in the mirror again and sigh. I slide off the jacket and go to pack it away in amongst the other garments: classic Italian vintage. They could be great for getting my business off the ground. I'll ask Giuseppe if I can buy them . . . or at least give him a percentage of every piece I sell.

There are some handbags here that would sell really well. Small clutch bags and over-the-arm everyday bags, fifties classics. I love them. I open one up and feel the lining. There's a rustle from inside one of the pockets. I put my hand in and pull out a postcard, folded up. I unfold it gently and straighten it out. There looks to be a recipe written on the back of it. I try and decipher it, but can't really make it out. I think it's something to do with lemons.

Suddenly I feel like I'm intruding on someone's private belongings and memories. This is obviously all very personal stuff and I don't feel I should be rummaging through it like this. I'll go and see Giuseppe, I decide. I can't look through any more of it without his say-so.

I slip off the dress and pack it away. A light green velvet ribbon slips to the floor. I bend to pick it up, but have no idea where it came from, which dress. I roll it up and tuck it into the handbag.

I carry the box with the handbag in it downstairs, where Valerie is drinking water with Barry.

'Here, love, I was just bringing this up to you. Lennie has gone into town to ask around about work. And Tabitha is up in her room, contacting moving-abroad magazines, trying to see if she can do some writing for them. Ralph's gone to buy a cash box, for the B and B business, so there isn't all that cash lying around. How did you get on? Did you find anything else in those boxes?'

I shake my head. 'Nothing that's right for a wedding. Besides, to be honest, it feels a bit personal. I think I should ask Giuseppe who it all belongs to and what he wants to do with it. This is his family home, after all.'

'Quite right,' agrees Valerie.

'I think I'll go and see him now.'

'So what are you going to do about a dress? You need something to get married in.'

'Actually . . .' I have no idea why I'm hesitating. 'Actually, I've been offered . . . well, someone has offered to make me one.'

'Make you one?'

'Yes, to say thank you for staying and wanting to get married here.'

'There's this old legend, you see,' Barry informs Valerie. 'Unless the town sees a wedding every ten years, Etna isn't happy.'

'A legend?' Valerie laughs. 'Well, if it gets you a dress for free . . . What are you waiting for? Go! Go and say yes please!'

It's for the wedding, for Lennie and me and Città d'Oro, I tell myself as I walk into town. He's just doing it to make sure the wedding's a success and for the town. It's his gift to the town, I tell myself. He said it was a gift to apologise for his father's bad manners. I shouldn't feel guilty about accepting such a generous offer. There's no harm in that. He might be attractive and make me feel like a schoolgirl with a crush, but nothing is going to happen. I'm marrying Lennie, and Luca's helping me do that. We're finally starting to be welcomed into the town.

Chapter Twenty-one

'Giuseppe? *Ciao*,' I say, slightly out of breath from climbing the steep steps up to the town hall.

'Zelda!' He gets up from his desk and walks over to me, kissing me on each cheek. I'm surprised at how quickly I have found this a totally natural way of greeting people. 'How are you? I am so delighted you have decided to stay. And of course the farmhouse is yours as long as you need it. There is very little selling around here right now.' He tries to smile, but I can tell he's still worried about the town and its fortunes. He's running his hands through his hair again.

'Actually, Giuseppe, I have something for you. When we were clearing out the outside bedrooms, we found boxes full of clothes. They're lovely. I just wondered what you wanted us to do with them.'

I open up the box I've brought with me.

'Ah . . .' A tear springs to his eye. 'These are my late wife's clothes. I put them in the outside rooms after she died. I couldn't bear to see them. She was a beautiful woman, dressed immaculately.'

He smiles sadly and puts his hand into the open box, resting it there for a minute as if transported back to a time before she died.

'We were very much in love,' he says. 'But she was taken from me too early.' He sniffs and takes his hand from the box. 'I'll get them taken away,' he tells me. 'Try and find them a good home. Some of the clothes were her mother's.'

'Do you have any children who might like them?'

'Sadly, no. We didn't have a family of our own. Once upon a time, it didn't matter. This town felt like one big family. We all had each other. Nowadays . . . well, it's very different.'

'Actually, Giuseppe, if you don't have anyone to hand them on to, I could sell them for you. Vintage clothing was my old business, and the one I had hoped to set up here. I could sell them online and split any profit with you.'

'You could start a business with them? People will want to buy second-hand clothes from you?'

'Yes, of course. I mean, these are beautiful pieces. These days, everyone realises the importance of recycling, up-cycling, especially given the quality of the workmanship that went into these clothes. Lots of them are hand-made. Like this bag.' I pull the handbag from the box and open it to look at the lining again. The folded postcard is still in there, and the ribbon. 'Oh, and I found this,' I say, and hold out the card. 'I'm not sure what it is.'

He takes it and unfolds it.

'Ah . . .' Again his eyes fill with tears. 'Limoncello.'

'Your wife's limoncello?'

He shakes his head. 'Her mother's. And *her* mother's before that, no doubt. Nonna's limoncello. She must have written it down for my wife before she died. She was always very exact in her measurements. As the years went on, she wanted to make sure the recipe wasn't forgotten.'

He hands the postcard back to me. 'Sad to imagine what she would be thinking if she could see Città d'Oro now. It isn't the same place any more. We don't have the lemons like we used to. But Sicily has had many influences over the years: the Greeks, the Romans, medieval Arabs. We must move forward and make it a new town, new people, new families, and share the traditions that they bring. Like Marmite. I love Marmite!' He beams. 'And tea! Would you like some tea now? I can make some.'

'No, really, I have to be getting on. I'm going to . . .' I smile and think about being part of a new town, sharing new traditions. 'I'm going to sort out my wedding dress.'

I'm going to accept Luca's offer, his welcome present. I'm going to trust him. Offer to pay him what I can. I'm doing this for the town, for all of us. For our new beginnings.

I walk towards the lemon grove, down the steep cobbled lane on the outskirts of the town. The soft citrus smell of the blossom guides me to the gates. Lemon with a hint of sea air. I look at the initials engraved there, 'F' and 'A', and realise that it is Luca's grandmother who is the owner of some of those clothes. The owner of the handbag and the recipe. Nonna. I run my hand over the initials and then push open the gates and walk in.

'*Ciao!*' I call. 'Luca!'

A dog wanders out from the shadows of the lemon trees and barks, and I stand still as it trots over to investigate me. It's a big, thickly furred dog. Like a German shepherd but not quite. I let it sniff around me whilst I breathe in the scent of the lemon grove. It's like, well, heaven. Once the dog has carried out its security check, it goes back into the shadows, and I call out again.

'Luca! Hello? *Buongiorno?*'

The dog is barking again, urgently now, and I follow it through the lemon grove, stepping down the terraces. The trees look fantastic, full of big fat lemons like yellow cricket balls.

'Luca?' I'm starting to get anxious. What if something has happened to him? A falling-out over the lemons? A fight? 'Luca!' I shout, my heart pounding.

Suddenly a head pops up from, well, a hole in the ground.

'I see you met my dog. This is Rocca. She is a Sicilian shepherd dog. A *cane di mannara*.' He smiles and rubs her head as he steps out of the hole. 'This breed has been here since the Bronze Age, but sadly, like the rest of the inhabitants, they are dying out.'

I stroke the dog's head and it pants contentedly.

'What were you doing down there?'

'Ah . . . you caught me,' he says, brushing his hands together.

'Doing what?'

He sighs and pushes his hair back from his face.

'Can I trust you, Zelda?' he says seriously.

'Yes, I think so,' I say. Being trustworthy is something I definitely am. Too trusting for my own good. I think back to the ghostings.

'Something tells me I can too,' he says quietly, and my mouth goes dry. He pauses. 'I'm delivering lemons.'

I look at him quizzically.

'Down a hole?'

He nods and smiles lazily. 'Do you want to see?'

I frown. 'Do I want to go down a hole?'

'It's not just a hole.' His smile widens. 'They're tunnels. They were created by the Greeks, to store water, years ago. Do you want to see?'

'Tunnels,' I say.

'They lead out to the coast. There are a lot of them in Sicily, mainly round Palermo. But like most things, they have been taken over by the Mafia – secret tunnels that can get them where they want to be without being seen.' He shrugs sadly.

'What are you doing in them then?'

'Like I told you. Delivering lemons. As you might have noticed, no one else farms lemons round here any more. This little corner, my grandparents' first lemon grove, has been over-looked. I grow lemons here and then deliver them to be sent to my British agent. They get picked up away from town and shipped out from there.'

I look at him, not sure if he's telling the truth or teasing me.

'Do you want to see?' His eyes twinkle, and I know that if he told me the man in the moon was real, I'd believe him, and yet I hardly know him!

I shake my head. 'No. It's okay.'

'Why not?'

'I don't do confined spaces, sorry. Just . . . just something that happened, y'know.'

I brush it off, but the feeling of claustrophobia comes rush-ing up to meet me. The memories of my childhood hand in hand with the clammy feeling of fear. The nights I would hud-dle in my bedroom cupboard when I was still living with my mum, hiding from the chaos of her party lifestyle, the rude awakenings when she would fill the space with strangers there for a good time. It had felt like my safe place, until the day a boy locked me in a cupboard in the care home, bringing back all those feelings of fear and uncertainty.

I was sixteen, about to leave school. There was a game of hide-and-seek. I reverted to type and hid in a cupboard, and this kid Richard that I didn't get on with locked me in and left me there while they all went for tea. I was so frightened and angry when I got out, saw red and hit him. That was the day I ran away from the care home. I didn't fit in there. They were going to ask me to leave, I knew it. I couldn't cope with the rules and was forever getting into trouble and arguments. I'd been hanging out with the wrong crowd and this was the final straw. I knew it. Valerie saved me that day. And Lennie too. I've stayed away from small, dark spaces ever since. I thought I was going to die from suffocation, or go mad, one or the other. I will never let myself go back there again.

'Besides,' I joke, trying to shake off the memory, 'I don't know you. You could be taking me down there to slit my throat for all I know!' I laugh, at quite a high pitch.

'You're right. You will have to get to know me better. Then you will trust me.'

My stomach flips over and my mouth goes dry again.

There are several chickens wandering around the lemon tree I'm standing under, pecking at the ground. Luca notices me looking at them.

'Ah, they belong to my neighbour.' He points to two scruffy-looking birds. 'These two often seem to hide out here. I think they are, how do you say, bullied by the others.'

'Henpecked,' I tell him.

'Really, that's a word?' and he laughs.

'So, why is this the only lemon grove that actually seems to be looked after around here?' I finally ask the question I've been dying to know the answer to since I arrived.

He sighs. 'It's . . . well, it's why Giuseppe and my father will never see eye to eye. The town is dying, and whilst Giuseppe wants to bring people, so the town will thrive again, my father thinks the way to restore prosperity is to claim every EU subsidy going. That's why all the lemon groves are neglected. My father . . .' he swallows, clearly finding it hard to say, 'he bought them all up, or should I say, acquired them. He has the access to the water, the reservoirs. He wanted the groves so he could claim the subsidies on them.'

'What subsidies?'

'To give other countries a chance to sell their lemons. Here we grew lots of lemons, good-quality lemons, but it meant other countries didn't get a look-in. So they offered subsidies for us not to grow them. This was music to my father's ears. Money for no work! He held the lemon grove owners to ransom, cut off their water supplies from the reservoir, and so they rented or sold the land to him, or in some cases just walked away from it. For me, he can't stop my water . . . I have a supply of my own.' He nods down at the hole in the ground. 'When the rain comes, it fills the tunnels and collects in the chambers there, like water holes dug into the rock. So, then I make it last.'

'What, all those villagers have surrendered their lemon groves to him so he can get the subsidies?'

Luca nods.

'And so they have nothing and he has everything?'

He nods again.

'Including our relocation fund?'

He nods a third time. 'The banker needs him as a customer, or the bank here will close.'

'Let me get this right,' I say slowly, trying to control the anger that is building inside me at the tide of injustice. 'Your father, the man who stole our relocation fund for himself, has also put all these other villagers out of business? Taking all the bloody pie for himself!' My fury builds: something has to be done. 'It's not fair! He can't bully people like this! Why has no one stopped him?'

Suddenly there is a loud squawking.

'Hey!' says Luca, and claps his hands at the chickens. He rolls his eyes. 'The pecking order, I think is how you say it in England. Like I say, the others gang up on the weakest ones.'

'Like Giuseppe?' I say. 'Trying to bring the town back to life on his own. While the likes of your father bully out those not in their gang!'

Luca gives a wry smile and nods. 'It's hard to hear, but yes.'

We both stand and look at the chickens again, lost in our own thoughts. I am determined we won't be bullied out.

'Giuseppe told me about your aunt,' I say. 'He's let me have some boxes of her clothes. I'm going to start a business with them. Do you mind?'

'Not at all. I am a tailor. I don't need boxes of women's clothes.' Luca laughs. 'Giuseppe is a good man. A very good man. He has spent his life trying to stop my father ruining this town.'

'Can't you stand up to your father, Luca? Surely someone has to?'

'It's hard. As I say, he has a heart condition. He becomes unwell under stress. You know, when I returned here from Milan, it felt like the sun filled my soul. I was happy to be back and helping the family out. But the lemon groves are all but gone now. All my father cares about is making money. I think Giuseppe may be losing his battle to bring the town back to life, to make it how it was.'

'No,' I suddenly say. 'Not with all of us agreeing to stay. And the wedding! The town will prosper with a wedding, yes?'

'I thought you didn't believe in that superstition?' He smiles, and my whole body lights up.

'That's why I'm here, actually. About the wedding. You offered to make me a dress. Is the offer still open?'

He nods. 'I will make you a dress. Like I say, my gift to you. An apology, a welcome, and a thank you for staying and helping to keep Etna happy.'

'That's kind. But I can't let you give it to me. I insist on paying. I don't have a lot of money.' I wince. 'But I will pay you what I can.'

He's thoughtful for a moment.

'I tell you what. I will make the dress and you can help me here in the lemon grove, a couple of hours a day. My agent has just got me a new contract in the UK. A high-end chain of delicatessens. I need to be picking and packing and shipping out a pallet load every week. I can't do it on my own.'

'Yes! But I mean, are you sure that's enough?'

'Yes, it's fine. Besides, like I said, if I am to design and make you a dress, I first need to get to know you. Here in the lemon grove, I will learn about you, you will learn to trust me, and I will create a wedding dress to celebrate your marriage and the start of your new life with the man you love. But this place must remain a secret. If my father finds out, he will not be happy.'

'Of course. No problem.' A perfect exchange, I think happily. Life just got better.

A supply of clothes to wash and iron and get ready to sell, and a job to pay for my wedding dress, here in the lemon grove! A shiver runs up and down my spine; a shiver of excitement about my new life to come. Things are suddenly going my way.

Chapter Twenty-two

I stagger back up the driveway and into the courtyard, laden down. As well as my box of vintage clothing, I have a second box, and a bag of fat, juicy lemons.

'Billy, I have something for you,' I tell him, and carefully put everything down on the big kitchen table. Lemons roll this way and that and Lennie and I chase around to pick them up, laughing.

'In there,' I say to Billy, pointing to one of the boxes. 'A gift from Luca's neighbours,' I add, not quite telling the truth. 'To welcome us all and say thank you. But really they're for you. I thought you could look after them.'

He opens the box carefully. Two balding, scruffy hens stick their heads out and look around.

Billy looks at the birds, then at Sherise, and suddenly a smile spreads across his face. A smile I haven't seen since he's been here.

'It's not a herd of cows, but it is a start,' I say.

He's still smiling as he lifts one of the hens out of the box, carefully holding down her wings. Sherise is beaming. The second hen makes a bid for escape, launching herself up and out of the box and doing a couple of laps of the kitchen table, feathers flying. She has bald patches from where she's been pecked by the other birds. Sherise and Billy are laughing as they round her up.

'Think we'd better find you somewhere nice to live,' says Billy. 'Let's see what we can come up with. Barry, fancy giving me a hand building a henhouse?'

'Absolutely,' says Barry, getting up.

'Maybe we could let them have a run in amongst those trees?' suggests a grinning Billy.

'Can't see it would do any harm. You can't stop hens trespassing. They can't read the signs!' Barry laughs.

'We'll have 'em happy again in no time,' Billy says.

'Will they lay eggs? I love an egg for breakfast,' Barry asks.

'I expect so. They just need a second chance at life. Maybe we could get some chicks, grow the flock?' Sherise suggests, and the three of them disappear off in the direction of the overgrown orchard.

Relocators one, Luca's family nil, I think.

'That was lovely of you.' Lennie puts his arm around me and kisses the top of my head. Valerie looks on and smiles.

'Well, I thought they could cheer each other up, the hens and Billy.'

'Where have you been?' he says.

'Sorting out wedding things, and finding some work. You?' I smile.

'Been thinking . . .' He's got a look on his face that says he's had an idea. 'About the new businesses we're all hoping to build here.'

The lemons make another bid for freedom as I try and scoop them into a large wooden bowl I've found in a cupboard. Valerie doesn't even attempt to retrieve them. She's sitting at the table, fanning herself with a piece of paper Lennie has been making notes on.

'What are you going to do with all these?' he laughs. 'And where did you get them from anyway?'

'Luca gave them to me,' I say, picking a couple up off the floor.

'Luca? When did you see Luca?'

'This afternoon, when I went to talk to him about my wedding dress!'

'Your wedding dress?'

'Uh huh. He's a tailor. He trained in Milan. He's going to design and make my dress for me.'

'Oh that's wonderful news! A wedding dress made just for you. Much better than all that old stuff you were looking at!' Valerie joins in.

'I reckon he fancies you, that Luca,' Lennie says playfully.

'No!' I reply quickly. Almost too quickly, I think. 'And even if he did,' I say, looking up at Lennie and knowing that I absolutely mean this, 'it's you that I'm marrying. It's the pact. No more chasing castles in the sky. I want a life with you. I want everything we have together: loyalty, friendship, laughter and a new life mapped out together.'

This time, it feels quite natural to wrap my arm around his waist and hug him, putting my head to his chest. Little steps, I think. Like the slow-cooked meal.

'And a house full of misfits that now has two scruffy chickens who seem very much at home!' He points to Barry and Sherise chasing the birds around the courtyard, trying to contain them whilst Billy is sorting through wood from the open-sided barn.

'Perfect!' I smile and hug him harder, and he kisses the top of my head. I'm beginning to wonder if Lennie and I will ever actually sleep together. I mean, we're sharing a bed, and that's really nice. Having someone to talk to at the end of the day and drink coffee with in the morning. But so far, neither of us has felt the urge to pounce on the other. We're just really comfortable. Like an old married couple. How long are we going to wait, or actually, do we have to do it at all? Could this be it? Can you have a perfectly loving relationship without sex? Because I do love Lennie and I love being with him, and maybe, maybe this is enough.

I look around and catch sight of the lemons, and I suddenly get a flash of Luca cutting them from the tree with his penknife and passing them to me, our hands just touching, sending electric shocks around my body. He may fancy me, and I may, I admit, even fancy him a bit. But I'm marrying Lennie, I tell myself firmly. I am marrying Lennie and I won't be distracted from that.

'What *are* you going to do with them?' Lennie looks at the lemons spread out across the table.

I pick one of them up and smell it.

'What about lemonade?' he suggests.

'Oh, that would be cooling,' says Valerie, fanning away.

'No, not lemonade.' I walk over to the other box. Lennie frowns. I open the lid and pull out the handbag with the ribbon and the hand-written recipe inside.

'Please tell me you're not going to make lemon curd.'

'Oh, you used to love lemon curd when you were a boy.'

'I didn't, Mum, you just thought I did.'

And they both laugh, Valerie's face lighting up at the memory of her little boy.

I reach into the bag and pull out the old postcard. 'No, not lemon curd. I'm going to make this. It's a recipe for limoncello. Luca's grandmother's limoncello, to be precise. I'm going to give some to Giuseppe to say thank you for the clothes and for letting us stay on here.'

'Perfect!' says Lennie, hugging me again. 'That sounds like a perfect thank you.'

'And you can tell me what you've been thinking about,' I say, pointing to a chair and pouring out two glasses of red wine. 'Valerie?' I ask, even though I know she's not a big drinker.

'No, you two take time to chat. Think I'll go for a lie-down before dinner,' she says. 'What *is* for dinner?'

'Pasta!' Lennie and I say together, and laugh. We're experts on pasta now, and ways to make affordable and tasty sauces.

Once Valerie has gone, I sit down next to Lennie and we smile at each other.

'So tell me,' I say, 'what have you been planning?'

And as I start to decipher the recipe, with Lennie's help, and we chat and drink wine, everything really does feel perfect.

Chapter Twenty-three

'Luca!' I call as I arrive at the lemon grove the following afternoon. The smell of the lemon blossom once again seems to wrap itself around me in greeting.

'Hey! *Ciao!*' He raises a hand, then walks towards me and kisses me on both cheeks, just like Giuseppe does. Why, then, does this feel so intimate? Why do I feel the urge to touch my cheek where he's placed that kiss?

'I've come to work, as agreed. Where do you want me to start?' I say, looking around, keen to get stuck in.

'No rush, let me show you the place first,' he says, pointing to a long single-storey building.

'And I brought my measurements for you,' I say, opening my bag with a slightly shaking hand.

'No need,' he smiles. 'First I need to find out what sort of a dress portrays you, the real Zelda. What makes you tick. What made you fall in love,' he says softly. 'And then I can do measurements when we know what to make.'

I find myself giving an involuntary shiver at the thought of it, and grab my water bottle and take a big swig.

'So why did you come back?' I ask as I'm cutting the lemons from the trees.

'My father needed me. With my mother gone, he couldn't cope with everything, running the family business and the restaurant.'

'Your mother, did she . . . die?'

'No, she lives in another part of the island now. She . . . well, she and my father parted company. He needed someone to keep an eye on him, with his heart in a bad way.' He reaches up and picks a lemon from a high branch, his shirt flapping in the gentle breeze, giving a flash of his tummy button and the dark hairs leading down from there. I practically cut my finger off.

'Ouch!'

'Careful! You okay?'

'Yes, fine.' I suck my finger, hard, by way of distracting myself.

'So, tell me about you and Lennie,' he says.

And I throw myself into telling him about how the two of us met. The times we've shared. 'We've known each other all our adult lives,' I finish, 'and we realised that . . . well, it made sense.'

'Sense? When did sense ever have anything to do with love?' laughs Luca.

'We just realised that everything we'd been looking for was right under our noses. It was there all the time.'

'More a long, slow burn than love at first sight.' He smiles, a wide, lazy smile.

'Exactly! And you?'

'I met someone in Milan. But she didn't like it back here. Besides that, my father kept trying to introduce me to people from other families he knew. Like I've said, he's a very untrusting person. He likes to keep business in the family.'

'And for the family,' I can't help but say.

'Yes.'

'And now? Do you think you'll return to Milan?'

He looks at me thoughtfully.

'I don't know. Depends . . .'

'On what?'

'On what's here for me. My father is still very good at making us all feel guilty. He likes us to stay close. Right now, I'm happy. I have everything I need.'

'Apart from love,' I point out.

He shrugs. 'That may change,' he says, not looking at me, reaching up again to a high branch.

The following afternoon, as I finish in the lemon grove for the day and gather my belongings, Luca is getting ready to go to the restaurant.

'I'll give you a lift if you like,' he offers.

I raise a hand. 'It's fine. I enjoy the walk.'

'Okay, if you're sure. Same time tomorrow? I have to get the crates ready to be delivered.'

'Through the tunnels?' I feel a shudder at the thought. 'Luca, I can't . . .'

He looks at me and cocks his head slightly, listening.

'I can't go down there, into the tunnels. I . . . Enclosed spaces. Claustrophobia,' I manage to say.

He nods and smiles. 'I understand. It's not for everyone.'

'Actually,' I find myself blurting, 'I'm absolutely terrified!' I realise that my hands are clammy and shaking.

'It's no problem,' he says. 'You help me harvest them and put them in the crates, then we'll stack them here and I'll get them to the pallet in the tunnels. My contact will pick them up from there. That way, no one knows what I'm doing and my father won't find out. We all need our secrets.' He gives me a little wink, and just for a moment I think about me and Lennie and I have no idea why.

'Do you think your father will ever accept us?' I suddenly ask.

'Don't take him head on. He has to see the benefit to him. My father only agrees to things that work for him. But he does love this town and his family, so he will do anything to keep them all here.'

Chapter Twenty-four

'Something's not right.' I hold up one of the bottles of limoncello.

It's the last day of June, and June certainly is flaming here! I've spent the past few days cutting the lemons from the trees in the lemon grove with Luca. As the sun sets over the island, we pack them into crates and talk, about things we like, music, films that kind of thing. It's my favourite time of the day.

'It doesn't look or taste like anything special. I thought it would be, y'know, really different,' I say now.

We peeled the lemons and steeped them in alcohol and left them for three days. Then we mixed sugar and water, sticking exactly to the measurements in the recipe. We found the bottles in a cupboard under the sink in the kitchen and washed them thoroughly before filling them.

'Give it time . . . let it percolate,' says Lennie. 'A bit like you and me! We've turned out okay, haven't we?' He smiles.

I put the bottle back down on the table next to my bag.

'Think I'll go and see Giuseppe today,' says Lennie. 'There's still no joy finding any work, so we need to do something to try and get some business ideas up and running. The Airbnb has dropped off since the flights took off again.'

'Morning all!' says Sherise. She's followed into the room by Billy and Tabitha, who is looking stressed.

'You okay?' I say.

'Not really. I'm trying to get a writing job. Anything. But I can't work out what to write about or who to sell it to. I'm not qualified for anything else. I just have a degree in English and a postgrad in journalism. What else can I do?'

'I know what you mean. We were just saying how it's gone quiet on the Airbnb now. Thank goodness we have Lennie's mum here. We need to advertise the place,' I say, laying out bread on the table from the local baker, along with marmalade, butter, cheese and lovely big tomatoes, all gifts that have been left on our doorstep.

'Yes,' says Ralph, joining us in the kitchen. 'Investing to accumulate. That's the key.'

'The thing is,' says Lennie, 'it's all very well a single business advertising, but as we've discovered, it's hard work. When I was working at the estate agent's, we'd get together with other agents to create a place for people to browse. That way, you bring in more customers.'

'What, like Rightmove?' asks Tabitha.

'Exactly. Similarly, when we all moved here, the story wasn't about one person moving abroad. You wanted to write about us as a group. We were more interesting that way.'

'Some more scandalous than others.' Ralph's face darkens, and Tabitha has the good grace to look embarrassed.

'You're not suggesting she sell that story about us again, are you?' Sherise is appalled.

'No, no.' Lennie waves his hands. 'I was reading about this Canadian idea. It's not about selling one business; it's about selling the town, the destination. Here, people just drive through without stopping, but a town like this was designed for people to walk around. We need to get the tourists on their way to Etna to stop and browse and spend their money.'

We all look at him.

'Like people who go to a shopping centre. They go because there's a range of shops. They go for the day. Have lunch out. Buy lots of things they weren't intending to buy.'

'But we can't just open up lots of shops; we haven't got the money. We need the B and B to generate more income.'

'And once the town is doing well, people will seek out places to stay, like this one,' Ralph joins in.

'But how can we attract people?' I ask.

Lennie beams.

'We hold a street party!'

'A what?'

'Like we did for the Jubilee?' asks Sherise.

'Sort of. We put stalls out on the street, selling produce, fast food; get some music playing, set up a bar. People will come to the street party, to the town. And if they like what they discover, they'll want to stay here.'

'That does sound like something to write about,' beams Tabitha. 'Brilliant! Breathing new life into the streets of Città d'Oro.'

'But what will we sell . . . and how are we going to get the townspeople to join in?' asks Sherise.

'There is one way . . .' says Lennie. 'If we can get Luca's father on board, the rest of the town will follow. We have to somehow get him to support the plan.'

'Good luck with that,' grunts Barry. 'From what I've heard, he only wants to find ways of making a profit for himself.'

Lennie looks at me. 'Why not ask Luca if there's a way we can get to his father, win him over? The two of you have become friends.'

'You know what they say, keep your friends close and your enemies closer,' laughs Barry.

Is that what Luca is, I wonder, the enemy? I think about our chats in the lemon grove.

'I think I may know a way,' I say slowly. 'I think I know how Luca's father works.'

Chapter Twenty-five

On the way to town, there are one or two people with their doors open, sitting just inside in the cool. Others are going about their business, cooking inside. Net curtains that used to twitch are now pulled back as I pass. It's not so secret. I wave, and they raise a tentative hand back. They all know who I am. I'm the one who's having the wedding, and with it seems to have come some sort of celebrity status.

I'm passing a small walled garden when I hear a rustling from the other side. Suddenly an elderly man pops his head out of the gate and looks nervously up and down the street.

'*Buongiorno,*' he says. His wife, behind him, does the same.

'*Buongiorno,*' I reply, taken aback at this interaction. The first since we've been here.

And then he steps out and hands me a beautiful bunch of flowers.

'*Grazie. Grazie mille,*' they both say.

I look at the flowers and then back up at the elderly pair.

'*Grazie,*' the old woman repeats. '*Per il matrimonio . . .*' and she nods and smiles a watery smile.

'Oh, for the wedding. It's not for a few weeks,' I tell her.

'*Per l'Etna,*' and she turns and looks at Etna's smoking peak.

'Ah . . .' I say, understanding. She's thanking me for having the wedding, for keeping Etna happy, like all the other gifts we've been getting, left on the doorstep.

The man points to his wonderful flower-filled garden and I think he's telling me I can have as many flowers as I like for the big day. Then they both wish me a long and happy marriage, like theirs. That is exactly what I wish for Lennie and myself too. And we have all the ingredients to make it happen. I can see the two of us just like this in years to come, I think.

I thank them, feeling rather choked, and kiss them both on each cheek. Then I carry on walking into town, carrying my bouquet of flowers and a bottle of limoncello. It may not be as special as I was expecting, but it is still limoncello and home-made! The smell from the flowers is so powerful; there is definitely lemon blossom in there too. I would love something like this for my wedding bouquet.

I walk through the closed-up town, past the grocery shop, where I hear the canary singing. I see Carina inside. She stops sweeping the wooden floor and turns to look at me, giving me a dark stare. I lift my chin and keep walking, taking strength from the flowers I'm holding. I'm not going to be bullied out, I tell myself.

I keep focused straight ahead, looking at Etna and her smoky top, framed between the buildings either side of the narrow cobbled street. As I reach the square, a voice behind me says, 'Hello!'

I turn. It's Sophia.

'Hello,' I say.

'How are you this morning?' she asks.

'Where did you learn your English?' I say.

'I watch a lot of Netflix.'

How sad, I think: all this countryside and she's stuck indoors, doing schoolwork on her own and watching box sets and films online.

I carry on walking and she falls into step with me.

'Shouldn't you be getting back? To your studies?'

'This *is* study. I'm doing English. With you. Like you're my teacher.'

'But I'm not your teacher.' I smile at her tenacity. 'And I don't think your mum would like you hanging out with me.'

'My mum is just cross because my dad was English and she's brought me up on my own. Also, Il Nonno says that we can't have any more people moving into the town because it would take our jobs and what little money there is to go around. We need to look after the family.'

'Maybe Romano needs to be a bit more open-minded. New people will bring more businesses and jobs,' I say. Now I do sound like a teacher.

'He cares about his family and looking after us all,' she says, clearly repeating what she's been told. 'But I agree . . . he is very old-fashioned in his views. Next thing he'll be wanting us to pull out of the EU and be independent!'

I practically splutter with admiring laughter, not only at this young girl's language skills but at her handle on current affairs too.

'I'll see you later, Sophia,' I say as we reach the end of the square.

'Okay. I'd like that. And it's Sophie! It's great having a friend to chat to,' she adds as she turns back towards the shop.

I look up at the big villa and swallow. I could back out. But I want Romano to know we're not going to be bullied. In fact, I want him to come on board with us, help us organise the street party, see how it could benefit the whole town.

I take a deep breath and walk towards the big metal gates. I'm determined to make him see that us coming here is a good thing.

Chapter Twenty-six

I'm waiting by the huge studded front door of the villa, having buzzed the button by the gate and announced myself into the small speaker there. I look around at the big stone balcony, the lamps like lollipops dotted all around, the statues of naked men and women and the huge swimming pool with lions spouting water from their mouths at each corner. There's a pathway leading from the house towards the foundations of a new building that is obviously going to be the gymnasium. For the community . . . pah! For his own personal use by the looks of it!

I can feel the fury building up in me again. This man is doing his best to pull up the roots that we are all trying to put down for ourselves here. I'm not going to take it lying down, I tell myself, just as I hear bolts being drawn back and the door slowly opens.

Standing in front of me is the man I saw that first night in the restaurant. Today he is wearing a long-sleeved shirt that strains over his round belly and, despite the heat, a leather waistcoat. Without the black hat, his head is bald.

I look at him and see my own reflection in his dark glasses, and I lift my chin defiantly.

'I'm Zelda. Zelda Dickenson,' I say.

'I know who you are,' he replies flatly. 'Why are you here?'

I reply without missing a beat.

'To start a new life. To set up a business and hopefully bring customers to the town. We want to make Città d'Oro our home. I think we all have something to offer that will help you. The houses here are empty, the streets deserted. Even the lemon groves are dying. No one comes here. But we did. To start a new life. Not to take anything from yours.'

I feel slightly light-headed after my impromptu and heart-felt speech. Must remember to breathe, I think, but my chest is tight and my throat dry. Still holding my flowers in one hand, I grab the water bottle from my bag – the bag that I found in the box of clothes. Luca's grandmother's bag. Romano's mother's bag, I realise. He looks at it.

Finally, he speaks again.

'No, I mean, why are you here on my doorstep?' He looks at me. Well, I think he does. All I can see is myself, staring back at him in his sunglasses.

'Oh, right,' I say. With a sinking heart, I realise that nothing I said has made a difference. He's not suddenly going to invite me in for an Aperol and an olive. I suddenly feel very uncomfortable. But I have to make him see how brilliant this idea of Lennie's could be if we all joined in.

'We at Il Limoneto, the farmhouse, we all want to work and start up new businesses,' I say. He snorts, and I'm not sure I have much more time here to pitch this idea. 'We want to create an event in the town, a street party. Get people to come and browse, spend some time.' He snorts again. 'We'll serve street food—'

'Then you are competing against my restaurant,' he says sharply.

'No . . . we'll be working *with* your restaurant. People will come and want to eat. The more people who come, the more . . . I've brought you this.' I attempt to give him the bottle of limoncello I'm holding. Then, when he doesn't hold out a hand to take it, I add, 'And these,' offering him the flowers too.

He waves a hand at me, and I feel like I'm being shooed from his front door.

'If you get involved, agree to it, others will too,' I say. But I'm being dismissed. I try to stand my ground, but find myself taking a step back, being pushed out.

'You aren't wanted here. There is not enough business for all of us. It's a ridiculous idea, letting just anyone move to the town. There is little enough to go round as it is. I am just looking out for my family.'

He waves his arm at me again, and I'm at the bottom of the steps, being forced back down the path towards the imposing gates, which are slowly opening behind me with a creak.

'We don't want you here, taking our business. We don't have room for refugees, wherever you are from. Go home!'

I drop my flowers, but he's advancing on me and I don't have time to pick them up. Then I am out of the gates and they are whirring shut in front of me.

'Please . . .' I go to say. 'Just listen . . . We can help each other.' But the gates clunk, whirr and then go silent, and I am left staring at the brown-painted metal inches in front of my nose. 'We're not here to fight you!' I shout. But there is no response.

My blood bubbles up and boils over. I was pushed out of the business I loved by greedy landlords; I am not going to be bullied out of here. No way! Romano may be a narrow-minded bigot, but we'll show him. We can make this work. I think of my flowers, now strewn across his path. Lots of people want us here, for the wedding if nothing else. I'm determined to prove him wrong.

'I'll show you!' I shout furiously. 'If you want a fight, you've got one.'

As I turn away, I see a statue standing by the gates. I march over to the overgrown lemon grove opposite, pick up a fallen branch, carry it back to the gates and swing it at the mannequin. I watch as its head falls clean off. Then I look up, straight into the blinking eye of the CCTV camera there.

Cheeks burning with indignation and rage, I set off back to the farmhouse, which, strangely, is beginning to feel more and more like home.

Chapter Twenty-seven

'You did what?!'

'Swung a lemon branch at his statue and knocked its head off,' I say. My anger has turned to embarrassment and regret, and by the time I arrive back at the farmhouse, I am utterly mortified.

'Oh Zelda! You and your impulsive behaviour!' says Valerie, who was there for every argument I got myself into during my time at school and afterwards. She always saw my side of the story and supported me, even though she'd tell me I'd handled things wrong. When I started a demonstration on the high street with placards against the rising business rates, she didn't tell me to stop making a show of myself; she just picked up a placard and stood beside me. What has always enraged me most is injustice. I just can't bear bullies.

'I know, Valerie. I'm sorry,' I say, wishing I could tell her I acted with great dignity and that she could be proud of me.

It was Valerie who read a piece in one of the daily papers about ADHD in girls and women and helped me to get diagnosed. I thought it only affected boys and just made them run around a lot. Turns out not. ADHD sufferers are impulsive and chaotic, acting in the moment, seizing each day as it comes and throwing themselves into it. Which might explain why I was always the last person standing at parties and never really slept properly at night, my mind whirring away. Why I couldn't stay in any job, until I set up in business on my own. Taking risks was never an issue for me. I just did it, without a thought about what could go wrong. That's why I always found myself in trouble at school and later in life come to that. But it's also what gave me the courage to start up on my own. Starting my own business suited me so well: something different happening every day, only myself to answer to.

Valerie helped me to understand why I behave in certain ways and to learn how to deal with it. Although maybe not today. One day I'll make her proud. The wedding will make her proud, I think. I want to repay her for all she's done for me. But first, we have a street party to organise.

'Right, Ralph, what are your barbecuing skills like? We are going to have this street party whether Romano likes it or not!'

He looks at me and bites his bottom lip.

'Maybe we could ask Luca for some tips,' he suggests.

'I think it's a great idea. I'd love to be involved. The more people that come to the town, the more people come to my restaurant.'

'Exactly!' I laugh as we work in the lemon grove, picking fruits by hand and placing them in wooden crates.

'And Lennie came up with this idea? The street party?' he asks, reaching up to a high branch, his shirt lifting to give me another peek at his olive-skinned stomach. I look away quickly.

'Lennie is great at ideas,' I say.

'And is that one of the things you like about Lennie?' Luca asks.

'He keeps me grounded. Settled. So I don't act impulsively,' I say, reminding myself firmly that Lennie is central to my world.

'Like when you knocked the head off my father's statue?'

I try not to laugh, but fail, and Luca laughs too.

'That was very wrong. I'm sorry about that.'

'I wish I'd had the balls to do it myself. He and the statue deserved it.' We fall into silence. 'I'm sorry about my father, Zelda.'

'It's not your fault.'

'I should have stood up to him years ago. Shouldn't have let myself be guilted into staying here just so he could feel safe surrounded by family. But all the time he's ill, it's hard. I don't want to bring on his heart condition. He's getting older.'

'We all are,' I say.

'True.'

'You have to think about yourself too, Luca.'

'I know. But you're right, something has to change. At least now you're here, something has changed. I'm not being hassled into marrying my own cousin!'

'And talking of weddings, how's my dress coming on? Can I see the designs?'

He smiles and shakes his head. 'Not yet.' He smiles, and my stomach flips over. 'Now, about this street party. How can I help?'

'Don't suppose you could teach us how to barbecue, could you?'

'Are you going back to the farmhouse?' asks Luca when we have finished our shift in the lemon grove.

'To Giuseppe, to tell him we're going ahead with the street party idea, and to give him this.' I show Luca a bottle of the home-made limoncello. He nods, interested.

'I'll give you a lift,' he says, reaching up and handing me an open-faced helmet.

'What, on your . . . on that?' I point to the moped.

'Of course. How else?'

And suddenly I am living my own Roman holiday as I take the helmet with a smile. What harm can it do? It's just a lift! I tell myself. Just a lift, wrapped around the body of the man who sends me into excited stomach flips every time I see him. But maybe this is the way to cure myself of these silly thoughts.

'Yes, a lift, thank you. I'd like that.'

Luca tells Rocca to stay and guard the lemon grove, then we both climb aboard the green and white moped.

I make the decision to try and hold onto the bike rather than Luca, but as he sets off down the road, swerving round potholes, I throw my arms around him for dear life, my body pressed up against his, and it does nothing to throw cold water over my overactive hormones but instead fuels the fire in my stomach.

'Giuseppe!' I call out.

He's sitting in his office, looking stressed.

'Zelda, my dear, come in.' He smiles when he sees me, then stands and opens his arms to kiss me on each cheek. Luca follows me in, having parked the moped on the street outside.

'Everything okay?' I ask.

'Yes, yes . . . Still trying to work out how we can put some money back into the town's coffers. But there is nothing. Another balcony collapsed last night, narrowly missing one of our slower-moving elderly inhabitants. It's dangerous. We need to start renovating these buildings or the whole place will collapse in on us!' He sighs.

'We've had a few Airbnb clients,' I tell him, 'but they're few and far between and they never stay for more than one night. But I brought you this to say thank you for the clothes.' I hand him the bottle of limoncello. 'I made it. I thought we could serve it at the street party. We're going ahead with Lennie's idea. Luca's going to open the restaurant and serve gelato outside. And Ralph and Barry are going to barbecue.'

'A street party! Excellent news!' says Giuseppe. '*Grazie*, Luca,' he adds.

Luca nods. 'My father will just think I'm opening the restaurant that evening. But I want to try and help. It is good to have Zelda and the others here,' he says, and my stomach does that flipping-over thing again and my thighs burn like they're still on the moped, the wind on my face, flicking up bits of hair from around my helmet, my chin resting against his shoulder.

'I think we should all have a glass of this,' says Giuseppe. He goes to a dark-wood cabinet, which opens with a creak, suggesting it's been some time since it's been used. He comes back with three shot glasses.

'If it's any good, maybe I could serve it at the wedding,' I say, and swallow, my mouth suddenly dry.

'It is from the recipe you found in the handbag, *sì*?'

'*Sì*,' I say.

'This,' says Giuseppe to Luca, 'is your nonna's recipe.'

He begins to pour the yellow liquid into the glasses, and I see him looking at Luca, who raises an eyebrow. He hands round the glasses and we raise them and say, '*Saluti!*' Luca nods his approval at my attempt at Italian.

We all sip, and then I look at them and wait. It tastes better than when I first tasted it. It's improved, but still nothing special.

'It's . . . wonderful,' says Giuseppe hesitantly.

I turn to Luca.

'It's good, but . . .'

'There's a "but"?' I feel devastated. Is nothing going to turn out right for me here? I can't even follow a simple recipe!

Luca looks at Giuseppe and smiles knowingly, then turns to me.

'This is good, but it's not how we make limoncello here.'

'No?'

'Do you have the recipe?' He holds out his hand, smooth despite the work he does in the lemon grove every day.

I take the postcard from my bag and hand it to him.

'Ah . . .' A huge smile spreads across his face. 'It's fine, but it's not *exactly* how Nonna made it,' he says.

'Or her mother before that,' joins in Giuseppe, and they are both smiling as if they've had a visit from Nonna herself.

'These are just the quantities, the measures. There's

something missing,' Luca tells me. 'I watched my grandmother make this many times.'

'Something's missing?' I scan the recipe, but the words are all jumbled up. I try again, moving my finger under the words to help me focus on them.

Giuseppe laughs. 'You won't guess it. Tell her, Luca. Put her out of her misery.'

'It's the verdello,' he says rolling the 'r'. I watch his tongue fall on the 'lo', and to my shame, I realise I'm transfixed. I snap my gaze away, catching Giuseppe's eye.

'The small, unripened lemons,' Giuseppe explains.

'Come!' says Luca. 'I will show you.'

I travel back to the farmhouse on the back of Luca's moped, Giuseppe following in his battered old Fiat. As he glides and swings around the potholes in the road and swerves around two cars working out whose right of way it is, I let my body relax into his.

We park up and he looks for a way into the lemon grove.

'Oh, you can get in here.' Billy glances up from where he is sawing wood, making what looks to be another henhouse, and points matter-of-factly. Luca smiles, and the next thing, he and Giuseppe are there in amongst the long grass and wild flowers and butterflies. He picks one of the small, greenish, knobbly-skinned fruit.

'Remember I told you when we learned to make pasta? These are here in the summer, before the fruit has ripened, before they have taken water and grown. The lemon tree fruits three times a year, which really means it has fruit and flowers on it all the year round. But often trees that are starved of water have more verdello on them.'

'And since your father put up the price of water, the trees are starved and there are lots of these around?'

'Exactly! They're unripened, but they have an amazing citrus flavour.'

He looks around.

'Here, smell.' He makes a tiny mark in the skin of the little fruit and holds it up to me.

'Wow!' My nose and head are filled with the fantastic citrus fragrance. Like the most lemony smell I've ever smelled. He's holding the verdello to my nose and I'm breathing in the citrus aroma and the smell of him, making me practically melt inside.

'Maybe we should serve it at the wedding, Zeld.' I hear Lennie behind me having the same thought I had earlier, and turn quickly away from Luca.

'Smell this,' I say quickly, to try and make the whole experience a little less sensual and a lot more normal.

Tabitha joins us in the lemon grove. Luca holds up the verdello for her to smell too, like it's the most natural thing in the world. Why then did it feel so special to me?

Somehow my body just keeps turning towards him, like a magnet resetting to home . . . but I know that home is with Lennie. It will be fine once we're married, I think. It's just Mother Nature trying to mess with my head, wanting me to make sure I know what I'm doing, throwing temptation in my way. But I won't be tempted.

I look out at the abandoned lemon grove. *Ve–r–del–lo*, I repeat to myself, replaying the image of Luca's mouth moving.

And if I'm not mistaken, there are an awful lot of verdello here. Is this what we've been looking for? Could this be the answer to our problems? Are the answers here, in the lemon grove? I snatch a glance at Luca, who smiles at me, and my insides melt all over again.

Chapter Twenty-eight

'It's gonna be a hot one,' says Barry, back from his morning ride around the town. 'I've put out some new signs for the street party. Let's hope Mattco doesn't try and turn these ones round. I've attached them to signs for the restaurant, so he'll have a job without taking down Romano's signs as well.'

It's the day of the street party; just five weeks until the wedding, I think. Just as I've thought every morning when I've woken.

Everyone in the house is busy with their own jobs. Lennie has us all organised with a list, and Ralph looks to have made a spreadsheet.

'We'll take the barbecue into the town square,' says Ralph, looking at the big oil drum out in the courtyard.

'Shame we haven't got a car,' says Barry.

'What about that old minibus?' says Valerie. 'Bet I could get that going. I spent years driving one of those.' And the three of them go out to the open-sided barn to see if she can work her magic.

We haven't had any Airbnb guests for weeks now, but maybe people will drive through today and see how busy the place is and want to stay on.

Barry and Ralph have cleaned down the barbecue after

last night's cookery lesson from Luca, where we tried out some traditional Sicilian street food. The chargrilled artichokes and aubergines were to die for. And then there was the masterclass in arancini. Beautiful crunchy golden balls filled with soft fluffy rice with peas, mozzarella and any other leftovers we had to hand. Luca's going to make up a batch for Sherise to hand out outside the restaurant, while Ralph and Barry are going to be serving the barbecued vegetables. Billy is in charge of the drinks, including my new batch of limoncello. Luca told me to make it just the same as the last lot, but with verdello, and to be careful not to get any of the white pith in it. He also told me to boil up the sugar and water with a few sprigs of rosemary from the garden at Il Limoneto, for remembrance for his nonna.

Tabitha is going to photograph everything as we work so we can get a Facebook page going and tweet and encourage people to come to the town and hopefully to the Airbnb.

'This will make a great story, how the street party brought the town back to life,' she says. 'I'm sure I'll get it into *La Dolce Vita* magazine, and who knows, maybe some of the other will take it too.'

Valerie has been making up bunting at the kitchen table every evening, which she also plans to use for the wedding, even though I keep telling her it will just be a small affair. Lennie's going to be selling ice cream for Luca. Billy has acquired some new hens, and a cockerel was left on the doorstep. He's selling eggs, bird boxes and chicken houses.

'He's always been good with his hands,' Sherise smiles as he works away. 'He wants to expand into benches and chairs.'

So all in all, it's been a busy week at Il Limoneto.

As well as making limoncello, I've been working in the lemon grove with Luca every day, helping to harvest the lemons, loading them into crates and carrying them down to the tunnel entrance. From there he takes them into the dark tunnel ready for delivery. I still haven't seen his plans for my dress, and I'm dying to. We've been gathering all our paperwork to make the wedding official, and Valerie has been organising it and delivering it to Giuseppe. She's ended up helping him in his garden in town, harvesting tomatoes and onions, which they're going to serve on little plates at the street party, sliced and drizzled in glorious dark green, peppery olive oil.

Suddenly there's the roar of an engine from outside, and a cheer. Valerie, it seems, has got the old minibus started and is easing it out onto the potholed drive. Once it's loaded up with everything that needs to go to town, we squeeze ourselves in too.

'Is it safe?' asks Barry. 'I could always take the bike!'

'I think at the speed we'll be going, it'd be quicker to walk,' laughs Valerie, and as the minibus belches and farts down the lane to the road beyond the gates, we all let out a big cheer, like a coach trip to the seaside.

Valerie parks up just down the street from the square and we all get to work. She puts bunches of wild flowers from the lemon grove in jam jars on all the tables that Luca has already set out around the piazza, covered in checked cloths. The bunting swings gently in the breeze as Barry and Ralph string it between the lamp posts. The two men seem to have become good friends, I think, watching them. Luca and Lennie too laugh and joke as they fix speakers and cabling around the place. Music suddenly fills the square and they both beam like boys, and I feel my heart squeeze and twist, with love and pride . . . and maybe a bit of confusion too.

Giuseppe puts out bowls of sweets, almonds in sugary orange, lemon and pistachio shells and nougat in gold wrappers, like he's inviting his grandchildren over for a feast. He would make a wonderful grandfather, I think. The smoke from the barbecue spirals upwards and through the square. Sherise and Valerie light tea lights in jam jars and put them next to the wild flowers. It looks wonderful. Soon the air is full of the smell of caramelising aubergines and artichokes, making my mouth water.

Luca comes out with a tray of arancini.

'Try one,' he tells me, holding the tray at shoulder height on the flat of his hand. I bite into it, crispy on the outside and soft as you like on the inside. It's just heaven. I look around at the bunting, the flowers and the candles, and in the distance the big ball of orange sun just starting to set in the sky. This is exactly what this town needs, I think, and we all raise a glass of verdello limoncello and wait for people to arrive.

Sicilians always eat late, once the sun goes down, I tell myself as we wander around the square, hoping to entice people in. Cars pass and their occupants look at us with interest, but no one stops. An elderly couple in coats, bent over, carrying bags of shopping pause to inspect the bunting and the tables. 'Come and sit down,' I call to them. They nod, smile, and carry on with apologetic looks.

Nobody stops. No one is brave enough to stop. Nobody comes at all.

Chapter Twenty-nine

I've barely slept. That may be down to the banging headache I have. Which may be down to the volume of limoncello I drank, when all the glasses were left untouched. Nobody came to the street party. Only Sophia, who was quickly ushered back inside by her glaring mother, to sit with the caged canary no doubt. I stomp furiously around the lemon grove, picking verdello as I walk, because I can't think of anything else to do to take my mind off things.

I don't understand it. Everyone we've met has been happy that we're here and that a wedding is going to happen. But no one wants to be seen to be associated with us. No one will stand up to Romano.

I walk back into the kitchen, where the others are finishing breakfast, and let the verdello tumble from my arms and across the worn wooden table.

'Hey!' Lennie says, trying to soothe my bad mood as I bang around the kitchen. Everyone else makes themselves scarce with jobs to do, clearing up from last night.

'No one came!' I'm looking in drawers for something I can't remember. My head is in a complete muddle. 'Nobody, not one!' I repeat.

'Hey!' Lennie says again, and takes my wrists and pulls me

to him. At first I resist, frustration and fury pumping round my body. But he persists, and eventually I give in, letting my head fall into his chest and burying my face there, shutting out all the thoughts that are charging around my brain. Lennie knows me, knows what I need.

'All that work,' I practically sob. 'You had the idea and worked so hard. You're doing all this to make a new life for us. I just feel I should have done more.'

'You tried. We all did,' Lennie soothes.

'What are we going to do? If we can't make this work, what are we going to do? Back home to miserable lodgings and dead-end jobs?'

'Mum says we can live with her,' he says. I pull away and look at him and we both allow ourselves a little smile.

'Hardly joining the grown-ups' club!' I say. 'We have everything we need here, if they'll only give us the chance.'

I look for something to blow my nose on, and Lennie goes to find me a piece of toilet paper.

'Thank you,' I say, taking it from him.

'And blow,' he says, looking down at me as though I'm a child, and I blow, feeling like one. But I'm comforted by his kindness. I grab him and hug him once more, then look up and wonder how it would feel to put my lips on his.

I move my face slowly towards his. I have Lennie and that's what important. I'm not taking risks any more. I have Lennie, I repeat. I feel like I'm moving in for docking, like a spaceship, landing on territory I have only seen before and am now about to touch and taste for the first time. I reach up and he, somewhat jerkily, moves his head towards me and then shuts his eyes. I scan his face, his familiar face, and then finally our lips meet and just as quickly part again, and Lennie stands up straight, looks down at me and attempts to smile widely. I feel like I'm mid dance and the music has stopped. These things just need working at. If I said I wanted to be a pianist, I couldn't sit down and play Beethoven straight away.

'Something will happen. We'll make it work,' he says, and I'm not sure if he's talking about life out here, or our physical relationship.

'But it's all because of that man!' I'm suddenly infuriated again. 'How can Luca not stand up to him? Tell him to stop being so bigoted, such a bully?'

'Actually, why doesn't he?'

'Because his father has a heart condition. And if Luca does try and tell him anything, his father reminds him of his delicate state of health.'

'Could be the answer to all our problems!' Lennie laughs, and I swish at him with a tea towel.

'I'm going to clear up in town,' he says. 'See if I can come up with any ideas. You stay here, clear your head.'

'Okay,' I say as he bends and kisses me on the cheek, and I feel grateful that we're not going to do the rather wet-lips kissing again.

I turn back to the mass of fruit spread across the kitchen table and push up my sleeves. There's only one thing I can think of doing right now, and I don't stop until all the verdello have been used up, throwing my frustration into peeling them and steeping them in the alcohol Luca has sourced for me from an out-of-town supplier, hoping to think of something that will stop us having to leave this place; that life will hand us something other than lemons.

Chapter Thirty

I look at the bottles of verdello limoncello lined up on the kitchen floor. The bottles are a bright light green – the same colour as the ribbon I found. I pick one up and slide it into my bag, then hesitate and pick up another.

'I'm off to work,' I tell Lennie.

'Wish I was,' says Lennie, looking unusually fed up, his hands shoved into his pockets. 'Anything I can help you with?'

I wish I could think of something, but I can't.

Over the past few days, whilst the verdello had been steeping I got to work cleaning and pressing the clothes Giuseppe gave me. Valerie helped with any little repairs and Tabitha photographed them on her iPad, and set up a website to sell them on. Handbags, shoes, coats and dresses. The only thing I haven't put up on the website is Nonna's handbag, which I have started using on a daily basis. I love it. It sits over my arm now. I reach up and kiss Lennie on the cheek.

'Something will turn up,' I say, sounding more positive than I feel, ruffling his hair and then thinking that it's not a very sexy thing to do. I love Lennie; he's my best friend and I don't want to lose him. The fact that he has no interest in sex with me right now is something I can live with. Because I realise – if I'm being honest with myself, and with a certain amount of relief – that I don't have any interest in having sex with him either. But that does mean that us having a family is never going to happen and I'm going to have to get used to the idea. That part of my life is over, I tell myself, but it hurts trying to shut the door on it. And then I wonder if Lennie is feeling it too. I mean, family was one of the things we both wanted from the pact. Is he coming to the same conclusion as me? That this is as good as it gets? Is being with me going to be enough for him? I wonder if he feels let down in some way.

I walk into town, dodging what looks to be a fallen balcony. A pile of rubble that could easily have killed someone. This whole town is falling apart, literally. I wave to Sophia, checking that her mother doesn't see me, and she grins from her seat under the shop awning, pen poised over a book, and raises her free hand. I carry on to the lemon grove and call out to Luca when I arrive. Rocca stands stiffly and comes over to greet me. I pat her head as she gives me a polite sniff then goes and flumps under a tree out of the hot sun. It's nearly August. In just one month I will be getting married.

'*Ciao!*' I hear Luca's voice from the balcony of his apartment. 'Come up.' He waves a hand.

'*Ciao,*' I reply as I push back the beaded curtain and step into the cool interior. He has notepads and drawings spread out over the coffee table that he carefully gathers up as I walk in. He kisses me on both cheeks, and I can't help but breathe in his citrus aftershave.

'Coffee before we work?' he says, walking over to the kitchen area and taking down a Kilner jar of ground coffee from a shelf.

'Actually, I brought you this,' I say, feeling suddenly shy.

What if it's wrong? What if it shouldn't be that bright green colour? 'I don't know if it's okay,' I add. 'I'd really like to serve it at the wedding. We don't have lots of money for champagne, so I thought . . . Will you try it?'

Luca looks at the bottle, then goes to a dresser in the living room and takes down two glasses. I glance around. There is a large map on the wall with different-coloured pins in it.

'What's this?' I ask, studying it.

'Places I've been and others I'd like to visit,' he says, taking the bottle from me. 'The red pins are the places I've been to; the blue are the ones I plan to visit some day.'

'When your father . . .' I stop myself from blurting out the obvious.

He shrugs, opening the bottle.

'When I feel I can,' he says.

'Where would you go first?'

'I don't know. Maybe Paris, or even London. See if I can spend some time working as a tailor, get into one of the fashion houses there maybe. I have friends from college working there and asking me over.'

He opens the bottle and I suddenly feel nervous and a bit foolish offering him this drink that is the colour of alien snot.

'Maybe you should save it, try it when I'm not here. It's probably not quite right . . .'

'Let us try it now,' he insists.

'No, you don't have to . . .'

But he ignores my protests and takes the glasses and the bottle out onto the balcony overlooking the lemon grove and the sparkling sea beyond. He hands me a glass of the thick, practically neon-coloured liquid, and I hold it nervously.

'I wanted it to be ready for the wedding.' I look at it suspiciously. 'But what if—'

'Shh,' he says, holding up a hand to silence me. He perches on the edge of the table and raises his glass to his nose. As he sniffs, his eyes shut, as if he is drawing in the smell. Then he opens them and looks at me, giving nothing away. He holds my gaze and my insides twist, turn and melt. As he moves the glass to his lips, I find my eyes drawn like a magnet to them. It's completely different from watching Lennie's lips this morning. Those were comforting and familiar. These are full of promise; of what, I'm not sure, but the thought is exciting.

His lips part and he places the glass in between them and tips it slowly so the liquid slides into his mouth and onto the tip of his tongue.

I watch and wait . . . and wait.

Eventually he lowers the glass and looks down, as if the liquid is still sitting on his tongue. The light streaming onto the balcony highlights a few strands of silver running through his otherwise dark wavy hair. After a while, he lifts his head and looks at me, very hard. But still he says nothing.

'Well?' I ask. 'Oh, look, it's fine. Sorry. I realised from the colour that it probably wasn't right. I shouldn't have . . . I'll get on with the lemons.'

I go to put my glass down on the table and leave. He smiles at me, and suddenly I'm feeling cross and agitated.

'I didn't come here to be laughed at!' I tell him. But his smile just widens.

'I know,' he says. He takes another sip of the green liquid, then holds the glass up to the shaft of sunlight pouring onto the balcony, and it looks like a thousand light bulbs have gone on around him. 'This,' he says, 'is the taste of Sicily.'

'Really? You like it?' I say, like the light bulbs have lit me up too.

He nods. 'I don't just like it . . .' He stares at me, then lifts his chin and says, 'I love it!' and that lazy smile spreads right across his face. 'Try it!'

I look at my glass and take a quick sip. It tastes . . . I stop in my tracks and look back at Luca. He is still smiling, nodding, swilling the liquid around the glass.

I take a deeper and more considered sip. I let it sit on my tongue, where it fills my mouth with its zingy, lemony flavour. A taste of sunshine, warm soil and wild flowers, everything that I have come to find fills my soul here in Sicily and makes me feel alive.

'Oh my God! It's . . .' I look at the glass. 'Amazing!' My eyes widen along with my voice.

'It is, isn't it? It reminds me of everything this town used to be. It reminds me of Nonna.'

'I can't believe it. It really does taste of . . . well, the lemon groves. Green, fresh, citrusy, full of possibilities.'

We both sip again, the warming sensation of the alcohol filling my head and wrapping around me like a reassuring pair of arms.

'And now,' he puts down his glass, 'I have something for you.' He goes inside and returns with a big A4 sketch pad. 'Here,' he says, holding it out to me.

'What's this?'

'Open it,' he nods.

I flip back the cover and look at the pencil drawing there. On the next page are more sketches, closer pictures of detail. I catch my breath.

'It's your wedding dress. Like it?' he asks, and now it's his turn to look nervous as I glance from the pages of drawings back to him.

'I . . . I . . .' I'm lost for words, and his face begins to fall to a more serious frown. 'I love it!' I finally manage to say. '*Grazie mille!* Thank you!'

I feel quite teary. It couldn't be more me if he tried. And there, around the nipped-in waist, complementing the lace and the beaded trim, is the velvet ribbon I found in the box, the colour of the verdello limoncello.

'Something old,' he tells me. 'A little piece of the past passing on to the future,' and this time my eyes fill right up with tears and one plops onto the designs.

'Whoa!' he laughs, and moves the sketch pad out of harm's way.

What an amazing memento to have of the wedding – every page a detail reflecting me and who I am. The heart-shaped neckline, covered in sheer lace; the long-sleeved bolero jacket sitting just below my bust line, because he knows I may come across as confident, but I'm not confident enough to show it all off in a strapless look. Neither would my ample bosom stand the strain. Then there's the three-quarter-length skirt, because he knows I'm worried about falling over a full-length one. The nipped-in waist to draw attention away from my full hips. The lemon-blossom embroidery on the neckline. The satin shoes he's going to dye to match the soft yellow of the netting underskirt. And the bouquet of lemon blossom and yellow Etna broom tied with another green ribbon. The colours of the lemon grove, he tells me.

He sits back on the table and picks up his glass, studying my face as I look at the pages.

'You're sure you like it?'

'It couldn't be more perfect. *Grazie. Grazie mille.* Thank you,' I say, covering all the bases. I look at the pictures again. 'So what happens next?' I ask excitedly.

'I have to measure you. Are you okay with that?'

I suddenly feel quite hot.

'Of course, absolutely,' and my tongue twists like it did the first day I saw him.

He slips off the table and goes inside, returning with a tape measure.

'Ready?' he asks, looking at me with his dark eyes.

I glance down at the sketch pad and think of how beautiful that dress will be, and try not to think about how it will feel to have his hands working their magic over my body. I look at my glass, then take a huge swig of limoncello.

'Ready!' I croak, feeling very hot indeed.

'Arms out,' he says firmly, a pair of glasses perched on the end of his nose.

I can feel his hands brushing against my skin, and his warm breath there too. My nerve endings are like an electric fence running round my body, on high alert when he's close and sending shocks through it every time he touches me.

He works slowly, running the tape measure along my arms. Then he turns and writes in the sketch pad, checking his measurements against the pencil drawings there.

I try to focus on looking out to sea, where the setting sun is creating a glittering pathway across the water, like it's guiding me to a golden city, a place I long to be, a place I'd like to think is home. I look down briefly at Luca's head and try to think of something to distract myself. Like Etna, there is a fire building, waiting to erupt right in the heart of me.

It's like a strange torture that is both unbearable and delicious, and I want it to stop yet at the same time I never want it to end. What I want is for his hands to actually touch my skin instead of skimming it. It is taking all my mental willpower to not cave and crumble. The part of my body I thought had switched off and gone to sleep now that I have taken myself well and truly off the shelf and am happy and settled with Lennie is suddenly very much awake and demanding attention.

'How do you think Lennie will feel when he sees you in the dress?' Luca asks.

I look at him and then up at the ceiling, and I think about Lennie.

'He will . . . he'll feel like me. Like the stars have aligned. This is what was meant to happen all along. It's our moment.'

'You've certainly taken your time.' His hand runs from my waist down my thigh to my calf, and my stomach turns to molten lava.

'We wanted to be sure. I've spent my life making wrong decisions, following my gut instincts, acting in the moment and getting it wrong. Lennie isn't one of those impulsive decisions. We've always got on. Always been best friends. We made a pact . . .'

'A pact?'

I bite my tongue, wishing I hadn't said anything.

'What sort of a pact?' Luca raises an eyebrow. I take a big breath.

'When we were teenagers, at college, we agreed that if we hadn't met Mr or Ms Right by the time we were forty, then we'd marry each other and live contentedly together.'

He says nothing for a moment, then, 'You didn't find true love, so you settled for second best?'

'Lennie isn't second best!' I say defensively.

'No. But if you don't fancy each other . . .' He looks at me quizzically.

'A relationship is all about what you put into it. There's more to it than fireworks and excitement.' I'm aware that I sound like a schoolmarm.

'You don't believe in love at first sight then?' He's still doing the eyebrow thing and looking over the top of his glasses at me.

'I just don't think life is as simple as that: that you meet someone and fall in love and live happily ever after. Not at our age. It's about finding companionship, shared goals.'

'So, Mr Right didn't come along in time, so you went for plan B.'

'Something like that. It's a good plan. One that will work. You know, you're told in school, and in magazines and social media, that when you do this or that in life, you'll move on to the next stage. Pass exams, get a career, have a house and partner. I just want all those things that we're promised when we become grown-ups.'

'And what if . . . what if you did discover there was such a thing as love at first sight? Then what would you do?'

I am not in love with Luca, I tell myself. It's just a crush, an attraction.

'What if you discovered that there was a missing ingredient in your relationship? No one can say what it is. It's just . . . chemistry. Like the sun and the soil here in Etna, making the fruit more special than other places. No one can create it . . . it just happens. What if you found that chemistry with someone and realised there *was* such a thing as love at first sight?'

My mouth is dry, my head so light it feels like it might float off.

'I would say . . .' I think quickly, 'I would say that it's an illusion. It doesn't exist. There's no such thing as love at first sight. I know, I've looked!'

He nods and looks away. The atmosphere is so highly charged, it feels like an electric storm waiting to break, or Etna about to blow her top again.

'Maybe it was waiting until you weren't looking before it turned up,' he says. 'Now, bust.'

'Sorry?'

'I need to measure your bust.' He laughs, and then so do I. And I think it's fair to say that in just those few words, the molten lava has finally bubbled up and exploded in my stomach.

'Hello! Luca! Oh, hello, *scusi*. Sorry.'

The highly charged atmosphere bursts like a balloon and vanishes off into thin air.

'Hey.' Luca turns and smiles. '*Buongiorno*, Emily, come on in.'

The newcomer steps out from the cool of the apartment onto the sunny balcony.

'Not interrupting anything, am I?' She is slim, dark-haired, in a neat slip dress with a large smart leather bag over her shoulder.

'Not at all,' Luca says, his tone friendly, putting down his pen and tape measure.

He kisses her on both cheeks, and my feelings of just moments ago evaporate. Now, if I'm not very much mistaken, I'm feeling . . . could it be jealousy?

Oh get a grip, Zelda! I tell myself crossly. You're marrying Lennie. Lovely, loyal Lennie. Your life partner. I love Lennie, I do! I love that he knows I like my tea with half a teaspoon of sugar. I love that he lets me choose which side of the bed to sleep in. I love knowing he's there at night, making me feel safe. I love the fact that he's as happy as me that we've decided to make a go of this. I love the effort he put into the street party. I love being a team with him. We just fit together. Always have done. So it might not be fireworks and chemistry, but it's solid and real.

'What's going on here?' says Emily, looking at the tape measure and sketch pad.

'We are measuring Zelda for her wedding dress; the one I'm making for her.'

'Ah yes, of course,' Emily says, and I wonder how this stranger knows so much about me. 'The wedding that will stop Etna from being unhappy and erupting.' She smiles, a beautiful wide smile.

'Yes, we are very lucky. Very lucky indeed to have Lennie and Zelda here,' says Luca.

'May I?' Emily points to the sketch pad and looks at me.

'Of course,' I say politely.

She studies the drawings. 'Oh, these are just beautiful! Did you really design this, Luca?'

'I did. My work is mostly as a tailor, but at college we had to try other forms of design.'

'You're really talented. Gosh! Not just a fabulous lemon farmer, but an amazing designer. You should do more. I bet I've got some contacts.'

Luca glances at me.

'Emily is my agent, my UK agent,' he explains. 'She finds buyers for my lemons. She is very well connected.'

'Hi.' She finally looks up from the sketch pad and holds out a perfectly manicured hand for me to shake. 'I've heard a lot about you.'

'Have you?' I say, and wish I hadn't.

'It's brilliant you moving here like that, on a whim.'

'Well, not actually a whim . . .' Or maybe it was, I think.

'Emily bought a place here ten years ago, with her partner.'

'Oh?' Suddenly, and I have no idea why, I'm feeling warmer towards her.

'Yes.' She smiles. 'Came out here on holiday, and by our third visit we'd found a place down on the coast and bought it.'

'Lovely,' I say.

'Well, it was, until we split. But there was no way I was going to sell the place. I love it here. I love everything Sicilian.' She looks at Luca.

So, no partner and obviously very keen on Luca.

'Emily divides her time between London and here. She has contacts there, high-end shops and businesses, restaurants and consortiums that she sells my lemons directly into.

It's because of her that I can do this.' He nods to the lemon grove below.

Emily looks at the wedding dress plans once more.

'You'll have to do mine when I finally find Mr Right, Luca.' She smiles widely, and I could swear he blushes, before glancing at me and then at the floor, at a bit of dust he brushes with the toe of his shoe, his hair fallen over his eyes like curtains on the outside world.

'And what is this?' She reaches out a red-nailed hand and touches the bottle on the table.

'It's verdello limoncello. Zelda has made it for her wedding; for the toast, to long and happy lives together.'

And for a moment, I envisage us all raising our glasses, to each other and to Etna and her snowy, smoky top, happy in the knowledge that love is alive and well in Città d'Oro.

'Would you like to try some?' Luca picks up the bottle, ever the perfect host. 'Zelda, is that okay?'

'Of course,' I say, holding out a hand.

Luca pours the green liquid into a third glass.

'Zelda? Another?' He holds the bottle over my glass and his eyes sparkle, making me laugh.

'Oh, go on,' I say, and he pours one for me and one for him.

'To love,' he says, and nods first to me and then to Emily, and we all raise our glasses and then sip. 'Marriage should always be about love,' he says, arching an eyebrow.

But I do love Lennie. And the wedding will give us the home we want, the fresh start, the new life. It's about protecting what we have. Am I sounding like Luca's father? I wonder.

A silence falls. Only the birds in the lemon grove can be heard, and a donkey braying in the distance, along with a cockerel from next door. Luca looks at Emily, who looks at her glass. Then slowly she raises her eyes, and I'm ready to hear that it's nice, but not her kind of thing. She strikes me as a high-end Prosecco lady.

'This is amazing,' she says, her wide white smile lighting up the rest of her face. She takes another sip, and I can't help but feel pleased and much warmer towards her.

We all sip again.

'How did you make it?'

'It's a secret recipe.' Luca steps in. 'Handed down from my grandmother. It is the taste of home.' He lifts his glass and holds it up in the sunlight. 'It is Sicily in a glass.'

Emily smiles.

'Do you mind?' She reaches for the bottle, her glass practically empty.

'No, go ahead,' I say, and she picks up the bottle, puts the cork firmly in it and then slides it into her big leather bag.

What a cheek! I think, outraged. But I pride myself on not saying it out loud, and focus very hard on the glass in my hand. I guess that's Sicilian hospitality for you. I think of all the generous gifts of food we've had left at the farmhouse. I suppose it's just an accepted state of affairs, woven into the fabric of the island's way of life, and that, I remind myself, is one of the reasons I love it and am determined to stay and make it my home.

'I must be off,' Emily says. 'I just wanted to check that everything was okay with the orders whilst I was here.'

'Yes, of course,' says Luca. He holds a hand out to me. 'It's much easier getting everything picked now that Zelda is here to help me.'

'Great. And no problems with the family? They still don't know anything about it?'

He shakes his head. 'No problems at all. Zelda is very discreet.'

'Good, can't have the secrets of Sicily getting out.' She checks the bottle is safely secured in her bag, and I feel a tiny pang of irritation but manage to push it down again.

'Bye, Zelda. Good luck with the wedding preparations. I envy you that beautiful dress. Actually, I just envy you!' she says, and laughs. She kisses me on both cheeks and I clumsily knock noses with her. I'm trying hard not to like this woman, but failing. She envies me, and my married life here in Sicily. And that is why I came here. I found the pot of gold at the end of the rainbow, I remind myself.

'Which way did you come in?' Luca says as he sees her to the door.

'Through town. But I have a hire car. Everyone thought I was just a tourist passing through, on my way to Etna.'

'You could always use the tunnel,' Luca says. 'Park on the outskirts of town or down by the sea.'

'I know, I know. But it's fine.' She smiles at him, and I wonder if the two of them have history. She kisses him on both cheeks, and again I get a little spike of jealousy.

Once Emily has disappeared, Luca looks around at the sketch pad and the tape measure. 'I think we're all done here,' he says, and I get the impression that he's drawing a line under whatever it was that either of us might have thought we felt. 'You sure you wouldn't like to see down the tunnels?'

'No, thank you. I told you, tunnels, dark spaces, they're not my thing,' I say with a shiver at the thought of it.

I stand at the top of the steps leading down from the apartment and look around. For no reason that I can understand, I have a strange, uneasy feeling. It's as though I'm being watched, even though there's no sign of anyone here.

'I should get back,' I say.

'Hello. Where've you been?'

'Sophie! Hello, you made me jump!' I say, my heart lurching and then coming back to land again. I'm relieved to be out of the bright and very hot afternoon sun and in the shade of the old buildings just off the square. But I'm increasingly nervous of the crumbling balconies overhead, and I glance up quickly and move myself and Sophie out of the way of one that is looming over us.

'Where've you been?' Sophie repeats.

'Nowhere,' I say, smiling at her constantly inquisitive mind.

'You must have been somewhere? Nobody goes nowhere, it's not possible.'

'Just for a walk,' I say, still with that strange, uneasy sense of being watched. What if Luca is found out? What if his father insists he hands over the lemon grove for subsidies? I think about Romano with renewed annoyance.

'Where are you going, then?'

'Um, well, back—'

'Home?' she finishes for me.

'Back to Il Limoneto, the farmhouse, yes.'

'Can I come with you? You could teach me more English.'

'No,' I laugh. 'I have things to do.'

'What things?'

'Well, a wedding to plan for starters. I have to tell Valerie . . . my mother-in-law about my dress.'

'My mamma says there isn't going to be a wedding, not if she can help it.'

I stumble, almost like I've been tripped up.

'Does she?' I eventually say as evenly as I can. 'But we want to keep Etna happy, don't we? I'm sure your mamma wants that too.'

'She says she'd rather take her chances with Etna than have a bunch of foreigners move in here, like Il Nonno says,' and I realise she's talking about Romano.

'Your . . . Il Nonno should be pleased that people want to come here and bring new life to the area.'

'He says you'll be gone by the end of the month. He still hopes Uncle Luca will marry Cousin Enrico's daughter.'

'Does he now?'

We reach the shop and I stop briefly.

'Don't worry, Sophie, we're not going anywhere,' I tell her firmly, then I smile and say goodbye.

Whatever Il Nonno says, I tell myself, there will be a wedding. I have a dress, and a fiancé, and no matter what chemistry there might have been with Luca during that fitting, we will be getting married in four weeks' time. One thing I do know: I have to stay as far away from Luca as I can.

And with that, I run all the way home to Lennie and the safety of Il Limoneto, where all those chaotic thoughts will disappear.

Chapter Thirty-one

I go earlier to the lemon grove the following day, and the day after and the day after that, so I can get the lemons picked and packed into the crates before Luca arrives at the lemon grove after checking in at the restaurant, like he does every day, just to see if there are any bookings or tourists around. I check his clipboard and see how many crates he needs and then get to work so that they're all there, waiting for him in the cool of the barn, ready to be shipped out through the tunnels.

It's hot, really hot.

No wonder people don't work at lunchtimes here. But I have plenty of water, sunscreen, and a hat, a large straw one I found in the boxes of clothes, with a big floppy brim.

Today, I pat Rocca and make sure she's got plenty of water too, then get to work under the blazing Sicilian sun, trying to stay in the shade and focus on getting the lemons harvested. I carry a box to the barn. One down. How many to go? I swig from my water bottle and take a moment in the cool of the barn.

'Hey! Zelda! Where have you been? I've been looking everywhere for you.'

My heart jumps into my mouth and my stomach flips over and then squeezes very tightly at the sound of his voice. It's

Luca. And I look a mess, I suddenly think, sweating in the heat of the day. That's a good thing, I chide myself. This way I won't be worried about feeling attracted to him.

He runs over to me and holds me gently by the top of my arms, his skin on mine making me tingle as he kisses me on both cheeks. My stomach turns once again to molten lava and I step back quickly.

'Is everything okay? I haven't seen you. What are you doing working here at this time of day? I've been coming back and finding all the lemons picked and packed. Is everything all right? If you have another job somewhere else, you don't have to do this. I'll manage.'

'No, it's fine. I just . . . I have things on my mind. I wanted the peace and quiet,' and I turn to look out to sea. It is the most beautiful place in the world, I think.

'You come in, work and leave without me even seeing you?'

'I needed to think,' I say, and swallow. 'It's not looking good for us at the farmhouse. The others just can't get work. We have hardly any Airbnb bookings. No one wants to come and stay in Città d'Oro and there's practically no money left in the kitty.'

I don't tell him that I'm avoiding him because every time I'm around him I feel like I'm about to explode and I can't think straight about anything.

'The kitty? The cat ate the money?'

'No.' I manage to laugh, and it brings a strange release. 'Our money. It's nearly gone. And unless we come up with some ideas soon, well, we're going to have to leave.'

'Leave? What? Leave here? No wedding?'

I shrug, and feel my eyes fill to the brim with unshed tears.

'No one can get any work, Luca. We can't get business ideas off the ground and no one will give us a job. This town is dying and I don't think anything can save it. If only it was all like this.' I wave a hand around. And then I think back to the farmhouse. Actually, most of them are doing something. Billy has his chickens and is busy making bird boxes and chicken houses. Ralph has taken to sketching; apparently he always wanted to go to art college before the army and then the City sucked him in. Barry loves going out on his bike and cooking in the kitchen. Sherise and Tabitha have taken up yoga. Valerie talks nothing but weddings. It's just Lennie who is lost really. 'If only we had a project or a business that we could all help out with. We could do with some good news.'

'That's what I've been trying to tell you.' Luca grins. 'It's Emily!'

'Emily?'

'My British agent,' he reminds me.

Ah, Emily, I think. Is this why he's so happy? He has good news? Have he and Emily finally got together? Despite feeling pleased for him, I feel like someone has put a pin in my birthday balloon. But that's okay. Because not every day is a birthday. You have to go back to real life sometime. No wonder he looks so happy.

'I'm delighted for you. Thought there was something there when she came here before. Thought it might be . . . that you might—'

'Zelda, will you stop talking and listen!' He takes hold of my upper arms again and I do stop talking and look at him. He's trying to tell me something.

'Is it the dress? Is it ready for a fitting?'

'The dress is fine. I'm getting there. We'll do a fitting soon.'

'Oh, good. I was—'

'Zelda, it's not the dress. It's Emily!'

'You said. Are you worried about what your father will say, with her being British?'

He looks at me as if trying to read my feelings. I suddenly bite my bottom lip, trying to fight back the tears of frustration that I've been holding on to for so long now.

'The verdello. The bottle she took . . .' he says.

I look at him quizzically, my head tilted to one side.

'She loves it!'

'So she said. She took the bottle.'

'And she gave it to her customers to try.' He is beaming from ear to ear.

'Good. I'm delighted. Now I have to get on.'

'Zelda . . . she has an order for it. A high-end deli. They want to place an order! They'll pay half up front, half on delivery.'

'But . . . but I only have what I made for the wedding,' I say, not really taking in the information.

'Then make more!' He beams. 'You're in business.'

Slowly but surely, the information sinks in. I'm in business. I have an order, from Emily. Someone wants to buy the verdello limoncello! Suddenly my spirits rise from the floor like a plane taking off and a huge grin spreads across my face. I'm going to make this work. The wedding is going to happen, and maybe life here beyond it too! And I find myself beginning to laugh, as tears of relief roll down my cheeks, and Luca's too if I'm not mistaken.

He hugs me, and I can't not hug him back, despite being hot and sweaty. But as I draw away, I catch sight of a figure standing in the entrance to the barn, leaning heavily on a stick and casting a long black shadow.

Chapter Thirty-two

'So what happened?' I ask. I've been waiting for Luca at the restaurant, helping myself to gelato as instructed.

'He said he'd heard I was farming lemons.' Luca helps himself to lemon gelato too, scoops up a spoonful and lets it sit on his tongue.

'And?'

He pulls the spoon from his mouth.

'And that I was letting the family down. The land is worth much more as a redundant lemon grove and I was disrespecting him and the rest of the family by not leaving it that way. If the inspectors came and saw it thriving, it could jeopardise all the subsidies if they thought we were producing fruit whilst claiming.'

'And?' I push.

He shrugs, sits on the table and eats more ice cream.

'He says he'll make sure the water to the lemon grove is cut off. He'll get Matteo to check.'

'But you have the tunnels for water.'

'Sadly, you need rain to fill them up,' he says, and puts down the little glass bowl. 'We haven't had rain in ages.'

Not since we've arrived, that's for sure.

'The lemon grove is the only thing I have here. I love that

place. It was my grandfather's. He loved it too. I think I told you how he used to say that a man only ever becomes a lemon farmer for love. Sadly, lemons are never going to make you rich. And my father could never understand why you would choose love over making money. But I could.'

His words hang in the air. I want to hug him, but know I can't. I want to go and smash another statue, but know I can't do that either.

'What are you going to do?'

He drops his head and his hair falls over his face like curtains once again.

'He'll be keeping a close eye on me, on the lemon grove. Or rather he'll be getting Matteo to do it.'

'He is strangling this town, Luca. Killing off anything that is good in it. What are we going to do?'

'He won't be watching Il Limoneto.' Luca raises his head, smiling. 'We're going to make your limoncello and make sure Emily has enough bottles to meet the order. He's so busy starving this town, starving the trees, that the trees are making more verdello than ever before!'

His smile spreads right across his face, and I could kiss him. But I don't. And I won't . . . I won't. I don't want anything to ruin things here. Nothing must spoil this.

Chapter Thirty-three

'Right, everybody!'

I've called a meeting in the kitchen early the following morning and am channelling my inner Alan Sugar as he hands out the tasks in *The Apprentice*. There is a tray of cannoli laid out on the table, crispy, sweet tubes filled with cream. A gift from the baker, no doubt.

'We need to pick as many of those little green lemons from the grove as we can. Billy, you've made a way in, right? And it's still okay to get in there?'

'Certainly have. Farming and fencing have been my life. Yes, there's no connection to the electric fence there now.'

'So we'll all go out and pick, then we need to peel and I'll start to put it in jars. We'll bottle in three days. We need more bottles. Luca has plenty at his place. He's sorting them out now but we'll need to bring them over. Could you help, Barry?'

'Righto!'

'I'll take the minibus over,' says Valerie. 'Barry and me can go together.'

'This is brilliant. I'll take photos,' says Tabitha.

'I think you probably need to put the camera down and pick fruit with us today,' Ralph says, and it's probably the most he's said to her since we found out about the magazine article.

'Of course,' she says, and without any complaint, she puts her phone on the table.

'We'll all need a little knife or scissors. It's not easy to get the verdello off the trees,' I say.

'What if we're spotted?'

'Yes, what if Matteo is passing?'

'Matteo won't be passing, not at this time of day. He'll probably be working on the gym.' We all look at Lennie, impressed by his insider knowledge. 'He told me the other day, when I saw him in town. We talked. He was fine. He's just doing his job. It's Romano that has all the power around here.'

'He's keeping an eye on another lemon grove on the edge of town at the moment,' I say. 'But if he is passing, we'll just say we're rounding up some chickens that have escaped . . .'

We all make our way into the lemon grove, and the chickens seem to love the idea of company, trotting around us and pecking at the ground. We've got a selection of baskets and bowls. Even Valerie is with us as we step through the wild flowers, drawn towards the trees by the citrusy smell.

We pick until it's too hot to pick any more. Luca has joined us too. Every now and again, the two of us seem to look up at the same time, like magnets returning to home, and I find myself quickly averting my gaze and my cheeks pinking up. But it's the excitement of the deal, the prospect of finally making some money and being in business that wins out. It's finally happening.

Ralph and Barry bring out chairs and flatten down an area

of grass in the shade of a row of lemon trees. Barry has been working in the kitchen, making big bowls of pasta, just like Luca showed us that night. Valerie goes to help him carry them out, along with a board of bread and wonderful caponata that Sherise has made from vegetables she's been growing and nurturing in the overgrown veg patch.

'This is fantastic, Barry,' I tell him. 'Thank you.'

'Actually, I loved it. I always wanted a big family to cook for,' he says. 'But it never worked out for me.'

'Me too. For so long it was just me and Lennie. Now there are three of us.' Valerie beams at me. 'And who knows, maybe . . .' She looks at my belly, and I blush.

'You're as bad as Giuseppe,' I laugh. I'm nearly forty. I think my chances of having a family really are over, especially as Lennie and I haven't even got going on practising and probably never will. Our relationship is based on other qualities.

We eat, chat and enjoy, and when we've finished, Luca stands and says, 'Who's for gelato?'

'Luca has brought some of his lemon ice cream,' Valerie beams.

'Me, me!' everyone says, waving frantic hands in the air. It's like a family Sunday lunch, the sort I always wished I'd had.

'I'll help,' I say as Luca climbs off the bench he's sitting on, next to Tabitha. As I follow him to the kitchen, I notice that both Tabitha and Valerie are watching him. Barry and Lennie are busy topping up people's glasses with wine from a barrel that was left on the doorstep by the nearest vineyard owner, and teasing each other about who picked the most verdello.

Luca pulls the ice cream from the freezer as I grab bowls and spoons. None of them match – a bit like us in the house, I think with a smile. Then he picks up one of the bottles of verdello I've made for the wedding.

'May I?' he asks, holding it out to me. 'I think we should celebrate your order and your new business.' His eyes sparkle with excitement, and I can't help feeling it too.

'Sure.' I smile broadly. 'We need to celebrate the future.'

'Yes, the future.'

'What about you, Luca, what will you do now?'

He shakes his head. 'I'm not sure yet.' Then he laughs. 'I'm weighing up my options, I suppose.'

'What about the restaurant?'

He shrugs. 'Until more people come to the town, there just isn't enough business to keep it going, no matter how much my father would like that.'

'And what about your cousin, the one your father wants you to marry?'

'My second cousin,' he corrects. 'And I'd rather wait for love to finally find me than settle for a marriage of convenience,' he says, and I feel myself suddenly bristle. Is that what he thinks Lennie and me are?

'I love Lennie,' I blurt out.

'I know,' he says, and smiles gently. 'But are you in love with him?'

I open my mouth to reply, but for once, tellingly, the quick-as-a-flash answer isn't there.

'That's not the point,' I say eventually. Suddenly I remember what Lennie told me back at that terrible fortieth birthday party. 'Love can be like food. It can develop and grow over time, like the flavours of a slow-cooked meal.'

'True.' He nods. 'Something to be savoured and enjoyed.'

'Exactly.'

'And you still don't believe in love at first sight?' he asks quietly and almost tentatively.

'I think,' I swallow, 'that it could be easy to mistake it. Like a tempting snack when you're hungry; whereas the slow-cooked meal will hopefully stay with you for a long time.'

He nods. 'I agree. My mother was unhappy with my father. She went for the tasty snack. He was English, working here. My father found out. He was the last to know. It's why he hates the town so much. He feels he was betrayed by them all.'

'Is that why he can't stand outsiders coming in?'

'Sadly, history has a way of repeating itself,' he says, looking down and then up between the curtains of his wavy hair. 'Carina, my cousin, who runs the shop . . .'

I raise an eyebrow. 'What about her?'

He sighs. 'She too fell for a visitor to the town. An Englishman. But he left and didn't come back.'

I take a sharp breath. 'Sophia's father?'

He nods.

'That's why she's so fascinated with all things English?'

He nods again.

'And why your father doesn't like incomers.' I put the pieces of the jigsaw in place.

'He would rather die than let a member of his family fall

for the charms of a "foreigner" again.' He makes quote marks around the word.

I swallow. 'But what about you?'

He shrugs. 'I will follow my heart where it takes me, if I know it's right,' he says, and a piece of melting ice drops from the ice cream pot and makes a little puddle on the table.

'My father, he isn't all bad. He is protecting his family, doing what he thinks is best. He doesn't trust.'

'And that's why he wants you to marry your second cousin?'

'It's his way of looking after the family.'

I look at him, and he sighs.

'It's just not my way.'

'Well, like I say, I'm here for the slow-cooked meal,' I tell him with a dry mouth.

'As long as it satisfies you and leaves you feeling happy,' he says, looking up at me with those dark hazel eyes that I want to lose myself in forever. My stomach flips over and over, and there is a fire burning there that could outdo Etna any day.

'I hope it will,' I say, barely audible, finding myself inexplicably drawn closer and closer to him, my hands still holding the bowls and spoons. 'I suppose it will all be in the tasting,' I say, looking at his lips and feeling the draw of them, and before I can stop myself, my mouth is finally on his.

It's as if my internal satnav is shouting, 'You have arrived!' Like the golden path I saw shimmering across the sea to a place I thought might feel like home. It's an amazing homecoming, the best feeling in the world, and I never want it to stop. Everything else around me fades out, and it's just Luca and me in my golden, sunny bubble.

'Where's the ice cream?' I hear Barry's voice as he comes

into the kitchen, and it makes me jump and step back, breaking the moment. 'Valerie sent me in to check on it.' He laughs, and although I don't think he saw us, I suddenly find myself blushing, my cheeks burning with embarrassment and, if I'm honest, desire. 'Said you two were taking your time.'

Luca picks up the ice cream and slides off the table where he was perched before I kissed him. I kissed him! Oh God!

'Here, you carry the bowls, Barry.' I turn and hand them to him, and then Luca and I follow back outside with just the briefest of glances at each other.

Outside, my cheeks still bright pink, I avoid Valerie's eye. Guilt is wrapping itself around me and trying to suffocate me. I know this has to stop. I have to find a way for Lennie and me to connect in the bedroom; a way to find satisfaction from our slow-cooked meal and try and make it taste like that kiss did. Like the best meal I've ever had, one that will stay with me forever.

Luca is dishing up glistening white ice cream into bowls in the shade of the lemon trees. I go to hand them round as the little round balls begin to soften and melt at the edges.

'Wait!' he says, and he opens the bottle of verdello limoncello and drizzles the green liquid over the ice cream.

When everyone has a bowl, he takes the last for himself. He bends his head to breathe in the smell, then digs his spoon in and lifts it to his lips. He lets it sit for a moment in his mouth, then slowly draws it out and swallows. He looks down, eyes shut, and I hold my breath, fighting this effect he has on me.

The whole table falls silent and watches him.

At last he opens his eyes, wide.

'This,' he waves his spoon at the bowl of lemon gelato and verdello limoncello, 'this is Sicily. This is what fills and satisfies my soul. This place.'

I look at him, and there's a sadness in his eyes, as if he's yearning for something or somewhere he's got to leave behind. And as we all tuck into the ice cream, I too have a sense of something special that I may never get to taste again.

Chapter Thirty-four

'Ralph, how about it, you and me on washing-up?' says Tabitha.

'As long as you promise not to write an article about me whilst I'm doing it,' Ralph says with a smile, standing and gathering bowls.

'Promise!' she says, and I think a truce might finally have been called. 'On Billy's chickens' lives!' she adds, and Billy glowers. 'Joking!' she finishes, and as we smile in relief, there is a burst of squawking and flapping in the lemon grove. It looks like Billy's cockerel is ready to protect his flock.

'Zeld? Will you be okay if I go?' Lennie looks down at his phone. 'Matteo is giving me some work. His hod carrier, Paulo, is ninety-three, and, well . . .'

'What? He's too old to carry the bricks?'

'No, he's had to go and visit his sister on the mainland. Matteo has asked me to stand in and help out while he's away.'

'You're going to work for Matteo?' We all look aghast.

'Don't tell me you're working on the new gym!'

'Look, maybe this way we can get Romano onside.' Lennie looks at Luca. 'If he sees we're here to work and get involved . . .'

I harrumph.

'It's worth a try, Zeld,' he says.

'Of course, of course,' I agree, guilt washing over me again. Lennie is working so hard to make our new life happen. My heart is safe with him. There's no risk of me being left, or hurt again. I must never, ever forget that.

I smile, and he kisses my cheek, then grabs a bottle of water from the table, slings his man bag over his shoulder and pulls down his shades from his forehead. I love the way Lennie has embraced Sicilian life. I just can't see him moving back home.

Luca helps me gather and wash all the verdello. We're exhausted, but happy.

'Okay, well I think we have enough here,' I say, looking at the crates of fruit.

'I have more jars and bottles at the restaurant. Maybe collect them tomorrow?'

'Good idea,' I say.

'But if you are not going to make the limoncello until tomorrow, when the bottles arrive, you need to keep the verdello somewhere cool . . . and safe.' He looks at me seriously, and once again I feel the electricity shoot round my body.

'What about the barn?'

Luca shakes his head.

'How about an outside bedroom?'

He shakes his head again. 'What if someone books to come tonight? You'll have to move the fruit somewhere else.'

'Well, a booking would certainly be very welcome,' I say, thinking about our dwindling household fund.

He looks at me. 'What about the tunnel? It is cool. No one will look for them there, especially now my father thinks he has put a stop to my lemon exporting.'

'What, take them all to the tunnel? But how?'

'I can help.' Valerie is suddenly standing beside us.

'Valerie! Where did you come from?' I say with a burst of laughter. I feel like a child caught with their hand in the biscuit tin.

'Well, I saw you two with your heads together . . . again,' she says, and I feel my cheeks burn. She couldn't have seen us earlier, could she? Guilt and shame wrap around me like a python and squeeze until I find it hard to breathe. 'What are you planning?'

'We're trying to work out where to store the fruit,' I say. 'It's important to keep it cool.'

'And safe,' Luca adds. 'Lemon theft has always been a problem in Sicily. It's how protection gangs started up. Lemons that had already been sold were being stolen before they had been picked, so farmers employed security staff to guard them. These guys then became the middlemen between the suppliers and the customers, running, how you say, the whole racket.'

'The Mafia!' Valerie's eyes are on stalks.

Luca shrugs. 'No one mentions that name here in Sicily. But yes, it is a part of our history.'

'Doesn't sound that far from your father's business practices if you ask me,' I say, thinking about Romano shutting down the lemon grove, cross on Luca's behalf. Actually, on the town's behalf. We have had such kindness from some people, but I'm so angry they can't carry on their lives as they used to.

They live in fear of the bully that is Luca's father. It's so sad that they are grateful for us arriving, but no one can tell us to our faces. All the gifts of food and drink that arrive under cover of darkness, practically every day.

Luca nods his head sadly, his eyes shooting back to Valerie, as if wondering how much she knows.

'Like I say, I can help,' she says brightly, and I love that she's so keen to be involved. I need to assure her that I'm here with Lennie. I love Valerie as much as I do her son. I don't want to ruin this. I have to put things right. After Lennie and I left, I did wonder what she would do to fill her days. She loves having him living at home. The wedding has taken up all her time until now. I think it's good for her to be getting outside and doing something else. I owe her. I need to make sure that whatever that kiss was, it was just a blip. It doesn't mean anything, no matter how much it seems to have shifted my insides.

'We need to move the verdello to keep them cool and safe overnight,' I tell her.

'But no one must know where we're taking them,' Luca adds sternly, and I feel myself biting my bottom lip, hard, to stop the feeling that is creeping up on me. The feeling I have been working so hard to ignore since the day he measured me for my dress. The feeling of attraction and . . . yes, desire.

I can feel Valerie's eyes on me.

'Cool and safe sounds exactly what's needed,' she says, and I feel myself blushing again.

'So, how are we going to get them there without anyone noticing?' I ask quickly, focusing on the verdello and trying to forget how attractive I find Luca and how my heart races when

I'm around him. Once the wedding dress is finished, I won't have this problem any more. I wish I could feel happier about it. But Valerie's hard stare seems to help.

We load up the minibus with the verdello and make the bumpy journey to the other side of town. Valerie stops at the gates of the lemon grove and we unload.

'No one must know about this place,' Luca reminds her. 'No one must find out about the tunnels.'

I help him carry the crates down to the tunnel entrance. When they're all safely stowed away, we return to the minibus.

'What are you doing?'

The voice makes us jump. It's Sophia.

'You shouldn't be here,' I say. 'Does your mamma know where you are?'

'I saw the minibus. I wanted a ride. How come everyone else gets all the fun?'

'Okay, we'll give you a ride, but just back to your house. Your mamma will be worried.'

'Mamma is always worried. I'm never allowed to do anything.'

'Come on, hop in,' says Valerie with a smile.

Chapter Thirty-five

'Gone! What do you mean, they're gone?!'

Luca is shaking his head as he emerges from the tunnel's mouth. 'See for yourself.' He holds a hand out.

'I can't believe it!' I'm almost lost for words. 'I know your father wants us gone, and the town to go back to how it was, but this is . . . bullying! Intimidation! He can't get away with it!' I'm shaking, I'm so angry. How dare he?

The air is thick and heavy, the heat almost suffocating. I look up at Etna's smoky peak and wonder if she's in a dark mood again. If the fruits aren't found and I can't make the limoncello – if I can't meet that order – it's all over for us here . . . and I am not going to let that happen. I am not going to let Il Nonno stand in my way. I have had enough of this!

The sky has darkened to match my mood. I can feel the pressure in the air, like it's pushing on my skull, making my head ache. He's not going to get away with this.

'That's it! I'm going to have it out with him!' I begin to march towards the gates, Luca following me. 'Other people may be too scared to stand up to him, but I'm not!'

What have I got to lose? Nothing, because I *have* nothing. I have nothing here and nothing to go back to. I am nearly forty and I'm not going to let this bully of a man take the one chance I've got at making something for myself and my housemates.

I realise with a jolt that I'm including the others here, the people I was so keen to get away from when we arrived just a few weeks ago. But I care about them. I care about Ralph getting a new start and putting his mistakes behind him. About Tabitha creating a life for herself with her words. About Sherise and Billy finding a home and Barry putting down some roots. This is not just about me; this is about the funny, raggletaggle bunch we have become, and I'm not going to let him ruin my last chance at making things right for myself and for them.

'Just because he hasn't got over the fact that his wife left him all those years ago,' I say. 'Frankly, I don't blame her. I'd leave him if he was my husband!'

Luca stops and stands still, and I realise my words have hurt him. It's not just Romano's wife I'm talking about . . . it's Luca's mother!

'Sorry,' I say.

I'm still fuming as I pull the gate open and stride through. It slams behind me, swinging on its hinges, and Luca is left on the other side.

'Wait! Zelda! Come back!'

But I ignore him.

Suddenly there is a flash of lightning and a crack of thunder overhead, but I barely notice it, or the downpour that follows, soaking me, plastering my hair to my head. I am absolutely focused on where I'm going. I'm going to speak to Il Nonno and get my lemons back, and nothing and nobody is going to stop me.

Chapter Thirty-six

Actually, I have no idea what I'm going to say as I march up to the big gates of the over-the-top, pimped-up villa and stare the CCTV camera in the eye.

'Come on! I know you're in there!' I shout, pushing the buzzer and leaving my finger on it for the count of five. The rain is lashing down on me, my hair is stuck to my face, but I hardly notice it. Overhead, there is another flash of lightning and a crash of thunder. This time I shriek. My nerves are shredded and my reactions on high alert.

I look around me. The headless statue is gone. Probably in for repair somewhere. But the branch I knocked its head off with is still there. It seems there is only one way to get this man's attention. Hit him where it hurts. His precious ivory tower.

He knows nothing about this town or how the people here live in fear – of Etna, and of him and his family business. They are too scared to be seen to be mixing with us, let alone welcoming us. He doesn't seem to understand that we just want to build a life for ourselves and in turn help revive the community. How dare he try and chase us out! He doesn't have a God-given right to the place. It should belong to whoever puts the effort in to care about it!

I'm not running away any more. I did that enough when I was younger, when things got on top of me at school or in the care home. But that's all in the past. Now I want to put down roots.

I look the CCTV camera in the eye again, and I swear it winks at me, taunts me.

'Come out, Romano, come out and tell me what you've done with them!' I shout over the torrential rain, rivulets turning to rivers around my feet, which are soaked like the rest of me. I can see my reflection in the eye of the camera, hair stuck to my face, mascara running down my face to join the water cascading down my cleavage.

I look at the gate, waiting for it to swing into action with a squeak. But it doesn't move.

'Okay, Romano. You asked for it!' I draw the branch back like a baseball bat, eyeing the camera as if it were the ball careering towards me.

Suddenly the gates groan and start to move. I stop mid swing and slowly lower the branch to my side as an irate Romano appears at the top of the steps up to the front door.

'Get away!' he shouts. 'Go back to where you came from! You're not wanted here! Touch any of my property and you will pay for it. I warn you, young lady.'

But I'm not listening. Instead, still clutching the branch, I march through the gates and up the steps until I am right in front of him.

'Where are my lemons?'

He looks at me blankly.

'My lemons, the verdello. Where are they? You don't need them. You only want the subsidies from the land. I'm not trying to compete with you, just using what is otherwise going to waste. What is your problem?'

'My problem? You! You are my problem!'

There's another crash of thunder. There is no part of me that isn't soaked, but I don't care. I don't care at all!

'It's not me that's your problem,' I say. 'It's the fact that your wife left you. You're still taking it out on everyone else, dishing out punishments, keeping any spoils to be had for yourself.'

'I am providing for my family. Looking after them. That doesn't make me a bad man!' he shouts over the rain as it slams down from the sky and bounces back up, thigh high, from the ground.

'At the expense of everyone else . . . yes, it does!' I yell back.

'You know nothing about me or my family!'

'I know that Luca is a good man who has stayed here to support you, but he has dreams, and they're not about marrying his second cousin!'

'Luca will do what I tell him. Stay away from my son. This is business. Love has no place in a marriage. It's about protecting what we have and the ones we love.'

'He's a grown man; you can't blackmail him forever into thinking he needs to look after you. You clearly don't need looking after, you're obviously—'

Suddenly he looks down, and then holds his hand to his heart. He takes a step back and leans against the door frame.

'Oh, don't start . . .' But I stop myself. What if he isn't putting this on? What if he really is having a heart attack? I can't tell. He couldn't really be that manipulative, could he? 'Romano?' I say. Guilt rushes in and pushes out all my angry thoughts. Did I do this to him? I just wanted to make him see; I just wanted my lemons back! 'Romano!' I shout at the top of my voice. And then I hear another voice.

'Papà!'

I turn and see Luca running up the drive.

'Luca, I . . .' My heart lifts and twists at the same time. But he doesn't look at me, just touches my elbow gently as he passes towards his father. And I realise it's Romano who's important to him just now, not my guilt and apologies.

'If there is anything I can do . . .' I say, rooted to the spot.

'Papà! It's Sophia!'

Suddenly Romano's head jerks up and his hand slips from his chest.

'She's gone missing!' Luca says in English, turning back to me.

Romano stands up straight, his hand dropping to his side. So, it was just a ruse! But I'm not thinking about that right now. I'm thinking about Sophia.

'I saw Carina,' Luca continues. 'She's out of her mind with worry. Sophia was supposed to be doing her homework. But when Carina went to check, she had disappeared. She has no idea how long she's been missing, or where she might have gone.'

My heart feels like there's a vice around it, squeezing. I feel sick at the thought. How must Sophia's mother feel? And briefly I wonder if my own mother ever felt anything similar. If she did, she never showed it.

'I'll get my hat,' says Romano.

'What can I do?' I ask Luca.

He turns out his palms. 'We need to start searching. Anywhere we can think of.'

I look at him, the water pouring through his hair like he's standing under a shower, making it spring into curls. He has worry etched across his face.

'This is a bad storm. We need to get her back safely,' he says.

I nod, feeling his concern, and just for good measure, lightning rips across the sky and there's another crack of thunder.

'Her mum is frantic. It's just the two of them. Tell anyone you can,' he shouts over the rain.

I want to take him in my arms and tell him everything will be okay. But I can't. I can't touch him. He has to believe that kiss was just a mad, impetuous, impulsive moment. That there was nothing in it and it will never happen again. Even if it felt as if everything was in it. He can never, ever know that.

'I'll get the others from the house!' I turn to the gates.

'Good idea. And I'll tell Giuseppe to spread the word,' Luca says. 'What's your number?' He takes out his phone, and so do I, and we exchange numbers.

'No, you go and look.' Romano appears again in his hat, this time without his stick. 'I'll go and find Giuseppe. I'll ask him for help, and the villagers. They'll listen to him,' he says, and I realise how important it is to all of them if he is finally able to speak to the man he hasn't had any contact with for so long.

I just hope there will be good news soon.

'No one wants another burial in this town . . . especially not a young one!' Romano says what we're all thinking. I look at him. Right now, there are more important things to worry about than his fake heart condition and my missing lemons – way more important. 'We need to find her, quickly! The storm is getting worse!' and lightning cracks open the sky once more.

Chapter Thirty-seven

'Lennie!' I'm soaked and out of breath and I struggle to call his name. But he's there all the same.

'Zelda! What on earth's happened?! Look at you. Come on, let's get you inside and out of those wet things.'

More than anything I'd love to fall into Lennie's comforting and reassuring arms and let him tell me everything's going to be okay. But I can't. I shake my head.

'It's . . .' I drag in a big gulp of air. Sherise and the others are standing behind Lennie now. Sherise gets me a glass of water.

'Is it the lemons . . . the verdy things?' she asks.

'No.' I shake my head and take a swig of water. 'Much. More. Important.' I have another drink. Everyone is on tenterhooks. 'It's Sophia, the little girl from the shop. She's gone missing.' Another clap of thunder explodes overhead, making us all jump, and no one needs asking twice.

'I'll get our coats, Billy,' says Sherise.

'Let's stick in pairs,' Ralph orders. 'And swap numbers.'

We all pull out our phones and I give them Luca's number as well, just in case.

'I'll contact Matteo, see if he can check the abandoned houses,' Lennie says, stabbing at his phone.

Outside the farmhouse, we split up, our thin waterproofs totally ineffectual against the rain now filling the courtyard, and turning the track into a muddy river.

The others spread out into the lemon grove outside the farmhouse. I decide to head into town. Lennie veers off at the narrow cobbled street before the archway to help Matteo search the old houses there. I keep marching on, looking up and down all the little lanes, some no wider than the breadth of my shoulders, all gushing with rainwater pouring off the mountain.

'Sophia!' I call. 'Sophie!' But there is no response.

I turn back. Luca is coming out of the restaurant.

'I wondered if she might have gone there,' he says. 'She sometimes hides from her mother under the tables, usually when she's avoiding doing her homework.' He tries to smile, but can't. Worry is etched all over his face.

The town is the busiest I've ever seen it. Locals are out with coats clutched around their bent bodies, searching in sheds and in old cars. All of them nod a greeting, but everyone is looking worried.

'When did you last see her?' I ask.

Luca thinks.

'I'm not sure. What about you?'

'I don't think I've seen her since we gave her the ride in the minibus yesterday evening.'

We look at each other with dawning looks spreading over our faces.

'You don't think . . . ?' I swallow. Guilt washes over me. 'You don't think she followed me there this morning, do you? When I went to check on the verdello?'

Neither of us needs to answer the question. As if working in total sync with each other, we head up through the square towards the slippery cobbled street that leads to the lemon grove. The water is ankle deep, and Luca stops and turns back to me, holding out a hand.

'Take it steady,' he says as I bound forward. 'Slow down. We don't need another casualty.' But I carry on blindly, desperate to get to the lemon grove no matter what.

Suddenly there is an almighty crack overhead. Luca stops abruptly and I crash into him as he holds out his arms to stop me. Directly in front of us, an old balcony crumbles and collapses. The rubble hits the road, and the water quickly builds, bubbles and diverts up and over and around it, like a dam bursting its banks.

We both look up, and I know he's thinking the same as me: that we were within a fraction of a second of that coming down on us. Me and my bloody impulsiveness, never thinking about the consequences!

Come on, brain, engage! And I don't know if I've said it out loud or not.

'It's okay,' says Luca calmly, whilst my heart is thundering like a Duracell bunny banging its drum. He holds out his hand again. 'Just take it one step at a time. No need to rush. Just think about where you're stepping. Listen to the voice inside you; it'll guide you right.'

And whilst part of me is saying, 'Don't take his hand, you'll start to have those feelings for him again,' another part is urging, 'Do it. Work together. It's all right.' And as I reach out for him, suddenly all the pieces of the jigsaw slot into place.

Together we negotiate the pile of rubble and the torrid river now running down the cobbled street. On the other side, we stay holding on to each other. This time we're moving a little more slowly and steadily, as though we're sure of where we're going with the other there to support us, and it feels for the first time in my life that I'm working with someone as one.

I love Lennie, strong, reliable, dependable Lennie, but the little voice inside me tells me this is different, and I hear it. Luca and I are both scared, but we're doing it together. And I realise that I am falling in love with this man, and there is absolutely nothing I can do about it.

Chapter Thirty-eight

We're nearing the lemon grove when we hear a voice calling Luca's name. We both look round to see that an elderly man has fallen, and his wife is trying to help him up.

'Go!' I tell Luca. 'Go and help them. I can do this.'

'Are you sure? You're not just saying that?' He holds me by the elbow.

'I'm sure.' Somehow I feel responsible for Sophia coming after us yesterday, and maybe again this morning, and now she might have ended up in the tunnels, which will be filling with water. Because that's what they're designed to do . . . fill with water!

'I'll follow,' he tells me.

I stumble and splash my way over to the tunnel entrance. Something inside me tells me that this is where I'll find her. I stumble again and steady myself. My palms are sweating, my head throbbing as I remember all those feelings that came crashing in on me the day I got locked in the cupboard. I couldn't escape. I couldn't get out. I thought I was running out of air. But I have to find Sophia!

I look around for Luca. He's nowhere to be seen. The rain is falling in stair rods. The tunnel must be filling; I can't wait. Legs like jelly, I climb down into the dark opening. He'll come!

I tell myself. He will! I hold up my phone as a light and start to make my way through the tunnel, ankle deep in water and getting deeper. My breath shortens. I'm hot, despite the cold rainwater. I turn around towards the exit, but something inside me tugs at me. If I'm scared, how must a little girl be feeling? Call it impetuous, impulsive, whatever anyone has ever said about me, but as much as I hate small spaces, I have to do this.

'Sophia! Sophie!' I call, my voice shaking, one hand on the rough wall, the other shakily holding the phone as I pick my way over the uneven ground until suddenly there in front of me is a pile of stone, a landslide, with water building either side of it.

'Sophia!' I shout loudly, peering through into the blackness beyond. My heart is banging so loudly it's deafening. And then, above the din, I hear it.

'Zelda! I'm here!' cries a little voice.

'Coming, lovely. I'm coming. Hang on!' And this time I don't give the dark or my fear of small spaces a second thought. Sophia needs me! I plough on over the pile of rubble to the dark beyond.

She has some cuts and bruises that I can see by the light of the phone. She's perched on a narrow ledge. The water is nearly knee high here. She has a small dog sitting next to her. I put out my hand to Sophia and it snarls protectively.

'Shh, shh,' I soothe them both. 'Hold on, honey. I've got you.' And for once, I don't feel I'm crashing around in total chaos, but taking control of the situation very firmly and not letting go. I pick her up off the ledge.

'And the dog. I've called him Harry, after the English prince.'

'Of course, and Harry.'

I scoop him up and shove him inside my jacket. He seems to understand that they are both safe now, and stays quiet.

Sophia clings on to me, and I wade through the rising water with the child on one hip and the little dog in my jacket, carefully negotiating the fallen rocks. Sophia is still wrapped tightly around me, nearly strangling me, as I carry her out of the tunnel, both of us shaking with cold.

'Sophia! Zelda!' Luca calls out, and he's running towards me. 'You found her!'

He goes to take her from me, but she buries her head in my neck and sobs.

'Shh, shh . . .' I murmur again, and the rain seems to ease a little with my soothing.

'Come on, let's get her home!' Luca says, and puts his arm around us both.

'But what if Mamma and Il Nonno are cross with me?'

'They will just be happy to have you back. Everyone has been very worried about you, Sophia. The whole town has been out looking.'

'The whole town?' She looks at me.

'Uh huh,' I confirm.

She says nothing, but finally loosens her grip and lets herself slide from my hip, then walks beside me, holding firmly onto my hand. Luca rings Giuseppe to call off the search, and Lennie too.

'You leave Il Nonno to me,' he says. 'I don't think he'll be giving anyone a hard time any time soon,' and I know he's thinking about his father's fake heart flutter and that he has a lot to consider.

Chapter Thirty-nine

On our way to the big villa, we pass many of the locals, all of whom wave and call, 'Thank God she's safe!' It is only when Luca raises his free hand in response that I realise the other is still resting around my shoulder as if it were the most natural thing in the world, with Sophia tucked in between us, clearly feeling safe there, holding my hand.

'It was Zelda,' he tells them all, but I don't hear their replies. I just keep thinking about what might have happened if the water had risen any higher, if I hadn't got there in time. What might have happened, over and over in my head. My teeth are chattering and I'm shivering, as is Sophia. I wish I had something dry to put round her, but instead Luca and I just draw closer together around her to keep her warm.

As we approach the big gates, I feel our pace slow, all of us reluctant to walk up the drive. We're like Dorothy and her friends arriving at the Emerald City, not knowing what kind of a reaction they're going to get when they come face to face with the Great and Powerful Oz. But I know, and Luca knows, that just like the Wizard, Romano is a fake. We haven't had time to talk about what happened, but we both saw him try to pretend that he had a heart problem. We both saw him and I'm wondering how Luca feels, being lied to all this time.

The gates are wide open, and we're now holding hands with Sophia, a hand each. Luca is looking up at the villa as if he's seeing it for the first time, as if the scales are falling from his eyes. If it wasn't bad enough that his father has commandeered his lemon grove, he's now realising that he's been kept here all these years on some false guilt trip. An elaborate ploy to make him do exactly what Romano tells him.

'Sophia!' Romano and Carina are running down the steps, arms flung wide open to welcome her home. Sophia looks up at me. I nod, smile and let go of her hand, and she runs forward, throwing herself into her mother's waiting embrace. Romano wraps his arms around both of them, resting his chin on his great-niece's bent head, as if enveloping them in a protective blanket. Whatever his faults, he does genuinely love his family, I think.

'It was Zelda who worked out where she was and saved her,' Luca says directly. Finally Romano straightens up and looks straight at me.

'She was really brave! If she hadn't come . . .' says Sophia, and then she bursts into tears, and Carina, with a look and a nod to me that says everything she needs to say – thank you and sorry – spins her daughter towards the steps and into the villa, chattering away about getting her out of her wet clothes and something to eat and drink.

Sophia stops at the top of the steps by the front door and waves. I feel a sudden pang, and I'm not sure if it's a pang for the mother I didn't really have or the mother that I'm never going to be. But it hurts, really hurts. I know there won't be any children now with Lennie. And in any case, I realise with an ache in my heart, it isn't Lennie's children my arms long to hold. A huge lump forms in my throat.

'We should get you back. Lennie will be worried,' Luca says. I nod, and tears spring to my eyes.

We turn to leave.

'Thank you,' says a gravelly voice. '*Grazie.*'

I turn back to Romano, and we stare at each other wordlessly.

'You saved . . . well, she is like a granddaughter to me,' he says eventually. 'You protected my family. *Grazie mille.*'

I nod.

'Will you come in? Get dry. Have something to eat?'

'No, *grazie*,' I say. 'I'm glad she's home safe.'

'Name it,' he says. 'Whatever it is.' He takes a step towards me, and I look at Luca.

'He wants to do something to repay you, to say thank you. It's how things are done around here.'

I look at Romano, and then say slowly, 'I want my lemons back. That's all. I just want to be able to make a life for myself here.'

'By rights, all the lemons around here belong to me . . .' He cocks his head, as if not really understanding what I'm saying.

'And don't we know it,' Luca practically growls. I see his fists clench.

'It's business. Good business,' Romano says to me, but I know he's addressing Luca.

'Look, I just want to know where the verdello are,' I say. 'You said to name it. Well, I am naming it. The verdello we took from "your" lemon trees, just let me have them. I'll pay for them, just as soon as I'm paid for the limoncello. Just give me this chance.'

He shakes his head. 'I'm sorry. I don't know what you're talking about. I know nothing about any verdello.'

'Pfft!' I throw up a hand and turn away. There's no point. He's never going to give anyone what they want if it doesn't benefit him.

'Papà! It can only be you!' Luca's voice is slow and measured. 'You have run things around here for way too long. You control everything and everyone with your money, your bullying, your intimidation . . .' He swallows. 'And your lies. It may have got you what you wanted, control. But it will never get you respect . . . not real respect. And I cannot be a part of your world any more. I'm done with you.'

And having said his piece, finally telling his father how he feels, he turns to walk away.

'Luca! Wait!' Romano calls.

I wonder if he's going to try and fake his dicky heart again. But I don't turn round to find out. Neither of us turns around; we just keep walking.

'Wait!' This time it's Sophia's voice, and both of us glance back to see her leaning over the balcony above the front door.

'Take care of yourself, Sophia,' I try and give a cheery wave.

'No, wait. Wait there!' she says, and she turns from the balcony and darts back inside.

Moments later, she appears at the wooden front door, with its heavy, ornate knocker, and comes running down the stone steps. She's wearing a big fluffy white dressing gown

'Sweetheart, you've already said thank you. I'm sure Zelda doesn't need you to say it again,' says Romano, trying to guide her back inside.

'It's fine, Sophie,' I say. 'You're safe and that's all that matters. Take care of yourself, and no more hiding out in tunnels!'

'No, wait, you don't understand. I went back to the tunnels . . .' I hear her begin, but I'm not really listening. I need to get back to the farmhouse now. I need to see Lennie and tell everyone that Sophia's safe but that the verdello are gone and with them our chances of staying on here. I wonder whether to do the 'I have good news, and bad news . . .' line.

'And I said, don't do it again,' I say lightly, trying to make a joke of it. 'I might not be around to rescue you next time.' And the words catch in my throat as I realise that I'm saying goodbye.

'But Zelda . . .' I hear her take a big breath. 'I know who stole the verdello!'

Chapter Forty

I march home, furious thoughts propelling me there. I'm so enraged, even Luca's offer of a lift falls on deaf ears. I can't hear anything apart from Sophia's words.

I know who stole the verdello.

I keep walking, with Luca riding behind me at a snail's pace on the moped, clearly worried. But I need to walk. I need to clear my head. Because now that I know, I have to work out what to do about it.

Chapter Forty-one

'You're back!'

'We were so worried!'

Everyone is there in the kitchen, looking freshly showered and dry. I am still in my sodden clothes.

'Is she okay?'

All their questions and concerns blur into one.

'She's fine. A bit shaken and bruised, but otherwise all right,' I manage to say through blue lips and chattering teeth.

'Thank God!' says Sherise.

'Well, that was quite an adventure,' says Barry.

'I've never seen so many people in the town,' joins in Tabitha.

'And Giuseppe and Romano out searching together. Quite a day,' adds Lennie.

They're all pottering around the kitchen preparing supper together, as if they've been doing it all their lives. And I realise how long I've been out.

'So the verdello have gone?' Sherise asks me.

'Yes,' I reply, teeth really chattering this time.

'So that's it. We're going home. We can't find any other work.' Ralph stops peeling onions and looks at me with his pinny round his waist, and for a moment I think how strange it is that this seems perfectly normal here.

'Someone wanted to get us out really badly,' Barry says, putting water on to boil.

'Yes . . .' I repeat, and the word hangs in the air before I finally manage to say the words. 'Didn't you, Valerie?'

And as everyone turns to look at Valerie, my blood runs cold. The expression on her face confirms everything I've been told. The rug has been well and truly pulled from under my feet.

Chapter Forty-two

'How could you?' I say, frozen to the spot, hot, angry tears welling in my eyes.

'It's not what you think. Or maybe it is.' She suddenly bursts into tears.

'Just tell me where the verdello are, Valerie!' I try really hard not to raise my voice.

She stands slowly, the chair scraping across the floor, and leads us outside, around the muddy puddles and out towards the lemon grove . . . and the chicken hut. There, all around, are the verdello, cut in half.

'Mum!' Lennie says, looking around, astounded and bewildered.

'They didn't really like them,' she says quietly.

'That's not all of them. Where are the rest?' I say urgently.

Looking ashamed, she lifts the roof of the henhouse. It is stuffed with fruit, the hens perched and pooping on top of them.

'I couldn't get any more in, so I . . .'

'Yes, Valerie?' I'm slowly realising there isn't going to be any hope of saving the verdello now.

'Before you were all up, I drove further up the hill, towards Etna, where it turns into a blackened moonscape, and . . .'

'Yes,' I press.

'I stopped at one of the tourist vantage points and threw them down the hillside.'

She drops her head in what I'm hoping might be shame. As she does, a single verdello drops from the heap, making one of the hens squawk in surprise, and rolls out of the henhouse towards us, followed by another. It's as if they're handing themselves in.

Everyone is standing staring at the ruined fruit.

I'm shaking, not just because of the cold, the wet clothes clinging to my body, but from utter betrayal. I feel frozen to the core of my body, despite the sun attempting to come out and warm things up.

'Mum! What on earth have you done?' Lennie finally speaks as we all take in what has happened.

Lennie guides me back to our room and turns on the shower, laying out a clean towel for me. And as I step out of it, there is a hot coffee waiting on the bedside table. I am in shock. But I know that no matter what his mother has done, I can always rely on Lennie.

I take the coffee and go and stand by the window, pushing back the flaking shutters and staring over the lemon grove up towards Etna, where my verdello lie in an ashen grave. To the right, Città d'Oro looks like a terracotta toy town tumbling down towards the sea, where the tunnels lead to. Where anything could have happened earlier today. Because of Valerie.

Valerie, I repeat to myself. Of all people. The woman who took me in, made me feel I had a home. Always insisted I had tea and toast before I went out in the morning and always said goodnight before I went to sleep at night. The woman who made me feel safe. And then today put me in my worst nightmare. In a tunnel, with a young girl, reminding me of the awful nights I hid in my cupboard, too scared of the chaos going on around me to come out.

I take a slug of coffee and realise Lennie has put something strong in there, probably for the shock. The shock of discovering that the one woman I thought I could rely on in life is the one who has let me down; and not just let me down, but tried to ruin everything. I feel absolutely lost. I thought coming here was going to be a fresh start, a new beginning; that I had finally made a sensible decision and was working at making a life for myself and joining the club of happily marrieds with homes and businesses.

I wipe away the tears rolling down my face. It's not the first time I've felt let down by the people I thought were meant to love me. And at least I still have Lennie, I think as I look away from the view and at the dry clothes he's laid out on the bed. We have each other and I know he won't let me down. Or will he? I would never have believed Valerie would. It suddenly feels like I'm walking on soft sand.

I dress and splash my face with cold water, and then, slowly and as calmly as my jittery body and mind will let me, I make my way downstairs, where the whole house has gathered.

'Oh Zelda!' Valerie gets to her feet. She's clearly been crying, and the rest of the house are standing round her, hands on her shoulders. I feel my own shoulders stiffen. They may have forgiven her, but I haven't. I stand and stare at her. The face that has meant so much to me.

'Please, love, let me explain. I've been so stupid.' She goes to take my hand, but I drop it limply by my side.

Lennie steps forward, tall and reassuring, and I allow him to lead me to the kitchen table, my face set. Luca is there, but I don't look at him. I can't look at him. Every time I do, my stomach feels like a merry-go-round and my heart starts beating at twice its usual speed. Perhaps it is a good thing we're leaving, because I can't be around him feeling like this.

I keep my eyes away from him. Whatever it is that makes him have this effect on me, I have to put a stop to it. Maybe this has all happened for a reason. Lennie and I aren't meant to be here; we're not meant to be getting married. It was all just a stupid, impulsive idea. Dreaming that I could be like other people, growing up and having a family life. My mum didn't manage it. She made mistake after mistake. Looks like the apple – or rather, the lemon – hasn't fallen far from the tree.

'Yes, I took the lemons,' Valerie says, sitting and sniffing into a hanky, and I focus on her rather than Luca. She looks around the group, who have obviously heard the story and are willing her on. I check whether Tabitha is taking notes. Gratefully, I see she isn't. 'I took them . . .' Valerie swallows, 'because . . . I wanted to go home.'

I stand and look at her, confused.

'I wanted you and Lennie to come with me, move into my house. It's far too big for me. I knew this day would come, when he would want to leave. I'm as lonely as anything. At least with Lennie there I had someone to cook and wash for. But I knew you wouldn't agree if I just asked you.'

I say nothing. I see her eyes flick to Luca and back to me.

'I didn't want anything to get in the way of you and Lennie getting married.'

My heart starts galloping. My mouth goes dry. Did she see us? Oh, stupid, stupid me! Why do I always spoil everything good in my life?

'I thought if the verdello were gone, you'd think it was Il Nonno. That you'd've had enough of being here and would come home with me.'

'But what about Etna? The wedding?' Sherise asks.

We all look at each other.

'I'm so sorry. I've ruined everything.' Valerie dissolves into her hanky again.

'But how did you do it? Move all the lemons?'

'I took the minibus back, early this morning. I saw the little girl, Sophia. She was on her own. I waved.'

'She must have followed you. She must have wanted a ride in the bus again.'

Valerie lets out a loud sob. 'I'm so sorry. It was such a stupid thing to do, I realise that now.'

'We've all made mistakes, Val love. We wouldn't be here if we hadn't,' says Barry.

I look at him, and a cold feeling of realisation washes over me. He's right, I think. We've all made mistakes, but I don't want to make any more. I think about the kiss, me and Luca, and the way it made me feel like I'd finally found everything I'd been looking for. But now I have to put it into a box and shut the lid, because I can never make that mistake again.

'I'll go if you want me to,' Valerie says.

I don't reply. I can't. What do I say? 'Go if you want?' I'm not making that decision. If she wants to leave, it wouldn't be the first time I've ended up on my own.

Just then, Giuseppe arrives.

'What is going on? What's happening?' he asks.

Everyone starts to explain, like a noisy Sicilian family all wanting to pass on the news. Look how far we've come, I think, and I can't help but let a little smile pull at the corner of my mouth.

'But the wedding?' Giuseppe looks aghast.

'There will still be a wedding.' Lennie smiles and ruffles my freshly washed hair. But there are no merry-go-rounds in my tummy. There's no passion. I'm settling for hugs and cups of coffee by my bed, and knowing he will always be there for me and will never let me down. There will still be a wedding. But a voice in my head whispers that it is a wedding for all the wrong reasons. 'But first, we have a batch of limoncello to make . . .' and he slaps his hands together.

'But the fruit is useless!'

I sit down, exhausted. 'Tabitha's right. The verdello are useless.'

Luca looks at me. '*These* verdello are, yes . . .' A thought seems to be slowly evolving in his mind. 'But because all the lemon groves round here have been starved of water, there are many verdello.'

'So . . .' I realise what he's saying. 'We need more fruit. Your father has the fruit.'

'Yes.' He nods. 'I'll go and speak to him.'

'No!' I say. 'I'll go. He owes me one, remember?' And I grab the handbag that has been my constant companion since

I found it, still with the green ribbon and the recipe inside, and somehow now they feel like my lucky charms.

'Here, take this,' Luca picks up a bottle of the verdello limoncello.

'But that's for the wedding.'

'If you can pull this off, you'll have more than enough for the wedding.' He smiles. 'Let it do its magic.'

'And for God's sake don't tip it over his head or anything daft like that,' Lennie says with a mixture of humour and concern. 'Matteo says—'

Luca cuts him off. 'You and Matteo, you're like an old married couple.' He throws his head back and laughs, and then, missing only a fraction of a beat, Lennie joins in. I look at the two of them, the good friends they have become, like two brothers teasing each other.

Then Lennie turns back to me.

'Just be careful, Zelda, that's all I'm saying. We all know what you're like.' He looks concerned, and I know it's because he cares.

'I think Zelda will do just fine. I think my papà may have met his match!' Luca laughs, and I can't help but smile as I take the bottle from him. As I do, our fingers touch and it's like I've been charged with an electric shock. Oh God, I think, I am in love with two people. I love them both, but differently. My head feels like it's suddenly full of cotton wool. Like all my thought processes have turned to mush. Like I'm right back where I was when I was a kid at school, confused, unable to sort out my feelings and thoughts. I have to choose! But how?

I grab the bottle and practically run out of the house and up the lane, dodging around the big muddy puddles filling the potholes, trying to clear and order the thoughts in my mind. There is a banging in my head, getting louder. But it's not in my head, I realise. It's in the town. And as I pass, I see a sight for sore eyes – building work, on the houses. Our houses! And Matteo raises a hand in greeting.

Chapter Forty-three

I love Lennie! I do! I keep repeating it to myself, and then an image of Luca smiling and saying 'I think Zelda will do just fine' keeps popping up and replaying over and over in my mind. On the one hand, a man who cares about me and worries; and on the other, one who seems to get me and isn't worried, because he knows I'll be fine. One who helps me breathe; the other who takes my breath away.

But I know I can't have two men in my life. There can only be one, and I know which one that has to be. There can't be any other way, can there?

Chapter Forty-four

'I'm sorry. I shouldn't have accused you of taking the verdello,' I say, lifting my chin and staring Romano right in the eye as I stand in front of him at the top of the steps to the villa.

He nods, and I'm wondering if that will be that and he'll turn and shut the door on me, as before. But instead, he stands aside and holds his hand out.

'*Prego.* Come in,' he says, and I suddenly feel nervous and try to line up my thoughts, which keep jumbling up like abandoned knitting.

I step into the hallway. Big dark furniture, huge silver lamps and shades, tall green ferns and a sweeping marble staircase to the balcony above.

I find myself looking up and around. Compared to the other properties I've seen in the town, this is . . . well, certainly very different. Not rural and rustic at all. The house is a bizarre mix of old and new.

He leads me across the marble floor to a large veranda. The view is incredible, so much so that I practically catch my breath as I step forward and lean on the mottled light-cream stone wall. I stand taking it all in. The town hall and church below, the main square with its palm trees and pale-salmon-coloured houses and green wrought iron, and in the distance, the brilliant blue sea. In the other direction is Etna, looming over the town, the centrepiece of every picture, her slowly smoking top like low-hanging cloud.

Running riot over the top of the veranda is a beautiful-smelling cascading wisteria. It all feels a lot like paradise. The only thing to ruin the view is the part-built gymnasium in the far corner of the garden, and suddenly I'm reminded of every-thing this man has done to try and get us out of this town, and to keep his son in a place he doesn't want to be. I feel my hackles rise.

'Coffee,' he says, and I turn to see him lifting a cafetière from the table behind me.

'*Grazie*,' I reply. I'm surprised how quickly I've slipped into Sicilian mannerisms. I couldn't imagine going back home now.

As I sip my coffee, I lean against the stone balustrade and look out again at the amazing view, and then remember the balcony that fell the night of the rain and step away from it.

'Please sit.' Romano gestures to a rattan chair.

I'd rather be standing – frankly, I like to pace when I'm thinking and talking – but I know it would be bad manners to refuse, so I sit and let the Sicilian sun on my shoulders take away some of the tension there. Romano sits opposite me.

'I haven't had the chance to thank you properly for sav-ing my great-niece. She is like a granddaughter to me, as I explained. The only child in the family. I . . . It's important I don't lose any more of my family. It's why I work to keep them, and to keep them safe.'

I look around and spot CCTV cameras in the corners of the veranda and dotted around the garden. I try my hardest not to quip back that he's created a prison rather than a safe haven. One that at least one member of his family is desperate to leave.

'I should have come to see you earlier. I'm sorry. I still haven't repaid you,' Romano says.

'You've allowed the building work to start on the houses,' I reply, sipping. 'Thank you for that. It's me that should be sorry. Like I said, I shouldn't have accused you of taking the verdello. It wasn't you.'

'We all make mistakes,' he says, and it's not the first time I've heard those words today. 'Finding the words to say sorry is the hardest part of all. Thank you.'

'Forgiveness is hard too,' I say without thinking, remembering what Luca told me about how Romano hadn't been able to forgive his wife. Immediately I wish I hadn't. I wish I had some sort of an edit button. He looks at me and I glance down and sip my coffee in order to stop my mouth saying anything else it might regret.

'I brought you this, by way of apology.' I pull the bottle from my bag, realising that getting down to business is the best way out of the hole I'm digging for myself.

He takes the bottle and looks at it, studying the hand-inked label that Ralph has made and stuck on.

'This looks good. Did you do it?'

I shake my head. 'I couldn't have done it,' I say. 'I'm dyslexic. Dyslexic and impulsive – it was never going to be a winning combination.'

'Maybe those are the very things that have made you who you are,' he says evenly.

I remember Luca's look again, and think about all the

things I've beaten myself up over throughout my life, all the mistakes I've made. Maybe they have actually made me who I am. I am impetuous, but then I wouldn't be here now if I wasn't, and I wouldn't still be fighting to keep this idea of staying here alive. I'm dyslexic, but that meant I did more practical things, like buying furniture and clothes for the shop, shifting it all myself, getting stuck in. But it's also why I couldn't hold down a job. Other people always telling me what to do just rattled me, confused me. That's why working for myself was so great and why I can't let this chance slip through my fingers now. My heart is banging so loudly in my chest, I worry Romano can hear it.

He holds the bottle up to the light and looks at the colour.

'But you made this, right?'

I nod. 'Luca told me how.'

He stands and goes to a dark-wood dresser and takes out two glasses, then comes back to where I am sitting. My heart, if possible, is now banging even louder, and I feel like I'm in the amphitheatre waiting to be thrown to the lions.

He picks the bottle up and studies the colour again.

'By rights I should have charged you for the lemons, the verdello ... a local tax for helping yourself to what wasn't yours to take in the first place.' He looks at me, and I hold his stare.

'By rights I should point out that you've been holding people to ransom around here for most of their lives,' I say, unable to help myself, as if the floodgates have opened once more.

He doesn't reply, and instead focuses on pouring two glasses. He pushes one towards me.

'Your family,' I find myself continuing, thinking of Luca

and wishing I could stop, 'and the locals. This town is dying on its feet, and not many years from now, the last person will have to turn off the lights and shut the door behind them when they leave.'

He concentrates on the green liquid in his glass. I hold my breath, waiting for him to ask me to leave. Damn it! Blown it again! Why can't I just keep my mouth shut?

I gather up my bag and stand. But as I turn back to him, he is raising the glass to his lips. He tips it back, the black hat that he seems to always wear nearly falling off his head. I can see him shutting his eyes behind his sunglasses.

He lowers the glass, but says nothing, just rolls his lips in on each other again and again. Then, to my surprise, he takes off his hat and pulls off his sunglasses, and I see his face properly for the first time. There is a look of Luca about him, no doubt.

He covers his eyes with a hand, then pushes a thumb into one and rubs.

'Are you okay?' I ask, instinctively reaching out to him then quickly remembering the fake heart attack and snapping my hand back. I feel, well, bemused. What is going on? I'm standing here waiting to be told to leave. I'm ready. I'm used to being told to go.

Slowly he lifts his head and opens his eyes.

If he's going to tell me that I know nothing of his life or his business, he's right. But I am going to tell him what I think of what he's done to Luca and the town.

I take a deep breath, and then stop when I realise that tears are trailing down his cheeks. He's actually crying.

Chapter Forty-five

'This,' he says, lifting the glass, 'this is how my home town used to taste. Where I grew up, where I brought up my family, where all my hopes and dreams were. This is it. This is Nonna's recipe, isn't it?'

I nod. 'It is,' I say, 'and your home town could be like this again. I have an order for this limoncello. But the verdello we picked yesterday are ruined. I need more, and since you own or rent all the land around here, only you have the lemons I need.'

He stands and walks over to the view, as if seeing it again for the first time in a long time. 'That is how this place should taste. That is the place where I belong, in that bottle.' He holds up the glass, and the light shines through the vibrant green liquid.

He looks at me.

'Take the lemons, as many as you need. Get Matteo to help you cut the fences around the lemon groves. Start with the one here. Tell Giuseppe to invite the villagers. You will get the picking done quicker that way. None of them moves very quickly these days, but there may be help in numbers.'

It takes me a moment to realise what he's saying. He's saying yes! And I beam. 'Thank you, Romano!' I exclaim. '*Grazie mille!*' and impulsively, grinning like mad, realising our plan is back on track, I grab his wet cheeks in my hands and plant a kiss on his cheek, and I'm not sure who's more surprised, him or me, as I run out of the house, down the drive, through the gates and all the way home to tell the others the good news.

'I'll let everyone know,' says Barry, climbing on to his push-bike, his constant companion now. 'I'll cycle into town and tell anyone I see to come and help.'

'We'll start in the morning,' I tell them.

'I'll be there,' says Ralph.

'And me,' says Tabitha.

'Okay, tell everyone we'll meet at the lemon grove on the top of the hill,' I say.

'What? Il Nonno's?' asks Lennie.

'Yep,' I smile.

'Knew you'd do it, Zeld!' he says, pulling me to him and kissing the top of my head. He looks at his phone. 'Matteo is coming to take down the fences. He's just finishing up at the houses. Looks like there could be plenty of work for me now!'

Early the following morning, as the last of the verdello are gathered in, I'm standing right at the top of the hill, looking out at the orange sky over the sea and the golden path across the water there. Behind me is Etna. It's an amazing view, the lines of lemon trees crowded with people working and chatting.

Giuseppe and Valerie have paired up, and Il Nonno and his great-niece are a team; him carrying her on his shoulders and Sophia picking the fruit. Matteo has arrived, and he and Lennie have gathered the high fruit that the older, bent-over members of the community can't reach. The couple who gave me the flowers are holding hands and helping each other from one tree to the next. Harry, the little dog that Sophia found in the tunnels, is running with Rocca through the overgrown grass and wild flowers. Rocca has found a whole new lease of life since Harry turned up. The sun is at a comfortable heat, just warming the soil and our souls before the intense rays of the day kick in.

Luca comes to stand with me. I can smell him before I hear or see him. I know he's there and my heart starts racing.

'Good to see,' he says, looking straight ahead at the lines of lemon trees. 'If only it could always be like this.'

He's right beside me, our hands next to each other; barely touching but enough for me to feel connected to him and the moment.

'Yes,' I say, my heart banging away. 'If only it could always be like this.'

We say nothing more until Lennie turns to indicate that they're finished and are taking the last of the verdello to Matteo's truck to drive them to the farmhouse.

'Don't forget we have the fitting for your wedding dress,' says Luca, the moment broken and real life beckoning. 'Meet me at the lemon grove once you've finished making the limoncello.'

I nod, knowing it will be the last time we will be alone together. The wedding is only two weeks away. *If only it could always be like this.* His words repeat in my head as, with one last deep intake of breath, as though drawing in the moment and making it last, imprinting it in my memory, I step forward in the soft soil, a basket of verdello under my arm.

As we reach the truck, Il Nonno is waiting there. He slowly lifts Sophia off his shoulders, smiling and laughing.

'Had fun?' I ask her.

'It's been great! We never come into the lemon groves. I love it!' She beams, and I think about the little girl I first met, sitting at home doing her studies. Never allowed any further than the town square. All this land around, and yet she has been as caged as the bird that keeps her company.

'It seems I am in your debt again,' says Il Nonno. 'You have worked a little magic here today.' He smiles as he watches the child running around in the long grass with the dogs. 'What can I do to repay you this time?'

'Really, there is no need. I have everything I need right here.' I gesture to the basket of verdello.

Carina walks over to us.

'Zelda,' she says, and I lift my chin warily. 'Thank you, for everything. For finding my daughter and, well, bringing a little fun back into our lives. You are welcome here. I'm sorry for my earlier ... apprehension.' She smiles at me, and suddenly I feel a big ball in my throat.

Giuseppe and Valerie are chatting together, bouncing off each other's shoulders as they make their way from the lemon grove. Then Valerie looks up at me and her smile drops. There is still a lot of pain there between the two of us.

'Is there nothing I can do to repay you?' Il Nonno asks again.

'Really,' I say, 'just the chance to make the limoncello, to try to find a way to stay, is all that matters.'

He smiles, a long, slow smile.

'I tell you what, that street party you put on a few weeks ago ...'

'What, the one no one came to?' I raise an eyebrow.

'Put it on again. Tomorrow night. What do you say, Giuseppe?' he calls over.

Giuseppe looks up from listening to Valerie, her big hips swaying through the long grass as though she has spent her life picking lemons.

'What's that?' he calls back.

'Tomorrow night, a street party in the square, to welcome the new arrivals.'

'A magnificent idea! And to celebrate the soon-to-be wedding!' He grins broadly, but I don't return his smile. I am full of nerves. Pre-wedding nerves. Or should it be pre-married-life nerves?

'Tomorrow, after the limoncello has been made,' I agree.

'And after your final dress fitting,' Luca says, looking at me, and the nerves bubble up like a shaken bottle of Prosecco, fizzing and spilling and spoiled.

As the sun starts to rise higher in the sky, the last of the lemons are loaded. This time, I think proudly, they're leaving not through a secret tunnel, but right through the heart of the town, where they belong.

Chapter Forty-six

The next day, with the verdello safely steeping in alcohol in large jars and everyone busy preparing for the street party, I walk into town. The sun is like a huge orange in the sky. In the main square, Sherise is potting up geraniums with Valerie.

'They're lovely,' I say.

'Yes. Carina gave them to us. They weren't selling, she said. Thought they would brighten the place up for this evening.' She smiles. Valerie attempts a smile too, but I can tell she's still feeling bad about what she did and is keeping her head down. I can't stay cross at her, though. It was my fault too. I should never have kissed Luca. I should never have let my guard down. I should have learned by now to stop being so impulsive. Marrying Lennie is all about finally growing up – and helping this town that I have come to love, I think as I start down the twisty cobbled street towards Luca's place, passing the little houses on either side of me, and various locals who all raise a hand and wish me *buongiorno*.

I wave back and wish them a good day too.

When I reach the lemon grove, I push the gate open and the dogs come rushing from their shady spot under one of the trees to greet me. They have been devoted to each other from the moment they laid eyes on each other, inseparable, as if it was love at first sight. And who said there was no such thing? I try and laugh at myself, but the painful truth is that I've come to realise that I was wrong.

I make my way up the steps to Luca's apartment and knock. Every part of me feels as nervous as a child on its first day at school. Telling myself it's because I'm going to see my dress, finally finished, I take a huge breath and tug at the scarf around my neck. I have to go in. It's now or never, or I will just turn back and then I won't have a dress to wear in two weeks' time.

'*Buongiorno*,' I call through the beaded curtain over the door, and I slide my hand in and push it back with a tinkling sound and step onto the cool tiled floor.

Luca, glasses perched on the end of his nose, is standing next to my dress on a mannequin, and I'm not sure which one takes my breath away more.

The dress is everything I could have hoped for . . . and more. I begin to walk around it as the sun streams in through the big open doors. Luca pulls off his glasses, his hair parting naturally in the middle and falling down across his forehead. He pushes it back with one hand, the hands that have made this dress just for me; the dress that says: this *is* me.

I feel tears prickle my eyes and wish I had someone here to share this moment with. But who? Not my mother. It's Valerie who has always been there for me, more like a mum than my own ever was. She hasn't left me. She was just frightened of us leaving her, of being lonely, on her own. I remember how lost and alone I felt before she scooped me up. If anyone should understand, it's me. I vow to put things right with her as soon as I leave here, at the street party tonight.

'Let me make some coffee,' says Luca, giving me the space he can see I need just to take in the dress and what it means. I walk around it, taking in the detail: the lace, the lemon netting and lemon blossom embroidery.

He comes back with coffee and a plate of small cakes.

'Cannoli?' He smiles, holding the plate out to me. I reach out a shaking hand and take one, then turn away, biting into the soft pastry and its creamy filling and letting the delights of it melt in my mouth and distract me just for a second.

When I turn back, he's looking at me.

'So, are you ready to try it on?'

And I swallow, hard.

He takes the dress into his bedroom, where three suits are hanging, presumably for Lennie, Ralph and Barry. They're so smart, sharp and pressed. The bed is neatly made, and again, I swallow, realising that this is where this man was lying not so many hours ago. There is something very, very sensual about that thought.

'If you need any help, just call me,' he says as he goes to close the bedroom door.

I definitely won't need help, I think. There is no way I can ask him for help. I just wish my shaking hands would work with me on this one.

Finally dressed, I look into the full-length mirror and catch my breath. Can this really be me? How have I changed so much and not noticed? There's a slight tan on my face and a glow about me, and the dress seems to enhance every good bit and gloss over the not-so-good.

When I step out of the bedroom, the expression on Luca's face brings tears to my eyes all over again. It is the look I have always dreamed someone would give me, like I was everything they had been waiting for in life.

'You look *bellissimo*, just beautiful,' he says, and I can hear a crack in his voice.

'It's the dress,' I say quickly, trying to bat away the compliment as I blush hotly. I look down at the soft waves of satin. 'I don't know how you did it. It's everything I could have wanted.'

'I had hoped it would be. I have got to know you so well over these past few weeks, it was easy to make a dress that described you.'

We both look at it.

'Now, let me just make the final alterations. Stand on this box and turn around. Do you have the ribbon with you?'

'Yes, here . . .' I take it from the bag and hand it to him.

'Something old, something new, isn't that what they say? A piece of Città d'Oro's past here at the start of your new life.' He begins to pin the ribbon around me, and his fingers touching my back send a thousand volts through me.

'Yes,' I try and say.

'As long as you are sure that this is what you want, it will be the best day of your life,' he continues as he pins. 'And turn,' he says, and I shuffle round on the box. And now, dear God, he is pinning just to the side of my right breast and I feel I'm about to explode and go into orbit. I look up at the ceiling, trying not to think about the sensation of his hands on my bare skin, the desire building and burning . . .

'I have a condition,' I say. 'It's called ADHD. It makes

me . . . impulsive.' God, I hate that word. It's how the doctors described me. 'I was always in trouble at school. Couldn't concentrate on the lessons, my head always somewhere else, maybe three places at once. I was forever forgetting homework, or losing it. I remember losing my school coat for the third time; my care assistant went ballistic. And I could get into an argument practically in an empty room. I always acted first, thought later. Lennie knows what I'm like. He keeps me grounded. Marrying Lennie is about me keeping my impulsiveness under control. He's my rock. He understands me and helps me stay out of trouble.'

'But it's part of who you are,' Luca protests. 'You wouldn't have come to live in a ghost town in Sicily if you weren't impulsive. It makes you brave. Braver than most of us. Maybe it's what gives you wings . . .'

He looks up at me, and right there and then, something inside me just slots into place. *Maybe it's what gives you wings* . . . I repeat in my head, and I think about my life so far and realise that he's right. It's made me who I am, and actually, I think I *like* who I am.

'You stood up to my father. No one else has done that.'

'That's because I just see red and don't think about the consequences.'

'And look how you got everyone at Il Limoneto to stay.'

'Again, heat of the moment.'

'And the street party, and the limoncello . . . It's fantastic. You make things happen. You have brought this town to life. You have made me realise what I'm missing in my life too . . . someone like you.'

We look at each other, and the impulsive me wants to just

move in and kiss him and stay there for ever. But it's him that turns away and focuses on the job in hand. I try and think about anything other than his hands on me. I think about what it was like when we first arrived here, when we all discovered we would be living in the house together. And then finding out that Tabitha was writing about us. Then Etna erupting, and getting the B&B up and running, and that first night when we learned to cook pasta. And Valerie arriving, and me realising how much she means to me and how much this wedding means to her.

I think about Lennie, and how he has embraced life here, working with Matteo; and the others, who all seem to have found their place too. Ralph has been sketching more and more. Billy is loving his chickens and Sherise the vegetable garden, and Barry has positively embraced pasta-making. Even Tabitha is a changed person and has lost all her prickliness. I think about finding Sophia in the tunnel, how everything that had scared me about life came back to me in that moment. I think about Valerie taking the verdello, and how she was worried about the wedding not happening.

The kiss comes back into my mind, and I push it away firmly. I think of the locals coming out to help us pick the verdello, and the town now preparing for the street party and the wedding. The curse of Etna staved off by Lennie and me marrying. How everyone seems to have found their happiness . . .

'Zelda?'

Luca's hands have stopped moving around my body, and I slowly start to open my eyes. I see him first, looking at me, and then the mirror he has placed in front of me. The ribbon is in place. He walks behind me and lifts my hair off my neck. I can feel his breath there.

'Zelda, this is what you want, isn't it?' he asks, looking at me in the mirror.

The dress makes me feel . . . well, like the person I have always wanted to be. Luca has done that. He has made me feel powerful, in control of my life for the first time ever. This is me taking charge of it now, my life, my future, my destiny.

'Marrying Lennie is the right thing to do for everyone,' I say slowly.

'Then I won't ask again,' he says, letting my hair fall and stepping away, and a part of me realises I will never feel like that again.

I look in the mirror. I know I have to do this. I have to marry Lennie, or I will lose everything I have here.

'I'm going to stay,' I say. 'Make more limoncello if I can. I can't leave. I love it here. After all, no one ever became a lemon farmer for anything other than love.'

Chapter Forty-seven

By the time I leave Luca's, the sun is setting and the sky is the colour of citrus fruits, brilliant yellows and vibrant oranges. Everyone from the house is gathering in the town square. Barry and Ralph are firing up the big oil-drum barbecue. There's a table with bottles of verdello limoncello to give everyone a glass or two to say thank you for their help. Valerie's bunting is hanging up, and Lennie and Matteo have strung the town's Christmas lights, which haven't been used in years, all around the square and zigzagging up the main street, softening the peeling cream and salmon-pink walls. Giuseppe has rigged up his record player and a speaker and is playing Frank Sinatra with a wonderful authentic crackle. Valerie is watering the geraniums, her hips swaying to the music, but her head is down and she's still very reserved.

The chef from Luca's restaurant is cooking porchetta on a big spit, and Sherise is laying up a table to serve it from. The air is full of the smell of herby slow-roasting pork, joined by the scent of caramelising peppers and onions. It smells like Christmas when everyone you love is there.

I look at Valerie. We've hardly spoken and I know she's feeling bad.

'Valerie,' I say.

'Yes, dear,' and she looks like she's terrified I'm going to finally tell her to leave.

'Valerie, what you did was wrong, but I also know why you did it.' I take her hands. 'I'm marrying Lennie. We're going to be a family. I give you my word. Just like I've given my word to the people of the town, who need a wedding to happen. This is a fresh start for us all.'

'Oh, I'm so pleased, love. It's what I've always dreamed of. And I'm sorry I was such an idiot and tried to spoil your lemons.' Her head drops again and she starts to sniff. My heart twists. She might not be my mother by birth, but she's the best one I've ever had. I reach out and wrap my arms around her.

'We all make mistakes, Valerie.' I repeat Barry's wise words quietly. 'That's why we're here. But we all deserve a second chance too. That's why we have to pull together and make this work.'

She looks up at me, takes my face in both hands and kisses my cheeks.

'You will always be like a daughter to me,' she says. 'I only want the best for you. I'm sorry I interfered. I just want you both to be happy. I know you won't be coming back to live with me in the UK, but at least I'll be able to picture you here whenever I want to.' She looks around at the town square, at the twinkling lights and the burning orange sun setting in the sky.

I feel something in me twist, and I think briefly of Luca and remind myself that marrying Lennie is the right thing to do for everyone.

'*Buonasera.*' A voice interrupts us. 'Is everything okay, ladies?'

'Yes,' says Valerie. '*Sì*. Everything is fine.'

Giuseppe hands us both a glass of limoncello from a nearby tray. He raises his own glass and we follow.

'Oh, wait! Let me take a picture,' says Tabitha, grabbing for her phone. 'I was thinking, if it's all right with everyone, there is one last story I'd like to write before I hang up my pen, so to speak. How about: "When life hands you lemons, make limoncello. How lemons changed our lives"?'

'*Saluti*,' Giuseppe says, and takes a sip. 'This is wonderful,' he says, and looks out at the setting sun.

'Well let's hope everyone else thinks so and joins us,' I say.

'And if they don't, well, we will have tried. You especially, Zelda. *Grazie mille* for believing in my dream,' he says, watery-eyed. He raises his glass again, and I shut my eyes briefly.

I wish it could have worked. I wish the town had accepted us.

And at that moment, we hear voices and Il Nonno appears at the top of the town hall steps in his big black hat, flanked by his family. Carina is there with Sophia, as well as Romano's cousin and his daughter.

The song comes to an end on the record player and there is just the sound of the disc spinning on the turntable.

For a moment, no one says anything. Giuseppe looks up at Il Nonno. I see his hand tighten around his glass, anxiously, and I step up to stand beside him. Valerie moves to his other side, and then Barry, brandishing his long-handled tongs, and Ralph, followed by Tabitha, Sherise and Billy. It has been a long time since this fractured community has come together like this, to socialise and eat and drink and forget their grievances. I hold my breath. I just hope they can.

Il Nonno walks slowly down the steps, the rest of the family following like flying ducks in formation.

Il Nonno finally comes to a standstill on the bottom step and looks at me, then at Giuseppe again. Then, they both break into a wide smile, and shake hands and kiss each other on the cheeks.

'I heard there was a party going on here tonight,' Il Nonno jokes. 'And that the limoncello is some of Sicily's best.'

And suddenly we all breathe a collective sigh of relief and the music starts up again, with Dean Martin singing about 'Amore'.

Tabitha steps forward with drinks and hands them round. Then Giuseppe steps up to Valerie and holds out a hand in invitation. She looks at it in disbelief, and I can tell she's about to say no and shake her head politely, so I step forward and place her hand in his. She looks at me, and then smiles like all her birthdays have come at once, and Giuseppe takes her in his arms and leads her in a waltz around the worn stones of the town square, in the footsteps of the town's past and the golden light of the setting Sicilian summer sun.

Then, like the Munchkins coming out from their hiding places when Dorothy lands in the land of Oz, the villagers begin to emerge from their houses, dressed in their best suits and dresses. They take the glasses of limoncello being offered to them before heading to the dance floor. And when the dance ends, the gentleman who gave me the flowers turns to me and holds out a hand, with his wife smiling and urging me on.

'Oh, I don't know if I can!' I blush.

'Go on,' says Lennie. 'Follow your instincts, you usually do!' and they all laugh.

Valerie dances again with Giuseppe, and Sherise and Billy dance and then swap partners with another couple of locals. Smoke is swirling skywards from the barbecue, and the smell of roast pork fills the air. There is wine from the barrel that Carina has brought out from the shop.

I'm standing eating roasted artichokes and porchetta from a foil dish when Il Nonno walks up beside me.

'Well, it looks like once again we are indebted to you, Zelda.'

'It was you who suggested we put it on again!' I smile.

'But you and your party had the idea in the first place. You could see what needed to be done here. You could see what none of us could. Me most of all!' He looks around. 'It has been a long time since Città d'Oro has come together like this. Not since . . .' He swallows and turns back to look at the big orange setting sun. 'Not since my wife left,' he says, the pain still clearly there, etched onto his face. 'You know she . . .' He bites his lip and looks out over the view.

'She made a mistake?' I finish for him.

'*Sì*,' he says quietly.

'And you've never forgiven her for that.'

He keeps his eyes on the sunset, not looking at me.

'*Non.*'

'And . . . it seems you've taken it out on the town ever since.'

'I thought . . .' He hesitates. 'I thought I was doing the best thing for my family. I wanted to keep them safe, and close.'

'And your heart?'

'Just broken, not ill,' he says, looking ashamed. 'I should never have used it as an excuse to keep Luca here. I should have let him go years ago. What is the expression, "If you love someone, let them go"?'

I nod. 'You're right.'

And we both take a breath and look at the now low sun on the horizon. At that moment, Sophia emerges from the shop carrying her caged bird, holding it high.

'I thought Montgomery would like to join the party too. It doesn't seem fair that he has to stay inside and not be out here with everyone else.'

'Quite right,' I say in agreement.

Before anyone can stop her, she opens the cage door and the little bird flies out and up.

'Isn't that what you said, Nonno? If you love someone, let them go?'

He puts his hand on her shoulder.

'It is, my love.'

He turns back to me.

'I was angry. I told her to go and not to come back,' and I know he's talking about his wife. 'I was angry with everyone. But I wasn't an easy man to live with. My brother had died. He was the older one, always looking after us all. And my wife had had enough of me ignoring her and what she needed. She needed to feel loved. Isn't that what we all want, to find our one true love? I had mine and I let her go.'

He looks around.

'She would have loved this,' he says quietly.

As we're all eating and drinking and chatting, a car drives slowly along the narrow street and then stops, just as we always hoped cars would do. The door opens and out gets Emily, Luca's agent.

'Oh, hi,' I say.

'Well this looks like fun!' she beams, looking around. 'May I?' She takes a glass of limoncello and holds it up, then sips. 'This really is fantastic stuff.'

'Are you looking for Luca?' I say, glancing at Il Nonno, who is clearly interested in the new arrival and why she's here.

'No,' she says. 'It's you I was looking for.' She takes another sip, and suddenly I freeze. Does she know about the kiss too? Does she think I'm stepping on her toes with Luca? Or is it the limoncello?

'Is something wrong with the order?' I ask. 'It's all ready for bottling.'

Suddenly everyone stops talking and turns to look at her.

'Actually,' she says slowly, 'word has spread. I have more orders, from a restaurant and another shop.'

'More? Oh God, that's brilliant! I'm in business!'

'In fact,' she says, 'I need four times the original amount. And more samples.'

I stand frozen in shock. How on earth can I make this work? I look around at the locals, who are all listening in silence.

'Il Nonno?'

He says nothing; just stares at me.

'This is how your town used to be.' I hold out a hand to the street party. 'This was the growing-up you had. This is what you want for Sophia, right?' And above us I can hear a canary singing from the rooftops. 'Look around. This is a town people will want to come to, because they have heard of the limoncello and the fabulous street parties. You said you owe me . . .' I try and keep my voice steady.

He nods once.

'Then let the townspeople have their land back.' I look around. 'Turn the water back on. Let the town grow lemons, then I can buy the verdello to make Nonna's recipe and sell it. Città d'Oro will be back in business!' I say. 'We will all be back in business! Let the town live again.'

Romano is silent for a long time. Finally he looks at his great-niece and nods.

'I will turn the water back on . . . and yes,' he shrugs, 'I will take down the fences.'

At first there is a stunned silence. I'm the first to realise what he's just said, and I throw my hands in the air and whoop with elation. Everyone else follows. A cheer goes up like a Mexican wave. Elderly couples cling to each other, just as they have clearly clung to the dream of this happening one day. Then they turn and hug us, the newcomers, kissing us loudly on each cheek. Giuseppe is brushing away tears as he embraces older residents and then bear-hugs me, thanking me in between great gulps.

'Where is Luca?' asks Emily amid the celebrations, and I realise that she might have needed to speak to me, but Luca is the one she really wants to see. I look around and frown. Where *is* Luca?

'He can't still be working,' I say, looking around the happy gathering, realising I haven't seen him since I left him finishing off my dress at the apartment. 'I'll go and find him, tell him you're here. I won't be long.' I realise too that I'm dying to tell him the good news about the order and Il Nonno finally giving the town back its lemon groves. He must come and join the party.

I skip over the cobbles off the main street and down to Luca's lemon grove.

'Luca! Luca!' I call out as I run up the wooden steps to the apartment. But the door is shut. I push down the handle and it opens. 'Luca?' There's no reply, and I step in tentatively.

There in the middle of the living room is the mannequin, and on it, my dress, finished, with a tiny piece of lemon blossom attached to the bodice. On the table is a note. I look down at it and read it with tears filling my eyes.

He's not coming. I try and practise saying it in my head, and big fat tears fall onto the page in front of me, because Luca has gone.

Chapter Forty-eight

I walk back up to the town square telling myself it's best for both of us. When I arrive, Lennie is dancing with Sophia, getting her to stand on his feet while he moves, and as he looks down at his feet and then glances up laughing, the happiest I have seen him in weeks, I see him look straight at Matteo, and Matteo smile back at him, like . . . like they only have eyes for each other.

I'd recognise that look anywhere, just like when I first saw Luca. Oh God! Is this what I think it is? How could I have missed it?

Chapter Forty-nine

The air is hazy and heavy again, just like when Etna blew up. There's a strange feeling everywhere, and the light is somehow weird again too. The wedding is just a few days away – three days, four hours and twenty-nine minutes, to be precise.

Lennie has been looking so preoccupied. I'm worried. I need to talk to him about what I think I saw at the street party. He's been helping to pick the verdello early in the mornings, then spending the rest of the day working with Matteo at the houses, which, from the sound of it, are nearly ready to move into. But every time I've attempted to talk to him about the wedding, whether he still thinks we're doing the right thing, he's brushed me off.

I tried again this morning when we got up, bumping into each other in his haste to get ready and out of the house to get to work. 'The wedding, Lennie – you do want to go ahead, don't you? I mean, if there was any reason . . . if you didn't want to, you'd say, wouldn't you?'

He was sitting on the edge of the bed to pull on his boots. There's a whole no-man's-land down the middle of the bed between us. An uncrossed line. He smiled at me, but I know there's a secret behind that smile. I'm sure of it.

'Everything is fine, Zeld,' he said, like he keeps saying,

and kissed the top of my head. 'The town is out in force getting ready for it!'

And he's right. Doors are being painted, front steps and streets swept, window boxes planted. The whole town is coming back to life. Ralph is opening a gallery to display his drawings and paintings in one of the shops in the main street. He and Tabitha seem to be talking about doing some exhibitions together. She wants to put up some of her photographs from the lemon groves. In fact, they're doing a lot together these days, I notice. Everyone is getting the town ready for the big day.

'But if you really didn't want to . . .' I tried again. 'If you were worried about anything, anything at all . . .'

'Zeld, it's fine!' he said firmly, almost sharply. 'I'm fine. Really.'

I'd like more than 'fine' for my wedding. But this is what I signed up for. The slow-cooked meal, rather than the blow-your-mind banquet. 'Fine' really means 'not fine'. I know that from my growing-up, when teachers or care workers asked if everything was okay. I always said I was fine when actually I was as far from fine as can be. I have to try and talk to him.

Later that morning, I walk slowly to Luca's apartment past people out on the streets, leaning on brooms, chatting with each other and waving and smiling and wishing me *buongiorno*, to pick up my dress that he's left there for me. Then I walk back through town to find Lennie at the houses – our new house.

'Zelda!' He practically jumps when I step in through the lovely wooden front door to see him sweeping the floor.

'Thought I'd come and see how . . . things are going,' I say.

I have to find out what he's thinking. If he really is in love with someone else.

'Brilliant! Let me show you around,' he says, and he does, proudly pointing out everything that he and Matteo have done. I get the full tour of the terrace. The houses are really lovely. Especially our one, with the balcony on the corner looking out to sea one way and towards Etna the other.

'Lennie,' I start. 'About the wedding . . .'

'Yes, Zeld,' he says, preoccupied, checking little jobs that need finishing up, making a mental list, not really listening to me. Or not wanting to, I think. But I have to be sure.

He leads me upstairs and I follow, into the bedroom, what will be our bedroom.

'You're happy that we're getting married in a few days?' I ask him directly.

'Yes, yes, of course!' He smiles and looks at me, then glances around the room. 'This is what we agreed. It's what we signed up for. Look,' he throws out an arm to the view. 'This is why we came here. I don't want to go back now, do you? I love it here. Everyone is excited about the wedding. Everything's fine.'

I say nothing and bite my lip. Fine again! But he's right. It's a bit late for thinking about all this now. A lot of people are depending on us marrying on Saturday. A town that has been dying is finally coming back to life and wants to celebrate. How can I take that away from them?

I glance at Lennie, and he gives me a quizzical look. I stare firmly at him. If we're going to make this work, we need to 'forsake all others', I think. I need to forget all about Luca, and I need to know Lennie wants to be with me. I need to know that it really is going to be fine.

We're standing on the balcony. I take hold of his elbows and he looks at me as if wondering what I'm doing. Then I place his hands on my waist. He starts to shift uncomfortably, but he doesn't run. He does look nervous, though. But I have to do this if we are to marry. I have to know that he wants this.

I move in closer, positioning my feet between his, and then look at his chest. I breathe in his familiar smell and slowly look up, hoping for something to ignite, for the slow-cooked meal to finally be the tasty feast it's been promising. I lift my chin towards him, trying to take in his face. We are standing in the house that is about to be our home. The setting couldn't be more perfect. I reach up. Understanding what I'm doing, he leans down, jerkily. I go to tilt my head, to miss his nose; he tilts his the same way. We both tilt it back the other way whilst moving in to each other's lips, and knock noses.

'Sorry.'

'Sorry.'

We both apologise and check our noses. Then I take a breath and we look at each other and move in again, more slowly this time. I tilt to the left, and he follows by tilting to the right, and then my stomach rumbles, reminding me it's nearly lunchtime. I put my hand on it and we both laugh a little. It is funny, after all. And love and lovemaking should be fun. It'll be okay, I think.

Eventually our lips meet and touch and stay there. He has lovely soft lips, but I know we can't just stop here; there has to be more to it. And then to my shame, I remember the kiss with Luca, and how he moved in deeper, our lips parting and the tips of our tongues meeting, wanting to explore, and as my lips begin to part now, it feels like . . . I'm kissing cold custard!

Suddenly there's a shout. I open my eyes to see that Lennie's are already open; I wonder if in fact they've been shut at all. His eyebrows shoot up and his eyes look from left to right and then fall quickly away from me, turning in the direction of the shout, and I swear he puts the back of his hand to his lips where mine just were. He seems flustered, almost blushing. Then he smiles, and I see the look on his face, and now I know for sure. It is the look I have yearned for all these years, and tried to find, and hoped I could live without, giving it up for a contented life with Lennie. I know that look because I tasted it briefly, the moment I met Luca.

So that's why Lennie has been so out of sorts. He's in love with Matteo! Now what? Without a wedding, the locals are convinced Etna will blow again. The town and the people I have come to care about. Città d'Oro has finally been allowed to come back to life, only to be threatened with extinction all over again.

Outside, Matteo turns on his heel and walks off. Luca goes to call after him, over the balcony, but then turns back to me, torn in two, knowing he can't follow. Instinctively, we hug each other tightly.

'It'll be all right, Zeld, it'll be okay,' he tries to reassure me, but I know it won't. How can it be? But there's nothing we can do now.

Chapter Fifty

I walk back through the lemon groves. The town is a hive of activity. Fences are being pulled down, weeds are being uprooted, hosepipes and watering systems are gently feeding the soil; even watering cans are being filled and poured, reviving the starved plants. Everyone waves and wishes me luck for the wedding with a huge smile on their face. They all look happy; all except Etna, who glowers in the distance, smoke rising from her peak.

The square looks amazing. I know Sherise and Valerie have been working hard, but there now seem to be even more flowers there, and I think Carina may have had something to do with that. There are extra fairy lights all around the square itself and bunting leading up the steps to the town hall, where Lennie and I will walk to make our marriage official with Giuseppe.

Rocca and Harry trot happily at my heels, having waited patiently for me outside while I spoke to Lennie. Luca asked me in his note to take care of the dogs, so they have moved over to Il Limoneto with us. I take my time walking through the trees, breathing in the scents as I did when I walked and talked with Luca. Am I doing the right thing? I wish Luca was here to talk to. I know he'd understand. I love Lennie, but I'm not in love with him. I love him like a brother, and Valerie like a mother. But I also love the town and my life here. I can't let them down. This is my home now.

I brush my hands against the long grass and across the lemon blossom, letting the scent fill the path that I'm walking. I think about Luca's note, in which he wishes me all the luck in the world but tells me he can't stay because he can't watch me marry another man. I wonder where he is now. Did he go to Milan to try and find work as a designer, or maybe to get back in touch with his ex there? Or maybe Emily has tracked him down now that she knows he's left the town and is free to marry whoever she likes.

My heart feels as heavy as my feet as I trudge over the newly turned soil, carrying my wedding dress in its bag over my arm. Luca's gift to me to wish me luck with my future, whilst he walks away from what he thought might have been his.

Chapter Fifty-one

'Oh, it's just stunning! Oh Zelda love, I couldn't be more proud!' says Valerie, her eyes brimming with tears. She brushes them away, but they just keep coming, and she wipes her hands down her hips, swathed in mother-of-the-groom pleats.

'I don't think you'll need that jacket, Valerie. You'll be boiling. This is summer in Sicily, not Cardiff registry office,' I say, distracting myself from the many thoughts tumbling through my mind and sounding much sharper than I meant to. I bite my tongue and look back at myself in the mirror. I'm standing in our bedroom in Il Limoneto, beside the open window. It's Saturday. Just two hours, nineteen minutes and eighteen seconds until I'm married to Lennie, forsaking all others, till death us do part.

I feel like everything is at odds. I feel like I am the person I should be in the dress, yet part of me is missing. I run my hand over the verdello-coloured ribbon. Valerie is looking at me, and I suddenly try and busy myself. This should be the happiest day of my life, and hers. I'm marrying her son, after all.

'Here, love, sit down, let's get this flower in your hair,' she says, taking me by the shoulders and guiding me to the little stool in front of the mottled mirror, and I wonder if this is where Giuseppe's mother sat before she got married too.

Valerie looks over my shoulder at my reflection in the mirror and holds my gaze. Then she picks up a hairbrush and runs it through my hair, saying over-brightly, 'I remember the hours before I got married. I'll remember them as long as I live. It was the most exciting time of my life,' and I see her watching me, almost as if she's testing me and how I feel. 'Everyone told me not to marry him, that he was too old for me. Twenty years my senior. But I didn't care. I knew he was the one, I knew it in my heart. And he was. I was madly in love with him from the moment I saw him, and that never changed.'

'But how did you know, how did you know it wouldn't change? How did you know you weren't just being impulsive?'

'You don't. You just have to trust your instincts. You may be impulsive, Zelda, but your instincts have always been right. You know your own heart.'

I scoop my hair up and twist it into a French pleat at the back, off my neck, like Luca showed me. As I clip it there, Valerie turns and picks up something wrapped in cream tissue paper.

'I brought my veil,' she says, almost shyly. 'I wondered if you'd like to wear it. You don't have to, of course, if you'd rather not. It's just . . . well, it's the only thing I've got that would fit in my case, and it does mean so much to me. If you'd rather just have the lemon blossom, that's fine, but I'd be honoured if you'd wear it.'

'Oh Valerie, of course I'd love to wear it. I know how important it is to you, how much you loved Lennie's dad. And I know you want to see Lennie settled and happy.' Tears spring into my eyes. Oh no! Not now! My make-up! But the tears don't listen. I try looking up at the ceiling as Valerie starts to place the veil on my head and pin it in place.

'I want to see both of you happy,' she says quietly. 'That's what life is all about. I want you to find the happiness you deserve because I love you. You are my family as much as Lennie is.'

As she fusses with the short veil, the first of the tears starts to slide down my face. Deciding that brushing it away will only do more damage and draw attention to it, I let it roll down my face and drop off my chin. I can't do this to her, I can't ruin her big day.

'Sometimes in life it's important to take a chance. You've spent so long trying to ignore the voice in your head telling you to act in the moment because you're worried it gets you into trouble. But that voice is right more often than not. More of us should be like you. Act in the moment and think about it later. Not be scared of what life might hold.'

I squeeze my eyes tight shut for a moment and try and will the tears away. I'm listening for the voice that says marrying Lennie is the right thing to do, but instead it's being drowned by 'I'm not in love with Lennie and he's not in love with me. We'll just make each other unhappy.'

'What about Etna, Valerie, do you think the superstition is true?' I say, trying to hide the crack in my voice.

'Load of old codswallop! A nice story, great to tell to tourists and to keep the town populated. Whoever came up with it was a genius, but sorry, I don't believe in fairy tales. Just like I don't believe in regrets. You do what you do at the time because it's what you feel is the right thing to do.'

I wish marrying Lennie felt like the right thing to do. I wish I didn't want to be with Luca, his lips on mine, feeling like nothing else matters.

'But the townspeople believe in the story about Etna, and because of that, I can imagine they are living in a constant state of worry. Sometimes we put our faith in the strangest of things, and they're not always the right things. We can only listen to what's in our hearts.'

My own heart plummets again, and the tears roll silently down my cheeks as I look back at myself in the mirror. How did I get myself into this? I thought it was the right thing to do, the easy option. Marry a man I know, trust and love . . . the slow-cooked meal, all the right ingredients and time to let it grow into something delicious. And then Luca walked into my life – well, I walked into his, to be precise – and bam! I knew it there and then. That was the elusive love at first sight, the thing everyone hopes for. Mine just turned up too late. And the tears plop into my lap.

'Oh my dear, you're crying. Let me get you a tissue,' says Valerie. 'It's an emotional day.'

'I'm fine, really.' I stand up quickly and turn away, to the window overlooking the lemon grove, where everyone has been hard at work. 'Like you say, it's just the emotion of the day,' I say. I'm with everyone I love and have come to think of as family, but I have never felt more alone.

'I remember that,' she says. 'I couldn't wait for my married life to begin. I wanted to make the most of our time together.' She looks at me again, then reaches into her bag and pulls out her phone, probably to check on Lennie, who is getting ready at the new house, with Matteo by his side.

With the terrace now ready, everyone is packing up and getting ready to leave Il Limoneto.

'I've never had free rein before,' Barry said when he saw his little house. 'Think I'll have a TV in the kitchen, and a beer fridge.'

Everyone is making plans. The relocation fund is even back in the bank, and work has stopped on the gym at Romano's villa. By this time next week, we will all have moved on. Luca already has. Today is the end of an era, but the beginning of a new one.

Valerie has gone to the bathroom to get me some loo roll. I look up at Etna. 'I don't know if the superstition is true or not,' I tell the smoky mountain. 'But these people deserve to be able to get on with their lives. I hope this makes you happy. I hope you leave them in peace now.'

'Here we are, dear.' Valerie bustles back in with toilet tissue in one hand, her phone in the other. 'Don't worry,' she smiles. 'Life has a way of sorting itself out. Look at the verdello and the mess I made there. Now you have a good little business going.'

She turns towards the door. 'Time for a Prosecco, I think. Giuseppe left a bottle or two for us downstairs. I'll get a couple of glasses.' And she leaves me looking out of the window, across the lemon grove to Etna, feeling like I've never been happier or sadder in my life, both at the same time. I love this place, I love Lennie, and I'm in love with Luca, but I can't have it all, I know that.

Chapter Fifty-two

I walk downstairs slowly, lifting my skirt to show off the shoes Luca left for me, exactly the same colour as the lemon netting. As I turn at the dog-leg, I start to hear the sound of clapping. My housemates are all standing there, staring up at me and applauding. My cheeks flush and I'm glad of the veil covering them and my teary eyes. Valerie is there too, checking over her shoulder out of the window.

It seems cooler today, the sun not quite so fierce, as if it's stopped putting us to the test. Or maybe it's just that August is on its way out, September and the autumn round the corner. A time to reflect on the summer that was: not quite the one I was expecting – a bit like life, I think – but an amazing journey, one I won't forget. And now it's time to settle and make the most of what I have got.

Ralph hands round glasses of Prosecco.

'*Grazie*,' I say automatically.

'*Prego*,' he smiles back. We have become so integrated in our Sicilian way of life, I can't ever imagine leaving here. But if I don't marry Lennie, the town will hate us and we'll have to go.

'I think I should start walking to the town hall,' I say.

'No, it's okay, there's a lift coming for you,' says Valerie, and I realise that's what she's looking out for.

We sip our drinks and talk about how smart everyone looks, and how they wish Luca was here.

'Here it is!' Valerie finally announces, practically falling over her own feet to open the door.

For a moment my heart leaps and I wonder whether Luca might have returned for the wedding, and then I see a red Ferrari pull up and we all gasp. The door opens and Matteo gets out, wearing a sharp suit and dark glasses, and my heart dips again.

I check the clock. An hour from now, I will be married to Lennie and life here at Il Limoneto will be over. I step out of the double doors into the courtyard.

'Il Nonno sent the car, to wish you luck and happiness,' Matteo tells me. 'He says he wishes you everything you wish for yourself,' and the words hang in the air for some reason and we all look around at each other.

I quickly scoop up the netting of my dress, grab Tabitha's glass from her hand and take a big slug of the Prosecco under my short veil before handing back the empty glass. I can't be with Luca, I think, but I can make the ones I love happy, and that will have to be enough.

My housemates wave me off, with the dogs sitting side by side in front of them, as if part of this big family. I clutch my beautiful bouquet, which was delivered to the house early this morning, as we drive in awkward silence, through the lemon groves and then into the cobbled streets of the town. Matteo's thick, dark-skinned arms are tense where he's gripping the steering wheel. It's the only clue to how he's feeling. I am about to marry the man he loves.

At last he pulls up at the bottom of the steps leading to the town hall. Città d'Oro is out in force; everyone is there, including Lennie, waiting to meet me, looking as nervous as a kitten.

Matteo goes to open the car door, and I put my hand on his arm, though I have no idea what I'm going to say. He freezes. 'I do . . . I do love him,' I say. 'I do want to make him happy.' Not what I wanted to say at all. I wanted to find a way to put this right. But I don't know how.

I step out of the car, hoping my shaking knees will actually hold me up, and look up at Lennie, so smartly dressed, so handsome. I feel immensely proud, as if I'm watching him marry someone else from the sidelines. Only I'm not; it's me, I remind myself. Matteo holds the car door, looking straight ahead, his wraparound glasses hiding his expression. I feel like I'm being led to the gallows rather than to my wedding day. This isn't right. For any of us.

'You look beautiful,' says Lennie, taking my hand.

'So do you,' I reply, and we both smile, gentle, affectionate smiles, before he holds out his arm to me for support, just as he always has.

We walk towards the steps leading up to the town hall, where Giuseppe is standing, beaming from ear to ear. Clouds have tumbled in and the sky is darkening, but nothing is going to dim his smile.

As we climb the steps, the townspeople following behind us, our housemates pile from the minibus, which is covered in ribbons and lemon blossom. Valerie has adopted Sicilian parking and left the bus where it stopped, bottom out, and is walking quickly beside us. Her face is worried, an expression that only the mother of the bride and groom is allowed to wear, but she breaks into a smile when she sees Giuseppe, as if here is someone to share the day with. And for a moment, I wonder if I'm seeing the same thing there that I saw between Lennie and Matteo, but for once I'm going to say nothing.

I look at Lennie again. Valerie checks over her shoulder nervously, and I wonder if she is worrying about Etna after all. The air has become quite heavy. Everyone looks a little anxious, keen to get into the town hall and get the ceremony under way.

'*Prego!*' Giuseppe stands aside to welcome us into the big room opposite his office. I look at the chairs laid out in straight lines, then back at Giuseppe's office and the disorder there: piles of paper and damp, crumbling walls. It feels like my life: on the one hand the world of marriage and home and the keys to being a grown-up that I've wanted for so long; on the other hand, comfortingly familiar chaos.

We stand in the hall, the wedding party behind us, keen to move in and be seated. Yet something won't let me walk forward.

'Would you like a moment?' says Giuseppe.

'Actually . . .' I try and swallow through my dry throat, and look at Matteo, glasses still on, hiding his feelings from the outside world as I have a feeling he must have done for a very long time. Everyone should be free to love who they want. Luca shouldn't have been bullied into getting engaged to his second cousin, and Matteo should be free to take his own path too. It's a basic human right. 'Actually, I would,' I tell Giuseppe.

I turn away from the beautifully decorated room – it's all for show, I think, covering over the cracks – and walk towards the comfort of Giuseppe's office, where I feel at home. Barry and Ralph usher everyone into the big room and put on some music, and I can't help but smile as Dean Martin starts singing 'Amore', reminding me of the bittersweet night when we held the street party and everyone came and I finally felt we were home . . . and Luca left.

Lennie follows me into the office and pushes the heavy door half closed behind him.

'You okay, Zeld? Nervous? Don't be,' he says. 'It's only me.'

'And only you is just brilliant. I love you, Lennie. I've never loved anyone more. You are my whole family . . .'

And then I take a deep breath and do the thing I've been trying not to do. I give in to my impulsiveness and finally open the floodgates, and it rushes out.

'I can't marry you, Lennie. I can't do this.'

'What?' His face does a strange thing of falling yet looking relieved at the same time.

Valerie slips in and stands by the door, but I keep my eyes on Lennie.

'But . . .' he stutters, 'we came here as a couple. The pact . . . being loyal to each other. It's always been you and me. This is what we wanted. A new life and this project.'

'And I want to stay, but as me. I want us to be true to ourselves. We took a risk when we came here; we need to take that risk again now, take a chance on life . . . and love. I love you, Lennie, but I'm not in love with you and you're not in love with me. We thought it was enough, but I can't let you marry me when I know you have a chance at real love with someone else.'

We both look towards the door, thinking about Matteo in his sharp suit, made no doubt by Luca. At least a little bit of Luca is still here, I think. I look down at my dress and imagine his hands working away at the stitching. They have handled every bit of this dress, with love and care.

'I was wrong,' I say. 'We shouldn't be settling for second best. Not that you or I are second best, but there is such a thing as love at first sight. I know it now, because . . .' I can't tell him that I felt it when I saw Luca, because Luca is gone. But I did get to taste true love, just for a while, and I know that it's real enough. 'Because I saw it in you and Matteo. We both deserve that chance and to take it when it comes along.'

He looks at me with sadness in his eyes.

'I thought if I could marry you, settle on somebody, then everything would become clear,' he says. 'I've been confused for so long. Not gay, not straight, neither one nor the other. I knew that if I married you, someone I care for very much, I could finally work out who I was.'

'What you needed to do was follow your heart and see where it led you.' I smile a watery smile. 'When we came here, when you suggested it . . .' I swallow, 'was it because of the man from your office? Marcus? The one who'd just split up with someone. The one who wasn't the settling-down type?'

He looks at me and nods. 'You know me too well.'

'It took a while to work it out!' I laugh.

Lennie looks at Valerie, who is still standing by the door.

'What I want is for you both to be happy,' she says. 'That's all I want. It's all any of us want; the ones who care about you. I was wrong to try and push you together, thinking of my own happiness. You can't find happiness in other people's lives. You must do what's right for you. That's what me and your dad did, and I have never regretted a single moment of it.' Her eyes fill with tears.

Lennie looks back at me. 'And what will you do?' he says, looking as if his heart is breaking in two.

'Stay,' I say. 'Become a lemon farmer, because no one ever . . .'

'. . . became a lemon farmer for anything other than love,' and Luca steps into the room.

'You came back!' I gasp.

'Yes.'

'Why?'

'I want to be a lemon farmer too.' He starts to smile.

'And I love you. From the moment I first saw you,' he says as he steps towards me.

'But . . . how did you know? How did you know I . . .'

'Someone contacted me and told me that if I really loved you as much as they thought you loved me, I should get back here now and tell you that.' He looks at Valerie, and I suddenly remember her taking her phone to the bathroom when she went to get me the loo roll.

'I had his number. From the day Sophia went missing.' Valerie looks choked and anxious, as if worrying whether she's done the right thing.

'I thought . . . I hoped to persuade you,' Luca says, gazing at me. 'I wanted to tell you that I love you. That I think of you all the time. I feel complete when I'm with you. Because I know you. And I know that you would go through with this to make everyone else happy.'

'The town . . . Giuseppe. The project. We promised them a wedding!'

'But like you said, Zelda, this is about being true to yourself, not thinking of others. This is about what *you* want.'

I look at Lennie.

'You can't choose who you fall in love with,' I tell him sadly. 'I really wanted to fall in love with you.'

'And me you!' He sniffs. 'Life would have been so straight-forward. Straight being the operative word!'

'I thought I was doing the right thing, the sensible thing. Trying to prove that I could grow up and be like everyone else. I was trying to ignore the impulsive voice that always gets me into trouble, saying, "Don't do it, don't agree to it." But I *can't* do it. I'm not in love with you, but I love you.'

'And I'm not in love with you, but I love you. I love you because you're brave, fearless . . .'

'I'm not brave! I'm terrified all the time. I was brave because I had you beside me,' I say.

'I'll always be here for you.'

'And me you. We're lucky to have each other. Friends?'

'The best of friends for ever!' And the world seems to slot back to how it should be.

I turn to Luca, tongue-tied and with no idea what to say. But it doesn't matter, because he takes my hands and looks deep into my eyes.

'I have loved you from the moment you walked into the restaurant, and I know you felt it too. I don't regret the kiss—'

'You kissed?!' Lennie looks momentarily affronted, and then shakes his head, smiling, and I know he and Matteo haven't been angels.

'I love everything about your impulsive, impetuous, spur-of-the-moment behaviour,' Luca continues. 'I love you *because* of it. You act in the moment. You wouldn't be here if it wasn't for that; you wouldn't have stood up to my father or done what you've done for this town. You are you and I love you for it. I never want you to change.'

I swallow hard, because if I did what I really want to do, I'd let out a great big sob and laugh at the same time. Oh, what the heck – and I do just that!

'No one can explain chemistry,' Luca says. 'But it's real. Love at first sight is real.' I nod emphatically in agreement. 'It's not just impulse; it's a real feeling right in the middle of your heart.'

'But the wedding!' I suddenly look towards the door. 'We have to have a wedding. It has to go ahead. Everyone is expecting it. Even Etna seems to be getting impatient.' I glance out at the darkening sky.

'Well,' says Luca, looking at me and then at Lennie, 'if this is what you want . . . if you still want a life here with the lemons, I think you're right, the wedding should go ahead. If it's what you truly want.' And I'm sent into a spin all over again.

Chapter Fifty-three

The wedding music is playing as I step out of the office. Lennie and Luca have left, and after checking that I'm really sure about this, Valerie has joined them in the room opposite. It's just me now. I take a deep breath and lift my chin and stand tall. I have butterflies tearing around inside my stomach, but I know I am doing the right thing. This isn't me being impulsive. This is me following my instincts, following my heart and taking a leap of faith all at the same time.

As I walk into the big room, everyone turns to look at me. Giuseppe stands, looking stately, behind a big wooden desk, and in front of him, illuminated by a sudden shaft of sunlight, I see Lennie with Luca by his side. I gaze at the two men I love most in the world. Luca is wearing a corsage made of lemon blossom, borrowed from Matteo, with a ribbon around it; the same colour ribbon he added to my dress: verdello green.

Every journey starts with the first step, and I put one foot in front of the other and begin to make my way towards them. Everyone that matters is here: my family, I think. Because family is what you make it. At the front stands Valerie, looking as proud as Punch. Giuseppe nods slowly, as if to say '*Perfecto*.'

The two men smile at each other and embrace, then Lennie

steps aside to join Matteo. Then Luca turns slowly to look at me, and I think my world might just explode as he holds out a hand for me to join him in front of Giuseppe . . . to join him in life, forever, on the lemon farm.

Because nobody ever became a lemon farmer for anything other than love.

Epilogue

One year on

'So how was your trip to London?' I ask Sophia. 'Did you see all the sights?'

'It was great. I saw Buckingham Palace, Downing Street, Pudding Lane and Big Ben. I went on the Eye and to the biggest toy store ever! But . . .' She tails off.

'But?' I ask, picking up Francesco from the pram and handing him to his new godfather, Lennie, and then handing Amelia to *her* godfather, Matteo, who takes her proudly in his strong arms. We all sit around the long table under the biggest tree in the lemon grove at Il Limoneto.

'Careful not to get anything on their christening gowns. Luca only finished them last night,' says Valerie, who has only been home once since the wedding – to pack up her house and put it on the market before moving out here to Città d'Oro. Although she seems to spend more time at Giuseppe's than she does in the little house Lennie and Matteo have done up for her.

Along the table there are sprigs of lemon blossom in jam jars on the white tablecloth, along with big jugs of wine and water. Everyone is ready for the feast that they have been preparing all morning, jostling for position in the kitchen, taking direction from Luca and Matteo. It's one big noisy group, just like after our wedding, when the whole town came back to help us celebrate, carrying bowls of salad, pots of pasta and trays of vegetables ready for roasting, all smiling and laughing as they walked from town to Il Limoneto.

'What are you writing now?' Valerie looks warily at Tabitha.

'Actually, Valerie, I've given up writing articles. I've spent so many years making stuff up, trying to make it sound like fact. I'm actually going to write a book. A novel, set on a lemon farm,' she grins. 'I mean, you couldn't make this stuff up!'

'And she's my new English teacher!' Sophia announces proudly.

Tabitha smiles. When she's not writing or teaching, she's helping Ralph, who has closed up his gallery in the main street for the day. He's preparing for an exhibition next week and his children will be joining him to celebrate. He and his ex-wife have been back on speaking terms ever since she saw the feel-good article that Tabitha wrote about a group of people who moved to Sicily and brought a dying town back to life.

Giuseppe hands round glasses of our latest batch of verdello limoncello and proposes a toast.

'To all of us,' he says. 'To home and to family,' and he raises his glass to Luca and me, and then to our children, Francesco and Amelia, named after Luca's grandparents and their initials on the lemon grove 'F & A'.

Il Nonno stands up.

'And to forgiveness. None of us would be here if we hadn't made mistakes along the way. It took an infuriating red-headed woman from the UK to make me realise that!'

'Hear hear,' says Barry loudly.

And Romano turns and raises his glass and tips his head softly at Luca's mum, who is taking a turn at cuddling one of her grandchildren.

'Still think you might find the woman of your dreams out here, Barry?' I ask.

'Do you know,' says Barry thoughtfully, 'I think I'm quite content to be on my own. When you've got a whole family around you, you don't really need to have just one person, do you?'

And we all nod and smile in agreement.

The breeze runs around the lemon grove, making the leaves whisper, and high up in the tree above us, the canary sings, never far from the family, returning to its cage each night, with its door wide open. Because when you love someone, you have to let them go. And if they love you, they'll come back.

We've all thought at one time or another about leaving, but in the end, we've all stayed. Matteo and Lennie are now restoring houses all across the town, with Matteo's designer eye and Lennie doing the hard graft. They have moved into the house with the balcony that Lennie and I were due to have. It was always their house, and now it's their home. Sherise and Billy are living happily with their hens in Luca's old apartment at the lemon grove on the edge of town, and Billy is expanding the flock, making more henhouses and, of course, growing lemons to sell to me. Luca and I have stayed on in Il Limoneto. Giuseppe wanted to see a family in it again, and here we are, living life in amongst our lemons with our children.

'But?' I ask Sophia again.

'I liked London,' she says, 'but it's nothing like I thought. It isn't like Città d'Oro. It's nothing compared to being at home.'

And we all raise a glass to Nonna and her recipe, and agree that when life hands you lemons, you make limoncello . . . because no one ever became a lemon farmer for anything other than love.

And as the big orange sun sets in the sky, Etna watches over us contentedly, the swallows swoop and dive as if preparing to say goodbye till next spring, and we all sit around the table to eat, because a family that cooks and eats together stays together.

Acknowledgements

This book wouldn't have been possible without the help of the fabulous Sarah Kearney who runs White Almond – Private Sicily, a travel, food and lifestyle blog all about life in Sicily. She answered so many of my questions and put me in touch with people she knew on the island. You can find her site here: www.whitealmond-privatesicily.blogspot.com

One of the people she put me in touch with was Matteo and his family at Agriturismo Il Giardino del Sole, just fifteen minutes from Catania airport. This is a wonderful family run organic farm where we stayed on our first night. It offers fantastic homecooked food, the children went horse-riding through the orange and lemon groves and we had an amazing cooking class where we learnt to eat and drink the Sicilian way! It was wonderful.

Sarah also put me in touch with Guiseppe who owns and runs a century-old citrus and olive oil farm (www.azienda brancati.it). We had a wonderful day visiting the lemon groves, tasting the oranges grown there and coming away with armfuls of fruit and olive oil. Follow him on Twitter @AziendaBrancati and Facebook @biobrancati. I have never tasted clementine's like it!! A real taste of Sicily.

And of course, I must thank James Villa Holidays (www. jamesvillas.co.uk) for my fantastic stay in Sicily at the wonderful Villa Viagrande in Trecastagni. It was simply stunning. I will remember two amazing things from our stay here. The first was swimming in a beautiful pool looking up at the view of Mount Etna as I did. The second was the sunrise over Sicily as I sat and ate oranges every morning on the terrace, like a big orange itself. Like I say, simply stunning.

My thanks to Jen Doyle and the team at Headline and lovely editor Celine Kelly. And as always to my fab agent David Headley.

And finally to the wonderful Sicilian people who made us feel so welcome, and their generosity wherever we went. We will be back!

Welcome to the world of

Jo Thomas

Hello,

I hope you enjoyed reading Zelda and Lennie's story as much as I enjoyed researching and writing it!

My great-grandparents were Sicilian so Sicily has always held a fascination for me. I'd always wanted to visit and write about the island. And it didn't disappoint.

Not only did we find everyone in Sicily so generous, but people who know and love the island are so generous with their help and time too. When I started researching Sicily, I came across a travel, food and lifestyle blog called White Almond Sicily that gave me a taste of what was to come. I contacted Sarah who runs the blog and she couldn't have been more helpful with her knowledge of the area. And that sums Sicily up. People who know Sicily want to pass on their love for the place and it didn't take me long to find out why.

Flying into Catania, we spent the first night in Sicily on an *agriturismo*, a working Italian farm. It is a fantastic way to see the countryside and meet locals. We stayed at Agriturismo Il Giardino del Sole and what a wonderful place it is. Totally inspiring and entrancing. We were surrounded by orange and lemon trees, horses and donkeys too. The children rode horses from the farm up through the orange and lemon groves and we could smell the citrus blossom in the air as we looked out over the island to sea. Then we did a cookery course on the farm and cooked and ate with the wonderfully welcoming family. It's one of my favourite memories, cooking and eating together like that.

For the rest of our trip we stayed in a beautiful villa, Villa Viagrande, in Trecastagni looking out over Mount Etna. It was truly gorgeous. Here too there were lemons growing in the garden.

Like everywhere we went in Sicily, our hosts were so generous and welcoming and we arrived to a table of wonderful home-cooked cakes, fresh oranges and sweet treats. Sicilians love their sweet treats. While we were staying here Sarah from White Almond Sicily arranged for us to go and visit an organic citrus farmer (**www. agricolturasiciliana.com**) where we walked through the fruit farm then sat and chatted over a huge bowl of the sweetest clementines I have ever eaten.

I had all the ingredients for my Sicilian story. Citrus fruit is at the heart of this beautiful island and its food; so too is family, generosity and the joy in feeding others with simple, sun-soaked ingredients. If you've been inspired by the Sicilian way of life like I was, you too could cook like a Sicilian. Rachel Roddy author of *Two Kitchens, Recipes from Sicily and Rome* has included some recipes for you here. So, get together with friends or family, get in kitchen and rustle up yourselves a taste of Sicily. I hope you love it as much I do now!

Until next time, ciao!

Jo xx

3 Recipes from:

Two Kitchens

Family Recipes from Sicily and Rome

By Rachel Roddy

Spaghetti with garlic, oil and lemon

Tagliatelle with lemon and Parmesan

Lemon pudding

Headline Home
A division of Headline Publishing Group

Lemons

Lemons, like so many things, were introduced to Sicily by the Arabs, whose farming and irrigation techniques changed the landscape of the island. In a tenth-century Arab treatise lemons are mentioned as part of ornamental gardens, and possibly they were used that way in Sicily too. In time, though, lemons became an essential part of the landscape, as much a part of Sicily and its food as the sunshine they personify.

Lemon juice is used in drinks, ices, on vegetables and on meat and fish, giving moisture and sharpness, and is used to balance the sweetness of other fruit, or simply eaten as fruit. My partner, Vincenzo, has inherited his grandfather's ability to eat a whole lemon like you or I would eat an apple, maybe peeled with a knife, maybe not. This is less surprising when you consider that Sicilian lemons are of a particular type. They have pale yellow skin over a thick layer of spongy pith which is more like aubergine flesh than the bitter-tasting white parts I am used to, and although sharp, it is fleshy, bright and edible, especially with a bit of salt. I can't, though. His mother, Carmela, also shudders. She prefers to do as her grandfather did: take a cup, rip small pieces of bread into it, cut very thin quarter-slices of lemon and add them to the cup, squeeze over the juice, add hot water, salt and pepper, and wait and wait. She makes this bread and lemon soup when she is jaded and needs cleansing and soothing.

My granny Alice had a way with lemon quarters too, tipping them from the jars that came from Schweppes into every gin and tonic she served in her pub. Of course, we tried them, then puckered. Alice also put empty halves on her elbows, to soften and bleach them. Aged eight, I was utterly confused as to why you would do this. At nearly 44 I understand.

Like sunshine in the kitchen, lemons – whether pulled from a tree or tipped from a yellow net bag – are beautiful, glorious and endlessly useful too, as a star ingredient, a quick dab of perfume, a seasoning or a quiet volunteer working away in the background. Lemon juice acts in much the same way as salt, bringing out flavours. It's the equivalent of a sound engineer, adjusting the balance, lifting, deepening, sharpening, brightening, filling out, making things taste more like themselves. When something is missing in a braise, stew, fruit pudding, soup or fruit puree, lemon is often the answer, pulling the dish together. A dish of lentils and hard-boiled eggs, for example, is transformed by a squeeze of lemon. You might not know it's there, but you would miss it if it wasn't. Lemon juice can also partially cook meat, fish, even vegetables, and its zest – as essential as the oils it contains – adds heat and intense fragrance.

When choosing lemons, look out for unwaxed ones with bright, unwrinkled skin; they should feel heavy in your hand. They're always available, but late November to March is when they are at their best which is excellent timing if you think about it: brightness and eternal freshness at the time of year we need it most. I like my box grater for zesting. For squeezing I use an old-fashioned plastic two-piece, with a cone top over a collecting dish. The secret is making sure the lemon is at room temperature and rolling it around on the work surface like a ball before you squeeze it.

Spaghetti with garlic, oil and lemon

Spaghetti aglio, olio al limone
Serves 4

2 large unwaxed lemons
a large handful of flat-leaf parsley
500g spaghetti
1–2 garlic cloves (depending on taste)
1 small dried chilli or a pinch of red chilli flakes
6 tablespoons olive oil

Two kitchens meet in this great Roman standby *spaghetti ajo, ojo epeperoncino* (spaghetti with olive oil, garlic and chilli), as it is known in Roman dialect, which is given a Sicilian lift with some lemon zest. It's a dish I crave when I haven't had it for a while, especially in the dark days of winter, when all the steady, starchy sustenance needs a slap. It is a simple meal, but full of flavour; the bright, clean oil, the pungent garlic, throat-tickling heat of the chilli, grassy parsley (a fleck of which gets stuck in your teeth) and the volatile aromatic oil in the lemon zest. Quantities for something like this are, of course, personal; you might decide to leave out the chilli or double the garlic.

Grate the zest from the lemons and very finely chop the parsley, then mix the two together and set aside. Bring a large pan of salted water to a fast boil, add salt, stir and add the spaghetti. Cook until al dente.

Meanwhile, very finely chop the garlic and chilli. In a large frying pan, very gently warm the olive oil, garlic and chilli over a low heat until fragrant, but do not let it burn. Once cooked, drain the spaghetti, or better still use a sieve or tongs to lift the spaghetti and add just a little residual cooking water into the frying pan. Stir, add the lemon zest and parsley, a pinch of salt and, if you like, a squeeze of lemon, then stir again, divide between plates and eat immediately.

Tagliatelle with lemon and Parmesan

Tagliatelle con limone e Parmigiano
Serves 2

220g dried or 350g fresh tagliatelle or linguine
75ml extra-virgin olive oil
grated zest and juice of 1 small unwaxed lemon
100g Parmesan, grated, plus more for sprinkling

If you whisk lemon juice with plenty of olive oil and lots of freshly grated Parmesan you create a thick, grainy, deeply flavoured lemon and cheese sauce that you toss with hot pasta. The flavours work beautifully together; the sharp, lip-puckering acidity of the lemon is tempered by the Parmesan and the olive oil lends it a silky, glossy texture. All the ingredients come together into a surprising sauce that clings to each strand of pasta and manages to be both soothing and vital at the same time.

It is important to whisk the ingredients together in a warm bowl, especially on a cold day. The modest heat helps the ingredients come together. The hot pasta continues what the warm bowl started and brings out the heady scent of the lemon juice, zest and the salty sweetness of the Parmesan. I have also added rocket and basil to this, which worked well.

Bring a large pan of salted water to a fast boil. If you are using dried pasta that takes about 8 minutes to cook, add that to the water now. If you are using fresh pasta, which only takes 2-3 minutes to cook, start making the sauce first.

Warm a large bowl under a hot running tap, then dry it. Add the olive oil, some of the lemon juice and a pinch of zest and beat briefly with a little whisk until it emulsifies. Now add the Parmesan, beat again, taste and add more lemon if you want it.

Taste and whisk again until you have a thick, grainy cream. Taste again; you probably won't need salt with all the Parmesan but if you feel the need, add some. Once the pasta is ready, drain it and quickly toss it in the bowl with the lemon and Parmesan sauce. Divide the pasta between two warmed serving bowls and add more grated Parmesan if you like.

Lemon pudding

Sbriciolata alia crema di limoni
Makes 8–12 slices

For the crumbs
300g plain flour
120g caster sugar
8–10g baking powder
a pinch of salt
100g cold butter, plus extra for greasing
1 large egg

For the cream
4 unwaxed lemons
500ml whole milk
6 egg yolks
150g caster sugar
35g plain flour
35g potato starch or cornflour

This is my friend Cinzia's recipe for *sbriciolata alla crema di limoni*, the literal translation of which is 'crumbs around a lemon cream', which really is the best description since none of the other possibilities are quite right. The lemon cream is typically southern Italian, and therefore thickened with a little flour, which gives it an old-fashioned and homely feel, especially if you are used to more elegant, butter-rich lemon curds.

Preheat the oven to 180°C/160°C fan/gas mark 4 and grease and dust with flour a 28cm shallow cake or tart tin. Pare the zest of 3 lemons in strips and squeeze the juice. Warm the milk and zest in a small pan. Leave to sit for 1 hour, then lift out the zest.

Meanwhile, make the crumbs. In a large bowl, mix the flour, sugar, baking powder and salt. Dice the butter and add it along with the lightly beaten egg, then use cold fingertips to rub the butter and egg into the flour until the mixture resembles fat breadcrumbs. Sprinkle half the crumbs over the base of the prepared tin to make a nice, even layer that covers the base. Bake on the bottom shelf for a few minutes, or until the crumbs are firm and very pale gold. Remove and leave to cool.

In another large bowl, whisk the yolks and sugar to a thick cream, then sift over the flour and starch and mix until smooth. Whisk in about 150ml lemon juice. Warm the milk a little, then, whisking constantly, add it to the egg and flour mixture in a thin stream. Return the mixture to the pan and cook over a low heat, whisking, for about 15 minutes, until it coats the back of the spoon. Grate the zest of the final lemon into the cream.

Spread the cream over the crumb base, leaving a 1cm border. Cover it with the rest of the crumbs. Bake for 25 minutes, or until the crumbs are firm and golden. It must be absolutely cool if you want to turn it out, and even then you must do so very carefully by inverting it on to a plate, then on to another plate so that the golden crust faces up. It is nice at room temperature or chilled.

Discover other books by

Jo Thomas

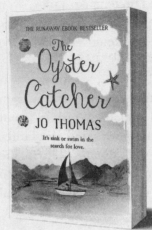

An irresistibly feel-good novel set on the charming coast of Ireland.

'A heart-warming tale full of Celtic charm, set against a beautiful landscape. What more could you wish for?' Ali McNamara

Can love bloom in the olive groves and vineyards of Italy?

'Romantic and funny, this is a great addition to any bookshelf!' *Sun*

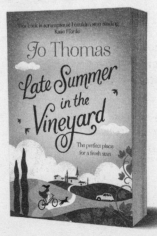

A gorgeous read filled with sunshine and wine in the South of France

'A fabulous French feast of fun' Milly Johnson

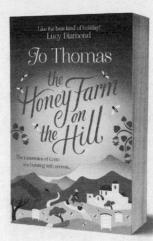

Let this novel transport you straight to the breath-taking mountains of Crete.

'Perfect escapist magic'
Good Housekeeping

Escape to the sun-drenched hills and cherry orchards of southern Spain

'Warm, funny, romantic with a terrific sense of place. I loved it!'
Katie Fforde

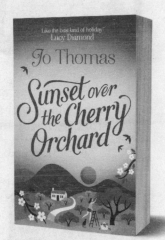

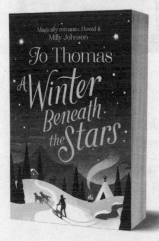

An unforgettable winter story set in the snow-filled world of Swedish Lapland.

'A sparkling, heart-warming hug of a story'
Miranda Dickinson

Jo's novels are available in paperback, eBook and audio

Discover the novellas

An irresistible romance filled with love and laughter amongst the rolling green of the Kent countryside

A sparkling, feel-good short story set in the picturesque beauty of a Welsh costal village.

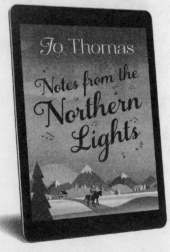

Dive into this gorgeous winter warmer, an irresistible winter tale set in Iceland that will melt the coldest of hearts...

Jo's novellas are available in eBook